# It was unlike anyplace they had ever known

Krysty lay on her back, staring around her, relaxing on a soft couch of deep green moss. "What you said, Doc, about how it used to be . . . was it really like this?"

"Oh, indeed. I swear it was like this. Of course there were cities. Great wens that soured the land and skies, blighting the environment. But there were billions of acres of unspoiled wilderness."

They were silent for a moment, each locked into his or her own thoughts. Ryan felt Krysty's hand on his. "Why keep on moving, lover? Why not stop here?"

Ryan breathed in, trying to find the words that would be an answer. "I guess . . . I don't know."

"There's valleys around here. We could build us a home."

"Us? Who's that, Krysty?"

"You. Me. All of us. We got the skills. Mebbe we could try and farm some of this green land. Raise a family."

Ryan remained silent for a long time. Then he spoke. "One day, Krysty."

"One day, lover?"

"Yeah. One day."

But not yet.

**Also available in the
Deathlands saga:**

# JAMES AXLER

# DEATH LANDS

## Crater Lake

A GOLD EAGLE BOOK FROM

# WORLDWIDE

TORONTO • NEW YORK • LONDON • PARIS
AMSTERDAM • STOCKHOLM • HAMBURG
ATHENS • MILAN • TOKYO • SYDNEY

*Cui dono lepidum novum libellum*
*Arido modo pumice expolitum?*

The question was asked by Catullus in 54 B.C.
And the answer is to Randall Toye, with
thanks for all his enthusiasm and guidance
thus far.

First edition August 1987

ISBN 0-373-62504-9

I, a stranger, and afraid,
in a world I never made.

—A. E. Housman

# Chapter One

JAK LAUREN'S EYES, pale pink, snapped open.

A fearsome stab of pain jerked through his narrow skull, making him moan and close his eyes again. His fingers curled, nails digging into the palms of his hands. As he moved, leaning against the thick glass walls of the chamber, the tiny shards of razored steel sewn into his clothes sparkled brightly.

"Was blind, but now I see." Why did the words of the old hymn come floating back into his mind at that moment?

He cautiously opened his eyes again, screwing them up against the bright light. There was a pattern of raised disks of polished metal that glowed faintly, the image fading even as he looked at it. The smoked glass walls were deep crimson. That wasn't right. They'd been blue. Blue. He held on to that fact. His head felt awful. Worse than the time—it had been his tenth birthing day just over four years back—when his father had been burrowing. Digging into the cellars of some of the derelict houses on the edges of West Lowellton, near Lafayette, in what had once been Louisiana, his father had found a bottle of something called Southern Comfort—a ribbed bottle of clear glass with a golden cap. He'd given it to Jak. The warm liquor had tasted of peaches and summer, and it had burned his throat. He'd drunk nearly the whole bottle and then been monstrously sick.

But that hadn't been anything compared to this awful swirling feeling. It was as if someone had sucked his brain from the caverned chambers of his skull, leaving only an echoing hollow, or pumped his brain like a pink-gray slurry through the twisted copper tubes of a moonshiner's still, then spat the results back into his skull again.

"How're you doing, Whitey?"

Jak leaned over and groaned. He felt like throwing up. His long hair, purest white, trailed like plumes of lace over his shoulders. He drew in deep breaths, fighting for control. He did not want to show any sign of weakness in front of his six new friends.

"Not 'friends,'" he whispered to himself. Friends would betray you. Or they could be used to try to make you turn traitor. "Companions" was better.

"What's that?"

He didn't realize he'd spoken out loud.

"Cold," he said, seeing the fog of his breath. Back home in Louisiana he'd never seen that. Never seen snow or felt the bite of frost. He hadn't really believed that this gateway place would actually work and transmit them somewhere else.

"Yeah. Just sit back and relax. It's a shit feeling, but it'll pass."

"First time's the worst, Jak." That was a woman's voice.

He risked opening his eyes again, keeping his head perfectly still. The armored glass felt cool against his skin. The others were strewn around the room in varying stages of recovery from the mat-trans jump.

Jak's eyes first focused on the girl called Lori. At six feet she topped him by at least nine inches. Her long blond hair tumbled over her shoulders and across the bright red satin blouse that clung to the soft swell of her breasts. The boy's

eyes were caught by the nipples, roused by the bitter cold
in the gateway, peaking under the thin material. Her long
thighs shone beneath the short maroon suede skirt. Jak
knew that Lori was only a couple of years older than he
was. He'd admired how she bore herself in combat situations, despite wearing the most absurd boots he'd ever
seen. They were made of crimson leather, well over her
knees, and had incredibly high heels. He had watched with
disbelief when she'd run like a gazelle in those boots. Now
she moved uneasily, the tiny silver spurs on each heel
ringing like bells. At her belt she wore a pearl-handled .22-
caliber Walther PPK pistol.

Next to her, one arm protectively around the girl's
shoulders, was the oldest of the party, Dr. Theophilus
Tanner. He looked around seventy, with grizzled hair and
a graying stubble on his cadaverous jaw. He was tall and
skinny and wore cracked knee boots splattered with Louisiana swamp mud. The pale blue denim shirt and stained
frock coat that he wore seemed like relics, something out
of an old, old picture book from well before the Big War.
A kerchief with a blue swallow's-eye design protruded
from the top pocket of his coat, and a battered stovepipe
hat was beside him on the floor.

"I trust you are feeling a little more like rejoining the
land of the living, my young friend?" the old man asked
in his rich, mellow voice.

"Better," Jak said, nodding.

Doc patted Lori companionably on the arm, dislodging
his walking cane from his lap. It was made of polished
ebony, with a carved lion's head in silver at its top. Jak
knew, because Finnegan had told him, that the stick concealed a rapier-thin sword. The old man also carried a bizarre double-barreled cap and ball pistol called a Le Mat.

Finnegan winked at Jak. The short fat man looked pale from the jump, beads of sweat dappling his sallow forehead. "Way weird, huh, kid?"

Jak nodded. He envied the way Finn dressed, though it did make him look a bit like a sec man—matching sweater and pants in dark blue and high black combat boots with steel-capped toes. One of the things that Jak Lauren knew a lot about was killing and all the ways of doing it. His father had often told him that killing was a craft like any other. And, like any other, it had to be learned.

Jak had learned it well.

In a soft leather sheath on his hip, Finnegan carried a long butcher's cleaver, its edge honed until it sang. In his belt was a 9 mm Model 92 Beretta. Finn's chubby hands cradled a Heckler & Koch submachine gun. Able to fire fifty rounds on either single, triple or continuous, it also sported a trim silencer. Jak had seen blaster catalogs in the undamaged houses where he'd been raised and recognized the weapon as a development from the HK54A2 from the late nineties.

Jak pushed against the wall, trying to stand up. The man next around the circle shook his head. "Give it time."

J. B. Dix, the Armorer, never used four words when three would be enough.

J.B. was the calmest, quietest man Jak Lauren had ever met. Lightly built, he weighed not much more than Jak's own one-twenty. Around forty years old, with a thin face and a yellowish complexion, he wore rimless glasses and habitually sported a battered fedora. Jak noticed he had the trick of never watching you when you expected it and always watching you when you weren't ready.

In a handmade canvas sling at his waist, he carried a mini-Uzi, complemented by a Steyr AUG 5.6 mm handgun on his hip. Jak suspected, though he hadn't seen any evidence of it, that J.B. also had a variety of hidden knives and other weapons about his person, perhaps under his leather jacket and nondescript pants.

"My first jump I thought I was going to die," a woman's voice said.

"Know what you mean, Krysty," J.B. replied, managing a wan smile.

Krysty Wroth scared the shit out of Jak. She was also tall, close to six feet, with a great body that fueled his adolescent fantasies. She had piercing green eyes and the brightest, thickest red hair the boy had ever encountered. Several times since their first meeting, he'd almost sworn the hair had had a bizarre life of its own, the vermilion fronds swaying gently in the breeze when there'd been no wind at all.

Krysty also had the power of seeing. He knew that. She could "feel" what was going to happen. Not like a full doomie, but enough to give a distant early warning of trouble. Also she had staggeringly good hearing and vision. Added to the fact that on occasion she was capable of feats of almost superhuman strength, it was enough to scare anyone.

She was sitting, knees drawn up to her chest, wearing khaki overalls tucked into a pair of beautiful western boots, which were made of dark blue calf with inlaid falcons in silver leather. The toes of the boots were chiseled silver points, making them both attractive and potentially lethal. She wore a holster that contained a silvered Heckler & Koch P7A-13 pistol that fired nine-millimeter rounds.

"Back with us, Jak?" she said, smiling at him. "By Gaia, but I shall never forget my first jump! Felt like my head was still a thousand miles behind me."

Jak nodded, pushing up until he was standing. The room swayed about him, and he staggered, nearly falling. With an effort he retained his balance.

"Don't push it, Jak," urged the sixth and last member of the group, the leader, Ryan Cawdor.

Ever since their first meeting, Jak Lauren had felt instinctively that Ryan Cawdor was a man he could follow. In the swamps he'd been leader, despite his youth, because nobody else killed as well as he did. Ryan Cawdor was something else.

Jak stared across the gateway mat-trans chamber at him. Ryan was stretched out on the floor, feet crossed, looking not terribly uncomfortable. He was the tallest in the party, about a foot taller than the white-haired boy, and lean-built, with broad shoulders and narrow hips. His hair was a mat of tight black curls, spreading over the white fur collar of his long coat of treated skins. Around his neck was a white silk scarf. Finn had once told Jak that there were lead weights in each end of the scarf that turned it into an excellent garrote.

The face was thin with high cheekbones. On the right side a long scar ran from the mouth to the corner of the eye, which was a chilling pale blue. The left eye was gone, the raw, weeping socket concealed by a leather patch. Finn had told Jak that Ryan's own brother had been responsible for the wound, but he didn't believe the fat man. Finnegan didn't always tell the whole truth.

Ryan wore a brown shirt and brown pants, with the bottoms slit so that they could slide easily over his combat boots. His right hand rested on the butt of a Heckler & Koch G-12 caseless fifty-shot automatic rifle with nightscope and silencer. Ryan, like Finn, wore a blade at his belt. But instead of a cleaver he carried a long steel panga, which was as broad as a machete. From the look of it, a strong man could behead an ox in a single stroke.

"You stare any harder at me, son, and you're going t'bore a hole through me." The words were said lightly, but Jak got the hint.

"Sorry, Ryan. Was looking at your handblaster."

The one-eyed man took the pistol out of his belt and lobbed it across the small room. Jak caught it easily in his right hand and studied it.

"Haven't seen one like this," he said. "SIG-Sauer, is it?"

Ryan glanced across at J.B. "You're the Armorer. You tell him all 'bout it."

In a flat, passionless voice, J.B. rattled off all the relevant details of the handgun.

"Model P-226. Nine mil. Fifteen rounds, push-button mag release. Barrel length 4.41 inches. Overall length 7.72 inches."

"Weight?" Jak asked.

"I'm coming to that, son. Keep your carriage behind the horse."

"Sorry."

"Weighs in at precisely 25.52 ounces. SIG-Sauer, like you said. Second half of the name's for J. P. Sauer and Son of Eckernförde. SIG is for Schweizerische Industrie-Gesellschaft. Anything else you want to know 'bout the blaster?"

Finnegan gave a great bellowing laugh. "You mean there's fucking more?"

Jak joined in the general laughter, feeling his strength flowing back now that he was standing up and his brains were settling back into his skull.

"How come it's so cold?" he asked, shivering in his tattered canvas-and-leather coat and breeches, dyed brown, gray and green for camouflage. He felt the weight of his trusty .357 Magnum, satin finish with the six-inch barrel, strapped to his thigh in its holster.

"Yeah, it is kind of cold," Ryan agreed, standing up with the easy grace of a large cat.

"Mebbe find some warm clothes in the redoubt," Krysty suggested, uncoiling at his side and rubbing her hands together.

"Bracing is the word I would use. So much more healthy than the awful humidity of the swamps, whatever they were called."

"Atchafalaya," J.B. said, reminding Doc Tanner where they'd been.

"God bless you," the old man replied. "Gesundheit is what we used to say."

The Armorer stared at him, blank-faced.

"Where are we now?" the boy asked, stretching himself and pushing his mane of white hair away from his eyes.

"We're here," Ryan Cawdor replied.

"We always here," Lori said, looking around at the others to make sure they realized she was joking.

"Yeah," Finn grunted. "Guess she's 'bout fucking right. We're always here."

Most of the other gateways Ryan had passed through had been clean and orderly. Once everyone was on their feet, blasters cocked and ready, he reached out and opened the door.

For several seconds nobody moved or spoke. Then Ryan said, very quietly, "Fireblast!"

It looked bad.

# Chapter Two

THE ROOM BEYOND THE DOOR was around five paces in length by three paces wide. The walls were painted a muted cream, faded with age. Virtually all the other gateways Ryan and his companions had been through had been thoroughly cleaned by the Americans nearly a hundred years ago. Kept immaculate and sealed, they had been so well hidden that nearly all trace of their presence had been long forgotten, all records lost.

But this one looked as if it had been vacated only thirty seconds ago. That was the first reaction from Ryan and the others.

Ryan's finger tightened instinctively on the trigger of the G-12, ready to spray the room with a veil of instant death. He could feel the tension all around him as everyone waited. He sniffed at the air.

"Doesn't smell right. Krysty?"

The girl was at his elbow, so close that her arm brushed against his. She shook her head slowly. "No. Can't hear anything. The air's stale. By Gaia, but it's years stale in here!"

There was a newspaper open on the plastic-topped table, with an aluminum can that once contained Coke resting on top of it. A plastic plate held the remnants of a meal, a maroon plastic knife and fork placed casually beside it, as if the eater had been interrupted moments before.

Several notices were pinned to a board near the far door, which, as Ryan saw instantly, was locked. A pack of chewing gum lay on the floor by one of the table legs. The room was totally, utterly still and silent.

"Looks like the Parody Club at five in the morning," Doc Tanner said, his memory leading him down some arcane corridor of his mind.

A large sign was screwed to the wall above the entrance to the gateway. Its message was the same as that of other redoubts: Entry Absolutely Forbidden to All but B12 Cleared Personnel. Mat-trans.

"All right, people, take care. Just a mebbe that something's boobied here."

J. B. Dix sucked at a hollow back tooth. "Don't see it, Ryan. No wires. No batteries. Nothing big enough to hide a gren. That's 'part from the cupboard there."

Against the wall next to the heavy vanadium steel door was a green metal cabinet.

"I'll look," Jak said, sliding past Ryan, eager to prove himself.

"Easy, Whitey," Finnegan rasped.

The boy moved slowly across the room. When he was about halfway to the cupboard, Ryan called out urgently for him to stop.

"Why?"

"Look at the floor."

None of them had noticed the dust. Jak's feet had left deep impressions in the velvet-soft layer, nearly a half-inch thick.

"Sloppy fucking housekeepers they got here," Finnegan muttered.

"Has to be untouched for years. Maybe decades," Ryan said. "Look at the table. It's everywhere."

The young albino flicked a finger at the door of the cabinet, as if he feared an electric shock. His fingers made the faintest pinging sound as it brushed the metal. He hesitated only a second, then grasped the handle and swung the door open.

It was full of paper.

There were six shelves on the left and five on the right, each filled with neat stacks of paper in different colors and sizes, along with folders and envelopes in cream and white and light brown.

All blank.

Jak pulled sheets off here and there, holding them up to show the others the smooth, untouched blankness. "Must be a store," he said. "Nothing used."

It was a disappointment to Ryan. As he moved through the Deathlands, he was always hoping to come across more information about the times before the great fighting. He'd seen books, films, vids, tapes, papers...but all of that gave only a glimpse through a tiny crack in time. He dreamed sometimes of finding some key to the past, some way of learning what madness had raced through the planet nearly a century back. Like a blinding virus, it had been an insanity that had torn apart the world, wrecking it beyond any hope of redemption. Too much had been lost for it ever to be put back together as it had been. The population had been decimated once and then again and again. Most science had been lost forever, and that, Ryan believed, was no bad thing. From what little he'd learned about the years before 2001, it seemed that the scientists should carry almost as heavy a burden of responsibility for Deathlands as the rabid politicians.

Now the best that he could hope for was that he and his friends would be like a single wave, beating upon a polluted shore, washing over it and withdrawing, leaving the shingled beach a little cleaner.

"Look at this newspaper," Krysty said, picking it up carefully. "It's like dried ashes." She laid it down again on the table, moving the drink can out of the way.

Ryan leaned over to read the faint newsprint. It was called the *Ginnsburg Falls Courier*, and was apparently registered at Ginnsburg Falls, Oregon. It was dated January 19, 2001.

"Day before Armageddon," Krysty said.

"What is it?" Lori asked.

"Newspaper from the last day of the old world," replied Krysty.

"Where's Oregon?" Ryan asked J.B. "Up north and west, isn't it?"

"Yeah. Lay 'tween California and Washington. Lot of mountains. Not much else."

"Never got there with the Trader."

"Nor me."

The two men had known each other for nearly ten years. Both of them had joined the wagon trains run by the man called the Trader. Ryan had become the right-hand man on the wags and J.B. had been Armorer. They'd roamed most of the central part of Deathlands, buying cheap and selling expensive. It was a profession with a high risk factor. Times you met folks wanted to pay less than your price. Times you even met folks didn't want to pay at all. That was why the ordinary trucks were guarded by war wags. That was why you saw a heap of dying when you rode with the Trader.

"What's it say?" Ryan asked.

Krysty stooped lower, her shadow almost obscuring the delicate newspaper. As she moved it with one hand, parts of the edge flaked away, turning instantly into dust. "Don't breathe on it, or it's going to fall apart," she said.

Everyone moved back a little, except Doc Tanner, who seemed almost hypnotized by the crumbling artifact from before the Big Chill. "What was concerning the good people of Ginnsburg Falls on the very day before most of them went grinning to meet their Maker?" he asked. "Or was this just for the mindless robots who ran these redoubts?"

"Front page says in big letters, 'Zoning Row Splits Council.' Doesn't say anything about there going to be a war or anything like that," Krysty told them.

"It must," Ryan said.

"No. Next story's about women picketing a porn-vid store on Red Maple Street."

Ryan shook his head and read more items from the front page. "'Councilman Hewer Promises Ped Xing Review.' And what's this? 'Shock Scam Threatens Thrift Store.' There's not a word. It can't be right. Doc? You know most 'bout the past. It can't be from the day before it started."

"Before the missiles darkened the skies and night eternal fell upon this land of the free?" the old man muttered. "Oh, yes. If one saw a bigger paper...the Los Angeles sheets, or the *Times* or the *Post*, they would have carried it for months. Building international tension. Threats and promises. Folks up here in rural Oregon wouldn't have been that worried. There'd been the talk before. There was Cuba. Sweet Jesus, but that was... Oh, such a yearning for small-town trivia that stirs my bosom, my dear friends."

"I can read," interrupted Jak. "This here is 'bout librarian...to do with books. Says got ban some foreign writers. Can't make out names."

Doc Tanner peered at where the young boy was pointing. "Tolstoy. Chekhov. Anton Pavlovich Chekhov. Dostoyevski. Fyodor Mikhailovich. Russian writers. She was banning them, was she? A short step from burning them." He gave a cackling laugh, muted in the small, low-ceilinged room. "Too late, she was. Oh, yes, I guess I was wrong. It had reached Ginnsburg Falls, after all."

Finnegan had been looking through the notices pinned to the board. The first one he touched disintegrated in a shower of fine dust, mingling with the pale gray powder that covered everything.

"Just rosters. Names and times for duties. Lotsa letters and numbers. Nothing fucking means a thing now. Lists watch times right through to the end of the month."

"No warnings? No clue that the world was going t'fall out of their bottoms?" the chubby gunman said, grinning.

"There," Lori said, pointing to a piece of paper that lay on the floor under the table. Even through the layer of dirt, the red writing, faded to a dull pink, was visible.

"Evac Nine Hundred," Finn read. "What the fuck's that mean?"

Ryan answered him. "Evacuate at nine in the morning. Story is that the last whistle got blown around noon that day. Where would they have gone?"

Nobody replied. Not one of the other redoubts had shown signs of life like this. For some reason that nobody would ever know, this mountain hideaway in Oregon had been left longer than most.

Most of the gateways had a small anteroom like this one. If this one was like the others then the master control room would be beyond the locked door, with its banks of electrical equipment, powered by either a solar or nuke generator, still ticking more than four generations after the last human had been there.

Ryan opened the door, flattening himself against the wall, ready for trouble. Trader used to say that if you kept ready for trouble, then it would never happen. Relax for a moment and you might get to be dead.

The air tasted less flat. Ryan exhaled, watching his breath as it misted in front of him. His guess was that the temperature throughout the complex must be close to freezing. Maybe well below in parts. The computers and control equipment wouldn't function once it dropped below zero.

Apart from a few sheets of paper and a pen, which had evidently been dropped on the floor during the evacuation, everything looked normal. He glanced across at Krysty, raising an eyebrow. "Empty, you guess?"

"Yeah. Think I can hear... No, it's gone. If it was there at all."

A piece of paper crinkled next to his boot, and Ryan stooped to peer at it. It was torn, showing only the words, "Host... Twin..."

It looked as if it had been some kind of food tab.

There was the background whirring and humming of the electrics. One of the overhead lights had shorted out, and it was spitting erratically, tiny sparks showering from the broken fitting. Wheels moved and lights of different color blinked.

Ryan entered the room, feeling the soft dust stirring under his feet. He wondered where so much dust had come from. None of the other gateways had had so much. The others followed. There was the familiar double armored door on the far side, which would probably open onto a large, wide corridor. If it was like the other redoubts...

J. B. Dix looked back at the mat-trans chamber. "Sure is a shame we can't control that bastard," he said musingly. "Be good to try and get back."

"Back?" Ryan echoed. "Back where?"

"To War Wag One. Back to Cohn an' Hovak. O'Mara, Lint, Hooley, Loz, Cathy... Where are they now? Dead or living?"

Ryan shook his head. "Actually, I guess only a few weeks have passed since we left 'em. But they could be anywhere now."

"We can't go back," Doc said. "I told you. The controls are random if you don't know the codes. We could try making jumps for years and never find the right gateway. And we'd probably hit on one that's damaged, and I swear I don't know what that would mean."

"If we got to a chamber that no longer existed, you figure we wouldn't exist either, Doc?" Krysty asked.

The old man shrugged his narrow shoulders.

"Somebody must know how they work." Finnegan muttered. "Just gotta keep asking, I guess."

The green lever on the outer portal was depressed to the closed position. Ryan moved across, eyeing the banks of disks and chattering contacts. There was a vaguely unpleasant, sticky smear on one of the consoles, as though some piece of fruit had been left there at the time of the evacuation and had rotted silently away into nothingness.

"They leave books of rules if in hurry, Doc?" Lori asked.

"I fear not, my dearest child," the old man replied. "I rather believe that there is no way anyone will ever be able to use the gateways as they were intended. And that may be no bad thing."

"What's this? Like a radio? Mike and speaker. Couldn't we try to raise War Wag One?"

"It's about a thousand miles out of range, Finn," the Armorer said.

Finnegan poked at a row of buttons and switches, one of which brought a startling howl of feedback that made everyone jump. Ryan was about to yell at Finn to leave it alone when the howling stopped, replaced by a faint crackling. And in among the tumbling static, it sounded almost as if there were words. Finnegan shouted in delight.

"Fucking sheep shit on a stick! You hear that? There's someone out there."

"Tune it in, if you can, Finn," Ryan called out, joining the others around the radio. "That dial there. Turn it real slow and easy."

The crackling came and went as though a directional antenna was turning. The words were sporadic and indistinct. There was an eerie quality to it that made the short hairs rise at the back of Ryan Cawdor's neck. He half turned and saw that Krysty's beautiful angular face was blanked with doubt.

"Something's not right, lover," she whispered to him.

He could feel it. He didn't have her power of seeing but there had been times that his life had been saved by some sort of second sight. A feeling for danger. A kind of prescience.

And he felt it now.

"...signal...help...tuned...to...willing...help...frequency...follow...north...fall..."

"Doesn't make sense," Jak Lauren spat. "Load garbage. Waste time."

Suddenly Finn's seeking fingers found precisely the right spot on the radio dial. The voice was clear, the message ungarbled.

"Anyone receiving this message who requires any assistance in any matter of science or the study of past technical developments will be aided. Bring all your information and follow this signal where you will be given help. Stay tuned to this frequency." It began to fade. "North of Ginnsburg Falls where...receiving...matter of..."

It was gone, though Finnegan frantically kept twisting the dial. The banshee howl of the static faded away, and the set was silent.

"Equipment malfunction," J. B. Dix said. "Probably not used in a hundred years. Burned out."

"But the message. North of Ginnsburg Falls. Where that paper came from. We follow it and mebbe pick it up again. Fuck it!" He banged his hand against the table, making the lights flicker. "Just another couple of minutes. We could of talked back to 'em."

"Loop-tape, Finn," Ryan said quietly. "Could have been set on automatic fifty years back. Mebbe even programmed with its own generator before the Big Wars."

"They offered scientific help," the Armorer said, rubbing a finger across his stubbled chin. "They might know how the gateways work. Couldn't they, Doc?"

"It's a possibility, Mr. Dix. I would concede that to you. But..."

His voice trailed away like the radio broadcast.

Ryan was tempted to hope. Was there someone who still had the skill and knowledge to operate the gateways properly? Or was it a voice from the tomb?

He couldn't even decide which he'd prefer—to find some place of long-dead science, or to find that scientists were still practicing their murderous skills.

THE LEVER THAT OPENED the main doors into the gateway complex was stiff. At first Ryan couldn't get it to move at all, then he threw all his strength against it and it grated upward. There was the sound of hissing hydraulics and gears meshing, somewhere buried deep within the reinforced walls.

As the doors began to move, Ryan turned to give the usual reminder to his group about taking all possible care. He was aware of the widening gap out of the corner of his eye with someone standing in the narrow corridor beyond.

Someone standing in . . .

Someone . . .

He swung around, his H&K swinging with him. A small man, in furs, face swarthy. Blaster of some sort at his hip, muzzle like the mouth of a bell. Too slow, too late.

Ryan started to say, "Fuck," which wouldn't have meant much in the pantheon of famous last words.

The boom of a gun, deafening him.

A scream, shrill and terrified.

And a heavy blow that spun him around so that he banged the side of his head against the wall.

Ryan was oddly grateful to reach and embrace the swimming blackness.

# Chapter Three

"TURN, TURN to the rain and the wind."

The mournful dirge was the first thing that Ryan Cawdor heard as he fought his way up out of the slimy-walled pit of unconsciousness.

He raised a cautious hand, touching the side of his head, finding a great bruise that felt soggy to his probing fingers. He gasped, opened his eye and looked around.

He was back in the room with the chattering electronic consoles. Ryan noticed that the heavy door was shut again.

"Better, lover?" Krysty asked. She was kneeling at his side.

"Yeah. Who hit me?"

"There was a mutie outside. You saw him?"

"Little bastard. In furs? Got a gun with a bell muzzle on it, bigger'n Finn's belly?"

"Yeah. Blunderbuss. Old homemade piece. If'n he'd squeezed off on it, he'd have blown you from here to tomorrow. But he didn't."

"I heard—"

"Me," Lori said proudly, but with a faint note of doubt.

"You shot him?"

Krysty grinned. "She's a tad worried because she realized afterward that her bullet must have missed you by about this much." She held her finger and thumb an inch apart.

"That's far enough, Lori. Thanks."

"It was more than that," she protested. "More like this." Her finger and thumb were at least two inches apart.

"But who in the long chill laid me out?"

"Sorry, Ryan. Had no choice."

"Jak?"

"Yeah."

"How?" Ryan found it hard to believe that the skinny little kid had sent him flying so easily.

"Kicked you."

Ryan closed his eye, shaking his head in disbelief. Krysty was grinning at him when he blinked up again. "It's true, lover. Damnedest thing ever. Hair flying like snow in a northern blizzard. Pushed off the side of the door with his hands, kicked you round 'bout shoulder high. Both feet. Bounced you out of the mutie's firing line. Your head was the first thing to hit the floor."

"Lucky it wasn't nothing fucking important," Finnegan cackled. "That was something, Ryan. Fiery little demon, ain't he?"

Ryan stood up, shaking his head to try to clear the muzziness. "Thanks, Jak. And you, Lori. There any more of those muties out yonder?"

"After Lori sent that one to go buy the farm, we checked a ways up the corridor," J.B. answered. "To the left's a dead end. Blank wall. No more doors. Other way's open, but the ceiling's real bad. Lot of places where it's collapsed."

"There's a big fall less than a hundred yards along that way," Krysty added. "Narrow gap's all. We figured best to come back in here with you sleeping so tight."

"Best we go look," Ryan said.

"Follow up that radio message," J.B. said, his voice holding just a hint of a question.

"Yeah. Why not?"

THIS TIME RYAN was a whole lot more careful. He kept flat as the lever was thrown, then moved out quickly, backed by Finn. The others came out only after the signal was given that the corridor was clear.

"See that?" Krysty said, pointing at the outside of the glittering metal door. It was deeply scratched and gouged, with scorch marks in places. "Someone tried real hard to get in there."

"Muties like him?" Ryan suggested, pointing with the barrel of the G-12 at the corpse of the little man. Lori had shot him with either a lot of luck or impressive skill. Bearing in mind how close the bullet had come to taking him through the back of the neck, Ryan chose not to think too long on which it had been.

The dead man was only about five feet in height and looked about thirty years old. His face was flat, with a coppery cast to the skin. The lips were narrow, peeled back to reveal long, curved teeth. The nails on the small hands were long and twisted, like horn. The man wore a coat of animal skins and furs, probably rodent. The gun had a hand-carved stock, while the barrel was iron, with the extra-large mouth riveted on. It was based on a primitive flintlock design.

"Rough old blaster," Finn said.

"Rip the belly out of even you," Ryan replied, kicking it aside with his foot.

The blood was drying, black around the neat hole just above the man's right eye. It had leaked over his face, filling the gaping mouth with a pool of crimson. A lot more blood had oozed from the exit wound at the back of the skull.

There was an odd weapon hooked to the belt of the dead mutie. It consisted of several narrow lengths of hollow wood, each about twelve inches long, ending in a sharp,

barbed tip of something like ivory. A rawhide cord ran
through the middle of the sections. J.B. bent over it.

"Interesting."

"What is it, Mr. Dix? I confess myself somewhat puzzled by it."

"Spear."

Doc Tanner smiled doubtfully. "You are teasing me, are
you not?"

"No."

"A spear only a foot in length? Perhaps for hunting the
inhabitants of the land of Lilliput."

"Where the fuck's that, Doc?" Finn asked. But his
question was ignored.

The Armorer unhooked the strange weapon from the
belt of the corpse. He held the cord and flicked it hard with
his wrist. Miraculously the sections slotted into one another, producing a lethal, six-foot-long spear.

"Gimme," Jak said, holding out a hand. He took the
spear, let it fall into its component sections, then whipped
it out to full length. Grinning delightedly, he said, "Be
good. I can keep it, Ryan?"

"Sure. Why not? Come on, let's go."

THE AVALANCHE COULD HAVE happened anytime. Maybe
only a month ago, maybe when the bombs had rained
down on the free land of America. Concrete, stones and
earth had slipped, blocking the corridor and leaving only
a small gap barely three feet high at its apex.

"Anything?" Ryan asked Krysty.

"No. Not close. But I can hear something, quite a long
way off. Maybe an engine. Maybe feet moving. Can't tell.
Blurred by the deeps here."

"I'll go look," Jak volunteered. "I'm smallest here for
it."

The albino scampered lightly up the earthslide on hands and knees, pausing a moment and staring into the hole.

"Does it go through?" Ryan shouted.

"Yeah. It's around ten feet. Easy. You coming?"

Finnegan had the most difficulty, wriggling along on his stomach, pushing his gun ahead of him, panting, red-faced, sweating despite the chill, but eventually he made it.

When Ryan himself was halfway through, bringing up the rear of the group, he was suddenly oppressed by the thought of how many trillions of tons of dirt hung above him. It had fallen before. One day it might fall again.

The corridor resumed on the far side of the dirt tunnel. It stretched out, ill-lit, curving gently to the right. The air tasted noticeably fresher, and it was much colder.

"Fucking freezing, Ryan. Got to get some warmer gear. Left most of mine along the way."

Finn was right. If it was as bitter as this deep down in the redoubt, it didn't much bear thinking on what it would be like if they got out into the open.

"If they evacuated in a rush, there could be some clothes around."

"If they haven't got to 'em first," J.B. said, pointing with his mini-Uzi at the many footprints that patterned the dusty floor.

"Must be hundreds of 'em," Finnegan said, bending to study the marks. "Most got skin boots on, like the chilled mutie back there."

"But they didn't get in the gateway," Ryan said. "Controls aren't hard. Just the number code on the panel. Figures they can't read. That being so, there may be other parts of the redoubt they haven't penetrated. We stay here, we freeze. We go back to the gateway and move on, then we never follow up that radio beam."

"Then it's onward and upward, my dear Ryan," Doc Tanner said, grinning and showing his oddly perfect teeth. "Let us carry our banner with its strange device and cry 'Excalibur!' to all we meet."

There were times when Ryan thought the old man would never get his full set of brains back.

EVERYONE WAS ON BATTLE ALERT.

J.B. took point, with Finn three paces behind him on the other side of the corridor. Doc and Lori walked together, followed by Jak. Krysty came sixth, and Ryan covered the rear, twenty paces behind her.

J.B. signaled for everyone to halt, then dropped to one knee, squinting along the barrel of the mini-Uzi. "Thought I saw somebody," he whispered. "Gone."

And once Ryan himself paused at a place where the corridor bent more sharply. He went around the curve, hesitated then suddenly retreated. Just at the edge of his vision, about a hundred paces away, two or three of the diminutive muties had seen him and had scampered out of sight.

They passed several rooms, most with open doors. Without exception, the rooms had been stripped completely bare. Some had carried signs over them, stenciled on wood, then affixed to the concrete. Though these were all gone, a few ghostly impressions of the lettering remained, in the same way that a picture on a wall will leave a pattern when taken down.

Orthodontal Surgery, one said.

Comsec R & R, another, more mysterious one said.

TR Manual 31C, a third said.

One door was much larger than the others, wide enough to get a war wag through it. It was simply headed Stores Subsec 9M.

"Stores sounds promising," J.B. said, beckoning to the others. "Worth a try?"

"How do we get in? Over, under or around?"

"Or *through*, Ryan?" the Armorer asked. "Looks like the muties have tried." There were ample dents and scratches in the dull matt-green metal, but no sign that the door had been opened in the past hundred years. "Control panel's not harmed."

Oddly, that was true. There was a palm-print indent in the control panel to the right of the door. A small digital display glowed faintly in the half-light.

"Any guesses?" Ryan asked.

"Probably not a sec lock system," Doc Tanner said. "No need deep inside the redoubt. Clean the dust off the panel and look at which ones are worn. Bound to show."

Ryan used his sleeve to wipe the display clear of gray dust. His breath fogged the transparent plastic, and he smeared that away. By squinting at an angle he could see that the old man was right. The letter *K* was marked, and so was the number 7. He pressed them, but nothing happened.

"Try the other way round. Seven and then the letter," Krysty suggested.

"Yeah," Ryan said. "Just going to."

There was the whirring of a motor, straining and grinding, then the door rolled about five feet upward and grated to a halt.

"Something burn," Lori said. A few wisps of smoke drifted out of the panel. For a moment, a tiny flame glowed red-gold, like the gleam in the eye of a hunting beast.

Finally the dreadful sound of mangling metal ceased, and the fire disappeared. Ryan looked at the heavy door, considering his next course of action. If there were sealed stores behind it, then it might be worth the gamble of ducking under. He touched the frozen metal; it was vibrating slightly, as if a motor were still turning over somewhere within it.

"It's going to fall," Jak said, spitting on the corridor floor. "If'n we go, best go now."

"Go," Ryan ordered.

A glimpse of the muties gathering behind them had helped him decide. There might be dozens more around the next curve of the main passage, and they'd be caught like nuts in the jaws of the crusher. They ducked under the trembling sec door, Doc Tanner having to stoop considerably to avoid knocking off his stovepipe hat.

They found themselves in a narrow corridor with a high ceiling. The lighting was good, and there was little dust. Ryan wasn't sure whether he imagined it, but it didn't seem quite so bone-chillingly cold.

Finn didn't agree. "Fuck a mutie rattler, Ryan! I'm colder than a fucking well-digger's ass."

"Then lets go see what we can find. J.B.?"

"Yeah?"

"Any way of fixing that door so it comes down? I'd feel safer with that locked at m'back."

J.B. stepped toward the ponderous steel shutter. Then he stopped, hearing what they all heard—a loud scraping noise, then the sonorous pinging of large cables snapping. Like the others, he moved away from the door. It fell a couple of inches, jerkily, then suddenly dropped to the floor with a massive crunch, making the stone walls and floor resound. Dust pattered from the ceiling, showering them all.

"Take the Lord Almighty to open up that sucker now," Finnegan said. "You wanted safe, Ryan. You got fucking safe."

IT WAS DISAPPOINTING.

Not so bad as some of the redoubts that Ryan and J.B. had found when they'd ridden with the Trader. Some of those had been stripped cleaner than charity, with nothing left inside but bare walls. At least the evacuation of this Oregon redoubt had left a little behind.

But it was disappointingly little.

There were no weapons at all, with those sections completely cleared. No blasters, no grens, no missiles. Ryan's group had better luck in the area of the redoubt where food and drink had been stored.

There were sealed containers of Colorado Springfresh Water. Finn peeled the ring off the top of one of the clearplas containers, and sipped cautiously.

"Not bad, folks. Come on, you guys, belly up to the bar and try some."

Ryan was suddenly conscious of the dryness in his throat and the dust that seemed to layer his lungs. He lifted one of the bottles from the opened case, tasting its contents, amazed that it was still good and fresh after so many years.

"Food here," Jak called out.

When the occupants of the redoubt had evacuated, they'd left all open cases and packages behind. There were some self-heats. Beans with bacon, beans with pork. Rice and stew, which looked good from the picture of a steaming banquet on the outside of the double-layer tin. Lori heated a can, waiting the approved three minutes, opened it and put it down on the floor.

"Ugh. Looks like shit," she said, wrinkling her nose in disgust.

"Probably tastes like it, too," Ryan said, grinning.

"What the fuck's this?"

"Tinned asparagus, Finn. Got lotsa iron."

"Sure, J.B., sure. Still looks like a can o' pickled muties' cocks."

The side room where the cases of food were stored began to smell good, with the steam from the self-heats misting the cold air. Everyone ate their fill, regardless of the odd gastronomical mix.

Ryan stuck to beans with diced pork, devouring three large cans before he felt satisfied. Krysty ate two self-heats of turkey, mixing it with cabbage. Finn managed nearly five of the chili beef, mixing in chicken-fried steak with rice. Jak would touch only the cans of fruit, sucking out the sweet syrup, licking his pale lips eagerly. Lori nibbled daintily at some mashed lobster with clam chowder, blowing on the bubbling mix to cool it enough to eat.

"Damned load of convenience clappertrap!" Doc Tanner moaned. "Time was we'd have found real food, not this syntho garbage. Art of cooking died in the United States around 1950. After that it was all damned packs and damned cans and add water and mix well and pop in the damned oven for three damned minutes at regulo three and... Oh, the hell with it all! I just hope that damned Sara Lee and her sisterhood are spinning perpetually in their urns!"

Doc ate only a tin and a half of long, obscenely pink frankfurter sausages, their skins glistening moistly in the half-light of the food storage chambers. But even he couldn't resist a large flat tin. When peeled open, after the obligatory wait, it revealed row upon row of small, circular blueberry muffins, deliciously light and mouth-watering. Everyone tried them.

Jak burped, grinning widely and holding his stomach. "Food good," he said. "Now feel like sleeping. What do we do, Ryan?"

"Sleep's a fine idea, Jak," Ryan agreed, glancing down at his chron. "I make it around late afternoon. Mebbe dusk out. Best we wait here. Move on in the morning. You agree?" Nobody spoke. "Well, you don't disagree. Best scout out the rest of this section, J.B., then set a patrol. If it's secure, we can risk a single guard."

"There's a pile of packing stuff. Plas sheets. Make good bedding," Finn said, pointing across the large room.

Ryan realized how tired he felt. The bang on the side of his head still throbbed, and the idea of lying down and closing his eye was exquisite. But sleep would have to wait.

Although their location in the stores seemed secure, and the door that had slammed down behind them was immovable, Ryan and J.B. scouted while the others got the bedding ready. There were several smaller storage chambers on either side of the central block, but there wasn't time to examine them closely. At a quick glance, it looked as if most of them were stripped bare, doors swung open. But a couple near the end were still closed. J.B. pressed his eyes to the ob-slit and whistled.

"This one was overlooked during evac, Ryan. Dozens of packing cases, all sealed tight."

"Check 'em tomorrow," Ryan said. "How 'bout that big end door?"

They approached it, noting its similarity to the entrance behind them. It was closed, with a control box dangling from an overhead cable gantry. Unlike the other door, this one looked as if it had only two modes. Red and green. Up and down.

"Try it?" J.B. asked.

Ryan took the control in his right hand, feeling the biting cold of the metal. He glanced at the Armorer, who stood braced, the mini-Uzi at his hip. "Ready?"

"Sure."

The green button was convex, fitting the ball of his thumb. He pressed it, immediately shifting his thumb to the red button, in case of danger. There was the faint hiss of hydraulics, and the door began to inch upward, a strip of light appearing under it.

"Hold it," J.B. said, ducking low to peek beneath it. "Nothin' there. I can see both sides. Concrete corridor that bends left. Must join up where the other one was curving right."

"Now? Go look or close it up?"

"Safe enough to close it. If it's shut after a hundred years, it'll stay another night for us."

Ryan pressed the red button, and like a massive guillotine blade of armored steel, the door paused a moment then began to descend again, landing with a barely perceptible thud.

"If this one failed, we'd have us some serious problems," J.B. said. "Take some high-ex to shift it. Probably bring the whole roof down if'n we tried."

It was a bleak thought to take to sleep.

# Chapter Four

HE AWOKE INSTANTLY, his body tense, then relaxed when he realized what had woken him. Krysty's fingers crept across his flat stomach, soft as the caress of a butterfly's wing as they reached the inside of his right thigh, then touched his penis, rousing him.

"Bitch nympho gaudy slut," he whispered, drawing his breath in sharply as her fingers closed and squeezed tightly, making him gasp.

"Not even as a joke, lover," she warned him, "or you'll be picking *this* up from the other side of the room." She tugged at his erection to heighten the warning, succeeding mainly in rousing him further.

Ryan reached across and laid the palm of his hand across her breasts, bringing his index finger and thumb together on the left nipple, feeling it immediately harden like a tiny, responsive animal. Krysty sighed with pleasure at the touch.

"Nice, lover. Keep the slow hand for a while, will you?"

"Sure. But if you're going t'pull my cock off, what would you find for pleasing?"

"From the satisfied look on Lori's face some mornings, I might ask old Doc Tanner for some sloppy seconds."

"He's fucking antique," Ryan protested, grinning in the semidarkness of the redoubt stores.

"Nothing wrong with some antique fucking, lover," she responded. "No substitute for experience, or hadn't you heard?"

"I heard, I heard."

As they busied themselves with the sexual mysteries of each other's body, Ryan and Krysty fell silent.

When she was ready for him, he lifted his hips so that she could guide him into her body. He gasped at the sensation as he slid deep into her waiting warmth, her arms locking around his neck, ankles pulling in the small of his back to deepen the lovemaking. She kissed him, with repeated, gentle brushes of her lips all around his neck and face. He lowered his face to hers, mouth open, tongue flicking against her teeth. Ryan could feel the delicate movements of her long, brilliant red hair, caressing his shoulders as he thrust into her.

The faster he moved, the faster and more urgently she rose to meet him, hips leaving the soft warm plastic of their bedding at each stroke.

"Now…now…now, now, now," she moaned, and he closed his eye, mouth open in a rictus of passion, driving in so hard that the girl cried out in shock at the way he filled her. He could feel the fluttering of her stomach muscles as her own climax rushed on her, and his body jerked and bucked with his own release.

THE LIGHTS IN THE REDOUBT were day-sensor controlled. At about five, according to Ryan's luminous chron, they brightened, flooding the pallid stone walls and sharpening the ruled shadows.

Ryan rolled away from Krysty, wincing at the dried stickiness that joined them from their lovemaking. The light and the movement woke her, and she eased away from him, shading here eyes with her hand.

"Time to be up an' doing, lover," she whispered, looking around.

"Yeah. Go look for these guys who sent the radio message."

"You think it's for real? Could be a trap."

He rose, pulled his pants on over his boots, then checked his weapons as if by instinct. "Could be a trap, Krysty, sure. But if there was someone around who knew how to work the gateways..."

"You want to go home," she said quietly, keeping her voice down so that the others, a few yards away in different side rooms, wouldn't hear.

"Home? Where...?"

She stood up and buckled her belt, smiling at him. "Don't try and shit me, lover. You know where home is to you."

"Front Royal ville, up in the Shens? Yeah. I guess home is always the place where you were born and raised."

"You said you didn't care."

"Care about home? I was wrong. Been thinking 'bout it for a few days."

Krysty stamped her feet into her boots, making the stone floor ring. "That's better. Got cramp in my toes. Front Royal? You could go back and talk to your dear brother and his wife."

Ryan's left hand lifted, seemingly of its own accord. He touched the leather patch over his ruined eye, brushing down the scar that furrowed the skin of his cheek. "Yeah, lover. Talk to my brother about paying some debts 'tween us."

Finnegan came striding noisily up. He'd been on the last watch of the night. "Thought I heard some noise behind the door over there," he said, pointing to the broken entrance to the redoubt. "Then it fucked off and there wasn't a sound. But have you seen the room along by the other door?''

''Which one?''

''Got an ob-slit in the door and dozens of cases, all sealed tighter'n a cherry's love nest.''

''We saw them last night. Figured we'd take us a good look this morning, 'fore we leave here.''

Doc Tanner approached. ''What might they be, my dear Ryan?'' he asked. ''I trust they are not some new and fearsome chemical poisons or some disseminators of hideous death.''

''I'd settle for some small grens. Lost most of mine along the way,'' J.B. said.

''Knives,'' Jak said, licking his lips in eager anticipation. ''Long, thin knives with edges that'll slit clean through a sec man's spine.''

''Bloodthirsty little bastard, aren't you?'' Krysty said. ''I'd settle for some clean underwear and a flask of brandy.''

''How 'bout you, Lori?'' Ryan asked. ''What would you like to find in those locked packing cases?''

The girl blushed. She shuffled a few steps to one side, reaching out to grip Doc Tanner by the hand. ''Theophilus tells me all 'bout weddings in old days. I'd like there are weddings in the boxes.''

Once again the arched bunker filled with the steam and aromas of the self-heats being opened. Ryan and the others stuck to more or less the same selections they'd taken the previous evening. Jak tried different combinations, gobbling some thimbleberries and smoked cod, following that up with some bottled water and topping off the meal with curried pickles.

Then he found an empty side chamber and noisily vomited up the whole mess. The others waited for him. There was a long silence, and finally Finn called out, "Hey, you all right, Whitey?"

"Sure, Fats. Sure. Just looking through this to see if anything was worth eating second time around." He waited for the yelps of revulsion. "But guess I'll open a coupla fresh cans."

When they finished eating, they packed up, each taking a couple of tins and a bottle of water. Ryan, heels ringing on the stone, led onward through the complex of rooms. Doc came second, arm around Lori, who was shivering again with the cold. She'd made a sort of cloak out of the plastic packing, and it rustled around her shoulders. J.B. followed, talking to Krysty about the relative stopping power of round-noise versus sharp-nose ammunition. At the back, Finn was using his fingers to ladle a sticky caramel goo out of an unlabeled tin. Krysty had warned him that it was probably either glue or a laxative.

"Don't give a fuck, long as it tastes good," was his reply.

Doc was singing quietly, his resonant voice echoing off the vaulted roof. It was a song that Ryan had never heard before. It sounded very old and mystical, not unlike the man himself.

"Western wind, when wilt thou blow,
That small rain down can rain?
Christ! If my love were in my arms,
And I in my bed again."

When he stopped, the concrete cavern seemed a lot emptier.

IT WAS FINNEGAN who found the racks of clothes. The part of the vast redoubt where they walked held dozens of lateral chambers, most of them empty and stripped. This one had its door half shut, hiding one side. Finn pushed it open with the flat of his hand.

"Hey, come look here!" he shouted, stopping everyone in their tracks. "Fucking furs."

Dozens of furs in all shapes and sizes hung on black plastic racks, with color-coded tags to indicate size. Some of them had fallen to the dusty floor. Perhaps they had lain there ever since some desperate order had halted the departure of the redoubt's garrison.

Lori dived in, vanishing among the serried rows of long coats. Occasionally they could see an arm stretching up as she tried one on, or a muttered curse when one wasn't the right size. Ryan was happy with his own suede coat with the white fur trim, but all of the others helped themselves to a new cold-weather coat.

Finn and J.B. picked identical coats in dark gray leather, with heavy collars in silky black fur. Lori seemed satisfied with one that was a dazzling white, until Doc whispered something in her ear. Looking crestfallen, she returned to the racks, eventually emerging with a more muted, gray coat in neat fur. Doc again whispered something to her, and her face became radiant, blushing with delight.

Doc Tanner picked a strange coat. It looked as if it had been stitched together from a variety of different pelts—some brown, some black, some gray. But its seedy grandeur somehow lent him a strange dignity, and nobody even grinned at him.

Krysty chose a coat that dropped just to the knees. It was a fine fur that was so black it was almost deep blue, the sheen reflecting the strips of overhead lights. Ryan made sure that no one picked an unwieldy coat that was too long or bulky.

Jak Lauren took ages, disappearing at the back of the room, where they could hear his feverish scurrying. Racks were overturned, and metal hangers rattled on the floor. Eventually he reappeared, wearing exactly the same clothes as before, except that now he wore, under his ragged camouflage vest and pants, a bizarre waistcoat of fur, with ragged holes where sleeves had been.

"Had to cut fucker with knife," he said, panting with the efforts of his exertion. "Arms too long."

THEY WERE STANDING outside the locked door. J.B. could hardly contain his enthusiasm for opening it and finding what wonders lay inside the rows of packing cases. "It's got to be good. Something real special that they left till last. Mebbe some secret blasters they were working on. Scopes. Missile launchers. Laser sights. Portable rail guns with megajoule power sources. Grens. *New* kinds of grens. Handblasters with heat sensors. Got to be good. All in neat rows, greased and packed, ready to take out and use."

It was an unusually long speech for the normally taciturn Armorer. His sallow face was alight with eagerness, his battered fedora pushed back off his high forehead. He squinted through the armaglass slit in the steel.

"Got to be good. Must be fifty cases there. All look the same."

They stared at the door. Ryan noticed that someone had scratched in the concrete, just to the left of the hinges, "Remember Charlie and remember Baker." He'd seen graffiti like that before in redoubts. Generally it was either names or crudely sexual.

"Move back and I'll blow the lock," J.B. said, leveling his mini-Uzi.

"Someone's tried kicking it in," Krysty observed, pointing at chips in the surround to the door. "Maybe in the rush they had to leave it, 'cos they lost the keys."

"Could be," Ryan said. He could feel a tremor of excitement that he always felt in redoubts. To be where no man had been for a hundred years was inevitably thrilling. And with those rows of cases waiting to be opened . . . The garrison of a large redoubt could easily have run to several thousand personnel, male and female. That meant a lot of armaments.

"Shall I blow it?" J.B. asked.

Ryan glanced around. The only danger was from bullets ricocheting off the door, spitting anywhere in the maze of stone and metal. "Got any plas left?"

"Little. Safer to do it that way?"

"Yeah."

Jak watched, fascinated, as the slightly built Armorer fumbled at the lining of his jacket and peeled out a small strip of colorless plastic explosive. He removed a tiny primer, with built-in rudimentary timer, from the cuff of his pants. Pushing them together against the lock, he pressed the start button on the timer.

"Set on fifteen. Go."

They scurried to an antechamber for cover, kneeling, hands pressed tightly over ears. Ryan instructed Jak to keep his mouth open to minimize the effects of the detonation in a confined space. He and Krysty crunched together, eyes shut, making themselves as small as possible.

The sound of the explosion was surprisingly soft and muffled. They felt the shock wave try to lift them from the floor. Dust billowed everywhere, making them all cough and splutter.

"Open," J.B. shouted as they rushed to join him. The plas-ex had been used with great skill. The force of the explosion had been just sufficient to take out a section of the doorframe, ripping the lock apart. The door responded to a gentle push from the Armorer's hand.

The crates were all identical, about four feet square, with a series of cipher letters and numbers stenciled along each side. But no clues were evident as to what they might contain. Ryan looked around the sealed room, seeing that a rectangular notice board on the left-hand wall had a frayed magazine cutting pinned to it. It had no heading and no date.

The others gathered around the wooden chests, discussing what they might hold. The consensus of opinion was that it would be weapons. Finnegan waxed lyrical about what they'd look like, saying, "Rows of blasters, in nests of grease and oil, stacked one a'top the other."

Ryan read the short cutting aloud. "'Straps have to be strong. Seen some men pull so hard against them that they've broken their own wrist and ankle bones. The first shock throws them forward. Folks don't know, less'n they've seen it for themselves. The eyes come out so far you think they're going to burst from the sockets. Tongue protrudes and starts turning black, and a few wisps of smoke come from it. Times the current doesn't do the job first time, so it takes a couple more jolts. Couple more rides on Old Smoky is what I call it. Hairs up the nose smolder an' all, and the teeth crack with the power. Fillings drop right out. Makes me laugh fit to bust when I think of that part. Worst is the smell. Land o' Goshen, it's terrible. Stench of burning, scorched flesh. Pungent, someone once said. I put Vaseline up my nostrils so I can't catch it so bad. But it gets in your clothes. After a bad one, I have to take my coveralls out back of home and burn them. I claim that on the County, you understand. Course, they always piss and shit themselves. Every one. You get used to it. I counted back the other day an' I've fried me over five hundred in the last four years. Beats all, don't it?' ''

"What's that you're reading?" Krysty Wroth asked, turning from the others.

"Nothing," Ryan said, pulling the paper off the board and crumpling it in his hand, letting the dry shards join the dust on the floor.

"Come on, we'll open 'em up." J.B. was more enthused than Ryan had seen him in a long while. Last time he'd been so eager was when they'd found a pile of old gun magazines and manuals in a redoubt near Billings.

"Sure," Ryan said.

There was a crowbar leaning against the nearest case. The Armorer took it up and started to jimmy open the closest chest, tearing the nails out, splintering the white wood. Inside was a layer of greased foil, and J.B. pulled that away so they could see what was inside.

They opened five cases altogether, but they were all the same. Ryan couldn't stop laughing at the look on J.B.'s face. There they were, all in rows, all in a thin coat of grease to protect them through eternity and beyond.

Something like three hundred thousand black plastic zippers.

# Chapter Five

RYAN WHISTLED SOFTLY between his teeth, considering all the options, failing to find one that looked even remotely worth trying.

The right fork of the corridor had finished in a blank dead end only fifty yards or so from the sliding entrance to the stores. Retracing their steps, they rounded the first bend to the left and found themselves faced with a dark section of the passage completely blocked by a massive earthslide.

That seemed to limit which direction they could go. The section of the stores where they'd found the fur coats led only to the totally wrecked sec door; Ryan knew they didn't have enough explosives to shift it. There was no other way out, and they could go neither forward or back.

It didn't look good.

"Figure there's enough stuff to eat an' drink to keep us alive for a week. Mebbe ten to twelve days if we're real careful," J.B. said.

"If we get through the slip, we should be somewheres round the place where the corridor passes the broken door. Should loop around," Ryan said.

"That looks like it's about a mile wide," Finn grunted, spitting in the dust.

Jak suddenly dropped to his hands and knees, staring intently at the floor where Finnegan's saliva had landed.

The others looked at him, puzzled, until Ryan also noticed what the boy had spotted.

"Fireblast! Look. Footprints. Those muties have been along here. Means there's some way in or out."

"And the air's fresh," Lori exclaimed, clapping her hands in delight.

"Let me," Jak said, not waiting for a reply as he scampered up the shadowed pile of gray-orange dirt and picked his way through the tumbled heaps of concrete and twisted steel. His newly acquired sectioned spear rattled on the stones as he went. When he reached the top, it was hard to see him, but his snow-white hair flared like a magnesium beacon.

"Yeah. Like other. Narrow, but dark. Can't see through." His voice was muted and they watched him disappear.

"Jak!" Ryan shouted. "Come back. We'll all go if'n it's safe."

The boy reappeared, his red eyes seeming to glow like rubies. "Yeah. Be tight for some." He stared pointedly at Finnegan. "But we can do it. Goes up at an angle. Seems to be another tunnel going off a few yards up here."

Ryan looked at J.B., seeing from his expression that he was thinking the same thing. "That mutie..."

"Yeah, Ryan. Small bastard. Dirt on his clothes. Spear like that ... useful in a tunnel."

"You reckon they're up there?"

J.B. nodded. "Could be. Waiting for us."

"One way to find out."

The Armorer grinned, thin-lipped. "Fucking right, Ryan. Fucking right."

IT WAS THE BEGINNING of one of the worst experiences in Ryan Cawdor's entire life.

At their highest the tunnels didn't reach five feet, and in places the group found it necessary to wriggle on their bellies. Mostly the tunnels were dry and dusty. But some of them were wet, with slimy mud that got all over everyone, making it hard to get any purchase on the rough floors with fingers and toes.

Most of the way, the tunnels were totally dark. But occasionally the black gave way to a dull gray light, which would fade away again as the tunnel dipped or straightened.

By mutual agreement, Jak went first, his lithe, skinny body folding easily around the sharp bends and inclines. Lori followed, with Finn struggling along third. Doc Tanner came fourth, his stovepipe hat cradled in his arms as he crouched and ducked like a rheumatic stork. J.B. was fifth, his Tekna knife in his right hand. Krysty was next, and Ryan brought up the rear. As the tallest of the party, he found the tunnels most difficult. He also got everyone else's dirt and mud pushed back in his face.

The only sound was panting and scrabbling, with an occasional curse or groan of discomfort.

It was agreed that Jak would stop every four minutes and that everyone would remain silent and still while Krysty listened for any warning of the muties.

At the third stop, at a point where the tunnel widened to about eight feet, and three other tunnels opened off it, they discussed strategy. Jak was for going on, picking every tunnel that seemed to go upward, on the assumption that eventually they'd emerge into the open air. Lori had become terrified, face glistening with sweat, voice high and thin as she chattered to Doc, begging him to take her back.

"I fear that we are in the land of no return, my dearest dove," he said gently, patting her on the arm in the way that one would try to gentle a frightened foal. "It is ever onward and upward for us all."

"Don't like dark, Theo, lover," she said.

"Get her to keep her voice down, Doc," Ryan warned. "If there's muties down here, they'll just have to sit quiet and tight and pick us off. Must keep as quiet as we can."

"Watch out for boobies, Whitey," J.B. urged the albino. "Sharp sticks, trailing wires, a deadfall in the tunnel. Anything like that."

"How come you know so much 'bout tunnels?" the boy asked.

"Read a book once. Found it in a ruined house, somewheres round North Platte, up in 'braska. Remember it, Ryan?"

It rang a distant bell for Ryan. "Sure. Tunnels in the Viet wars. You loaned it to me."

"And you lost it, you son of a bitch."

"Yeah, I remember that, too."

J.B. turned back to whisper to Jak. "There were tunnels in the Viet fighting. Place called Cu Chi. Lotsa little men being chased by bigger men. Naked guy with a bamboo spear killing a soldier with a dozen blasters strung all over him."

"Guess blasters no use in tunnels, huh?"

J.B. sniffed, wiping the sweat from his forehead. Despite the intensely cold clamminess in the tunnels, all of them were perspiring.

"Read of one. Smith an' Wesson .44 Magnum. Six-shot, cylinder load. Weighed in around two pounds. Exposed hammer on it. Fired fifteen-pellet round, starred like a shotgun. But they cut out most of the noise and the flash."

"Sounds good t'me," Jak said, smiling. "Could do with one of them here, case we run into muties."

"Keep that spear handy, son," Ryan warned.

"He's right," Krysty added. "Got me a feeling that we'll have some company real soon."

They moved on.

At one point the tunnel dipped steeply and then came up almost vertically so that Finnegan got stuck and had to be pulled by Lori and pushed from behind by a panting Doc Tanner.

When he was free, he hissed back to Ryan that they ought to abandon their bulky cold-weather coats. "Be best, after a fucking tight spot like that. Can't do that again, Ryan."

Despite Finnegan's almost limitless courage, Ryan heard the thin note of frayed panic that haunted the fat man's voice. Being in this twining, bending maze of darkness was like living one's worst nightmares. The walls seemed to close in, and the clumps of dirt that fell constantly from the roof kept the chilling fear of a cave-in fresh in one's mind.

"Keep the coats as long as we can. When we get out, we'll need them, Finn."

"Sure, Ryan. *When* we get out. Or maybe it's *if* we fucking get out."

"We'll get out, Finn. Air's tasting sweeter, and the light's not so bad."

A hundred feet farther along, they came to a dead halt. The tunnel had sloped down again, getting wetter and wetter, until they were crawling on hands and knees through clinging mud. Krysty whispered to Ryan that she thought she could hear the sound of running water.

"If it rains up top, then it's coming this way," he whispered back.

"I just love the way you reassure a girl, Mr. Cawdor," she said. "If these tunnels start to fill up with water, it'll be a million laughs."

Jak's voice floated back to them. "It goes under water. I figure it's mebbe a trap. I'm going through. If it's safe, or I can't get through, I'll come back."

Ryan pushed past the others and touched the boy's shoulder, feeling it slick with mud. "Don't try and be a fucking hero on this one, Jak. Don't push it too far. Remember that Doc and the girls, and Finn, won't be able to get as far as you can."

"Sure." The mane of tumbling hair, although matted and streaked with dirt, glistened white in the narrow confines of the tunnel.

Ryan, his eyes accustomed to the poor light, watched as the boy crawled to the point where the flat, leaden water waited. Jak took several deep breaths, then gave a quick thumbs-up sign. Slipping into the unknown deeps of the pool, he wriggled out of sight like an eel.

A feeble trail of bubbles burst to the surface, hung there for a moment, then vanished. To Ryan, the bubbles were a lingering reproach for allowing the lad to risk the dive. He counted fifty slow beats of his heart. Then he saw an ominous swirling in the water, as though some sinister creature were moving deep below them.

"There he is," Krysty said, pointing at a faint white blur in the darkness.

Jak burst out of the side of the pool, expelling air from his lungs in a wheezing gasp as he shook his soaking hair away from his face. "Easy. Go down coupla feet and swim straight for around fifteen feet. No more'n that. Air's fresher other side. Colder. More light."

"What about tracks?" Ryan asked.

"Can't see none. But I figure it's raining up top. Water streaming down passage."

"Best get it over," Krysty said.

"Yeah, lover. Let's . . . What's wrong, Lori?"

Huddled in her new fur coat, the girl shook as if she had an ague. When she tried to speak, her teeth chattered so much it was impossible to understand her.

Doc hugged her, then looked away from her to the faces of the others, seeing his own concern mirrored in everyone's eyes.

Finn broke the silence. "She can't fucking swim," he said quietly without anger. "That's it, isn't it, Lori?"

The girl began to cry, then buried her face on Doc Tanner's shoulder, which answered the question.

"I'll take her through," Jak suggested, standing up, muddy water pouring from his clothes. "But we best go quick."

Lori pulled away, backing against the wall of the tunnel, eyes wide and blank with terror, her right hand dropping to the butt of the pistol at her belt. Ryan saw immediately that she wasn't going to go through easy.

Which meant it had to be hard.

"Lori," he said, calm and friendly, stepping toward her, watching her fingers gripping the butt of the small Walther PPK blaster.

"No, no, no, no, no," she repeated, flat and dull, shaking her head.

"That's all right," he reassured her. "Nobody'll make—"

He watched her eyes, seeing her glance across to Doc Tanner for reassurance. That was the moment.

The punch jarred through his wrist and elbow, clear up to the shoulder. There had been no point in trying to pull it. The girl was in such an advanced state of panic that she could easily have gone for her gun. And then he'd have had to kill her. Better to lay her out cold.

Her teeth clicked together as she went over. His fist had hit her clean on the angle of her jaw, so that she was sent back up the tunnel, heels teetering, spurs jingling, before she crashed down, one leg kicking out in a residual gesture.

"You cowardly bastard!" Doc Tanner yelled, stepping toward Ryan and raising his sword stick.

"Don't do it, Doc," J.B. said gently. "Ryan did it for the best. We try and force her, someone'd get chilled. We leave her, she gets chilled on her own."

The old man turned away, eyes closed, shaking his head. "I had not thought...had not..." He turned back, moving to kneel beside the unconscious girl.

"Leave her, Doc," Ryan said. "No time. Finn, you and Jak drag her through. There's room?" he asked the boy.

"Easy. I'll hold hand over nose and mouth. Won't choke."

Finnegan and Jak plunged into the dark water, gripping the limp figure of the girl between them as they kicked their way out of sight. Ryan counted a hundred heartbeats, then gave the old man the nod.

"Go join 'em, Doc. And tell her I'm really sorry about hitting her."

"I accept that you were correct in your course of action, Mr. Cawdor, but you can scarcely expect me to relish it."

Hat jammed on his head, one hand steadying it, Doc Tanner vanished from their sight. Ryan, J.B. and Krysty waited for a few moments. The water at their feet swelled and surged, lapping at the toes of Ryan's combat boots.

"Fireblast!"

"What's...?" Krysty began, looking down. "It's rising. It's getting—"

"See you the other side," the little Armorer said, tucking his beloved fedora into the front of his coat as he jumped feet first into the pool. A trail of bubbles indicated his progress under the ledge of rock.

"The rain," Krysty said. "I can hear it. Hear it louder. Ryan . . . it's like thunder on—"

There wasn't time for her to finish the sentence. The pool began to foam and froth, a reddish scum appearing on its surface. Where it had begun to rise slowly, inching up the slight slope toward them, it now swelled wolfishly, clawing at their boots, forcing them back up the tunnel into the blackness behind them.

They hesitated. Already the water had risen at least two feet, pushing along a dozen feet or more. The power of the surge was frightening, bubbling like a monstrous cauldron.

"What d'you think, Lover?" Krysty asked. "Be difficult to swim through that now."

Ryan bit his lip in anger. Another half minute and they'd all have been through safely. It crossed his mind to wonder how the other five were on the far side of the pool. If the flash flood had this kind of awesome power, then what would it be like in the chamber beyond?

"Got to move back. No knowing how long this'll go on 'fore it subsides again. Could be a couple of hours. Come on."

He led the way. Now the light had virtually disappeared, and he felt his way along the slippery walls, hearing the thunder of the water behind them, imagining it pursuing them. The passage rose and fell, and Ryan wondered if the flood had sought out a lower level ahead of them where it would trap them.

He felt the tension of panic rising in his chest as his pulse and respiration thundered. His good eye probed the blackness ahead as he tried to remember the way the tunnel had gone and wondered whether there was any side trails to confuse them. Water lapped around his ankles, cold and glutinous, like the embrace of a dying sticky.

"You there, lover?" he called, shouting at the top of his voice against the rising roar of the torrent.

"Yeah, keep moving. Getting deeper."

The passage sloped down, and for a few moments the water was up to his waist, chilling his groin, making him gasp in shock. Then the passage jerked up again, so that the water only slurped at his boots. The floor was streaming, slippery and infinitely treacherous. The current was so fast that to fall would mean death in the shrinking darkness.

When the passage narrowed, he banged his head hard on the ceiling, stunning himself. "Watch your head," he screamed, hearing fear ride his voice.

Then the ceiling caved in, and someone fell on his shoulders. Fire lanced across his ribs from a knife or spear, as fingers clawed at his windpipe. The extra weight was enough to knock him off balance, and he slipped over, head plunging into the cold mud.

# Chapter Six

THE HECKLER & KOCH went clattering into the water. Ryan couldn't breathe. Something held his head under the slime, as a knife or spear sliced across his stomach and cruel fingers tried to rip out his throat. Feeling skins with his hands, he guessed it was an ambush from the stunted muties who had been trailing them since they had arrived in the complex. It had crossed his mind that the muties had probably built the maze of tunnels scaled down to their dwarfish bodies. This one had been hiding in a dugout in the ceiling when it had heard them back away from the rising flood.

Ryan's only edged weapon was the long cleaver that was sheathed at his belt, useless for such close combat. He half rolled, kicking out to try to gain a footing. Pushing against the walls of the tunnel, he threw himself back, feeling the satisfying crunch as he smashed his opponent into the jagged stone.

The grip on his throat loosened for a moment, and Ryan was able to reach behind him, grabbing under the skins between the man's thighs. Feeling the softness of the dwarf's genital sac, he squeezed and ground it as hard as he could, digging his nails in. In the noise and confusion he wasn't sure, but he thought he heard a scream. Finally the mutie was off his back, and Ryan straightened, his head at last clear of the torrent. There was a flickering yellow light from the hole above him where the ambush had been launched, and he made out the head of another man, staring down at him. A spear lunged toward him, and he dodged, seeing the first mutie approach again, face contorted with pain, mouth open, long wolflike tusks gleaming golden.

One of the strange sectioned spears was in his right hand, jabbing at Ryan's belly. The blow wasn't hard to parry with the side of an arm. Ryan blinked—mud had gotten in his eye. He watched his enemy. The water was just above his knees, swirling and tugging, making it difficult to maintain balance. The best thing to do, he figured, was to get in close and use his superior height, strength and weight in hand-to-hand fighting.

The lance darted out again, and Ryan took a superficial cut on his left hand from the jagged, barbed ivory tip. He felt the warmth of fresh blood trickling down inside his coat from the two wounds across his ribs, but nothing seemed too seriously damaged. Beyond the mutie's shoulder he caught a flicker of movement and the flash of brilliant crimson hair. Whatever problems Krysty might be having, there was nothing he could do to help her. Not yet.

"Come on, you evil little fucker," he breathed, watching the flat, blank face, seeing nothing in the mud-colored eyes.

Out came the spear, but he was ready, moving easily like a dancer inside the thrust, grabbing the wooden haft and pulling the mutie toward him.

Above the sound of the water, he heard the mutie utter a squeaky cry. Ryan swung a punch at the open mouth, but the mutie was quicker, ducking and grappling with him. A foot hooked behind his ankle, and Ryan fell again, dragging at his opponent's arm. Once again he swallowed a mouthful of the muddy stream, flailing and kicking at the mutie.

The creature tried to butt him, and Ryan turned, biting the side of the attacker's neck. His teeth slithered off the wet skin, and he tasted grease and sweat and wood smoke. He locked an arm around the scrawny neck, simultaneously managing to pull him closer and heave himself from the water, sucking in a great gasp of fresh air.

Despite being much smaller and lighter than Ryan, the mutie was a vicious and cunning fighter, throwing Ryan off balance for a third time, hands scrabbling toward his groin. With great effort, Ryan turned so that the clawing fingers tore at the side of his thigh rather than at his scrotum.

Again he dipped his head, seeking the mutie's throat with his teeth, finding flesh and clamping his jaws shut. An artery pulsed between his lips as he drove his teeth through skin into flesh. Blood, salty and warm, spurted into Ryan's mouth.

The mutie screamed like a pig being gelded, then thrashed and kicked. One hand came up toward Ryan's face, attempting to rip and pulp his one good eye. Ryan seized the wrist, squeezing it and feeling the thin bones flex and snap like twigs.

He clamped his teeth together with great force, spitting out blood from the corner of his mouth, working through the beating wall of gristle that protected the carotid artery in the throat. The mutie, even with a broken arm, wasn't down, and he nearly succeeded in kneeing Ryan in the groin, instead delivering the blow to his leg.

Ryan's head bobbed as he chewed into the man's flesh. As he finally severed the artery, there was a great burst of wetness and heat that nearly choked him. He opened his mouth and pushed away from the yelping mutie, seeing the lifeblood, almost black in the tunnel's dim light, spout clear to the ceiling.

The dying man was carried away by the surging torrent, his broken arm waving crookedly as he whipped around a sharp corner and vanished.

Ryan stooped to retrieve the fallen blaster, glancing at the trap in the ceiling, seeing someone still stooped there. Without hesitation he pulled the trigger, firing a short burst. There was a cry of pain, and the mutie fell backward out of sight.

"Any more?" a voice shouted from behind him.

"Can't fucking tell," he shouted back. Wading toward Krysty, who was stooping under the low roof a few yards away, it struck him that she was in a peculiar, lopsided position.

"Took your time there, lover," she called. "Getting too old for all this."

"Didn't know it took long. Shows how time hisses by when you're having fun. You hurt your leg?"

"No. Had a mutie come after me, but I neck-chopped the little bastard. Knocked him under water. Then, 'fore I knew it, I had the heel of my boot jammed tight on the back of his head. He's still down there. Figure he's 'bout had enough?"

"Let go and find out."

Krysty moved away, and the sodden corpse of another mutie rose slowly to the surface, face up, eyes and mouth open. It began to drift in a circle before the girl pushed it, allowing the current to carry it off and follow the other chilled body.

Ryan took Krysty's hand, holding her tight. "Done good," he said, leaning and kissing her on the cheek.

"You get hurt?"

"Some. He had one of them folding spears, like Whitey got. It caught me 'cross the belly."

"No serious damage...lower down?"

"No. Not that I noticed. Bled a little. The son of a bitching fucker tried to rip my balls off. That made me real angry."

Krysty stared up at the circle of yellow light. "Could be more of 'em up there?"

"I reckon they'll have had it on their toes when the shooting started. I'll lift you and you take the blaster," he said, handing her the gray G-12 caseless.

"Water's stopped rising."

"Yeah. But if'n that passage goes above, we can find a way out and mebbe link up with the others outside. Save us waiting down here. Truth is, I don't much care for this crawling on my stomach under five miles of mud and stone. I'm an out-in-the-open sort of person."

"Me, too, lover."

Ryan steadied himself against the wall of the tunnel, cupping his hands so that Krysty could step up, balance and stand on his shoulders. It would give her the height to look through the open mouth of the tunnel above and blast anything that moved.

If it didn't blast her first.

Her boots were slippery, and she nearly fell. She grabbed his head to steady herself, her fingers tangling in his hair, which made him yelp.

"Watch it," he moaned.

"Keep still. You're rocking around like an aspen in a hurricane."

Then she was up on his shoulders. Ryan braced himself, wincing in expectation of hearing the roar of a gun from some hidden enemy. But all was quiet. She half turned, the heels of her cowboy boots scraping his ears, which made him wriggle again. then she pushed upward, and her weight was off him. He looked up and saw her legs vanishing into the hole above, momentarily blocking the light.

"Anything?"

Her face reappeared, the long red rags of her hair dangling down, almost touching him. "Nothing. Come on up, lover."

She reached down, giving him a wrist to grip. In one steady motion, he hauled himself up to the higher level. Slumped against the far wall of the tunnel, which was wider than the one below, was the corpse of the third mutie, its head more or less pulped off its shoulders by the burst of lead from the G-12.

"Time we got out of this bastard warren," Ryan said, stooping and peering as far as he could into the dimness. The light at their elbow was a small clay lamp, with a wick floating in liquid fat.

"I can hear something," Krysty whispered. "Way we came. Could be J.B. and the others."

"Let's go, then," Ryan said, leading the way, finger ready on the trigger of the H&K.

IT TOOK THEM AN HOUR to reach full light and fresh air. Ryan stood in the entrance to the tunnel, drawing in deep breaths. "That is *so* good, lover. I wasn't meant to be a fucking mole. If we ever find another redoubt like that, I'm going to get right on back into the gateway and move along to the next stop."

"Me, too."

The sky was an unusual color—clear pale blue, with only a few wispy white clouds streaking across it. From the cold thin air, Ryan figured they had to be up a considerable altitude. From experience, it felt like around a mile high.

At first he saw no sign of another living being. There was the edge of what looked like a big lake, not too far away, and a lot of mountains all around, many snow-capped. The wind was from the north, clean and light.

"It's beautiful," Krysty said, putting her arm around his shoulders. "What Uncle Tyas McCann would have called 'God's Country,' I guess."

Ryan moved to the sharp-cut brink of a drop and looked down. He turned to Krysty, a smile on his face, and said, "They're here."

"Where?"

"Down," he told her, pointing with the muzzle of the mud-streaked blaster. "All of 'em."

Several hundred feet lower on the sharp, scree-covered slope of the mountain, five minute figures were visible. One with white hair, stark against the gray rock. One with yellow hair and one with a clumsy black hat. One round figure and one with glasses that glittered as he looked up toward Ryan and Krysty.

Ryan held his G-12 above his head, waving it slowly to and fro, signaling they were all right.

"They're safe," he said. "We all made it."

# Chapter Seven

"HE KILLED HOW MANY?"

Finnegan grinned. "Six."

Ryan looked at Jak Lauren, who was shuffling his feet like a kid caught with his hand in the candy jar. "How did you take six muties all on your own, son?"

"With spear," he replied, flicking the sections in his fingers so that they blurred into the full-length weapon. Ryan saw that the cane shaft was streaked with dried blood.

"All six?" It was hard to believe. "What the chill were you doing, Finn?"

"Stopping me from sinking in the water and being drowned. Thank you, Ryan," Lori said, with affronted dignity. There was a little congealed blood around the corner of her mouth, and a deep purple bruise on the left side of her jaw, making speech difficult.

"No other way," Ryan said, looking across at Doc to see if the old man understood.

*"Oh tempora! Oh mores!"* Doc replied. "Means when you're up to your neck in shit, you can't get along by smelling roses."

Lori nodded. "I suppose I know why you hit me, Ryan. Sorry I made trouble. But I still didn't like it very much."

Finnegan was eager to tell Ryan and Krysty about Jak's prowess in the underground battle. "I never seen nothing like the bleached-out little fucker. Like fucking poetry in motion, Ryan. One after another, like skewering fish in a pisspot.''

"Was easy. They came one at time, so killed 'em one at time." Jak's red eyes sparkled at the memory.

"You gut-rip 'em?" Krysty asked.

"No. Barbs on spears catch clothes. Snag on furs. No time rip clear. Had to stab at necks and faces."

"I swear he hit three out of the fucking six right splat in the middle of the fucking eye. They was down and thrashing in a row."

"Got no more brains than 'gator shit," Jak muttered. "Came together and I'd been chilled."

"I couldn't get my blaster to waste any of 'em for him. An' Doc and J.B. was bursting out the water, all pop-eyed. Real stiff in that river. Trying to tug you down and under."

"Sure," Ryan said. "We know it, Finn."

"It got fucking weird, you know. The light was real dark. Most times I could see his hair, like a whirlwind of fucking snow. Hear them screaming. The blade ripping them open. And the blood spurting every which way round the tunnel. I tell you . . ." His voice faded away into mute admiration.

There was a silence. Doc Tanner was hugging the trembling Lori, both of them still dripping muddy water from their new fur coats. J.B. squinted up at the sky.

"Could be a storm. Road down yonder. Mebbe best we head for it."


"ANYONE GOT ANY PYROTABS?"

There was a general shaking of heads and shrugging of shoulders. Jak looked at J.B. "What are they?"

"Pyrotabs? Self-igniting pellets. Start a fire quick and easy."

Ryan whistled between his teeth. "Going to get cold in a while. Need a fire."

"I got matches. Always carry 'em." Jak fumbled in the pockets of his jacket, pulling out various small, intriguing packages, most of them wrapped in clear plastic to keep them from getting wet.

"What's that?" Krysty said, reaching out as fast as a striking rattler to snatch a packet of fine white powder off the boy's palm.

"Give it back."

"Careful, son," Ryan warned, sensing trouble in the way the albino's body had tensed.

"Gimme, Krysty."

The girl eased open the self-seal top and dipped the tip of her index finger into the powder. She raised the finger to her lips then pulled a face. "Jolt."

"Can I try?" Lori asked. "I like jolt. Quint had some. And crack. Jolt was best."

"No," Krysty said. "Jolt's the worst. Mix of heroin and coke. Lift you up and knock you down all in one hard hit."

"Quint, my husband, said jolt was good. Gave me a lot all the time."

"Yeah," Finnegan said quietly. "And we know all about that poisonous little double-poor bastard."

"Give it back," Jak repeated. "I can handle it. Only do some now and then."

Ryan held his hand out, and Krysty put the packet in his fingers. They were all sitting on a wide ledge, overlooking the valley below. The sky was changing from pallid blue to vivid gold, with crimson chem-storms threatening from the west.

"You journey with us, fight with us, then you live by our rules. You don't like it, then get out, Jak. One rule is no drugs."

"I can—" he began.

"Handle it? I know. I've seen a lot of men and women say that. And I've seen a lot of fucking stoned corpses." Ryan's voice rose in anger. "You mess around with your head and your reflexes go, kid. Your reflexes go and I don't want you at my back when the muties come in at us. I want someone clean."

"So you're going to throw over cliff?" Jak asked with sullen anger.

"Wrong, Jak," Ryan replied, holding out the package. "You throw it over. And any more jolt you got on you."

"Don't have more."

"Then throw this away."

The boy reached for it, letting it lie for a moment on the white palm of his hand as he shook his head back to clear his hair from his eyes. "Waste, Ryan. Paid good creds for this."

"Waste of jack then, wasn't it?" Finnegan said.

They all watched as the slim-built boy rose to his feet and stood a moment on the edge of the drop. He peeled back the top of the plastic and then shook it so that the white hallucinogenic powder exploded like a tiny cloud in front of him, the rising wind dispersing it almost instantly.

"Satisfied, Ryan?"

"Yeah."

There was a light fluttering of rain. Toward the northern peaks they saw a jagged stripe of silver lightning, then another, the rumble of the thunder taking several seconds to reach them.

"I figure that'll pass by," J.B. said. "But night's not far off."

"You done a sighting on where we are?" Ryan asked. The Armorer carried a neat collapsible sextant with him, which could be used to determine their position. He also had an almost photographic memory for any map or plan. Once he'd seen it, then it was locked away deep inside his formidable memory.

"Yeah. Just 'fore you came down to join us. Where we figured."

"Oregon?"

"Near as I can tell we're to the south of it. Those big snow-tops were called the Cascades. See that spread of trees?" He pointed to where sharp-topped pines speckled the hillsides. "Called Rogue River Forest. Up to the north there used to be a famous place. Big, deep lake in the middle of an old volcano. Called Crater Lake. Probably nuked out of sight now."

"Radio message came from the north," Krysty said. "Mebbe we could head that way?"

"Good as any other," Ryan replied. "First thing to find is somewheres to shelter for the night."

Krysty joined Jak on the edge of the drop where he was peering down into the valley below. She shaded her eyes with her hand, holding back her coiling crimson hair.

"Looks like an old blacktop down there. Winds around the end of that small lake. Some kind of building. Can't make out more." Krysty squinted, then shook her head.

"Can we get down?" Finn asked.

Jak pointed. "Sure. There's a goat path or bear track round to the right. Comes out above the scree, near that stand of piñons."

THE PATH WAS UNEVEN, and several times one or another of the group stumbled and tripped. Doc Tanner found it the hardest going, relying on the steady arm of Lori to help him. On a level part he slowed to walk alongside Ryan.

"Time was folks paid good jack to do this sort of thing. Hiking they called it. Taking the air. Personally, I would happily dig deep into my own humble purse to pay not to have to hike these mountains."

As they progressed, the chem-clouds gathered in a furious array over the mountains, sending great stabbing sheets of lightning to burst against the dripping rocks. The Armorer had been correct in his forecasting. The storm was raging some forty or fifty miles away to the north, showing no signs of moving closer. Night was crouching to the east, ready to spring and spread its body across the land.

The path zigzagged across the slope, bending and twisting sharply. The stones underfoot were dangerously slippery. A red fox picked its way daintily across the trail in front of them, showing no fear. Generally this was a sign that there weren't that many human beings around. Far above, a solitary raven soared, riding a thermal over the valley, its beak catching the glint of the dying sun.

As they drew nearer to the road that curled lazily below them, the harsh rocks gave way to patches of scrub and meadow. The sides of the path became lined with a profusion of wild plants—the gold and cream of the butter-and-eggs flowers with the crimson spikes of the Indian paintbrush. They passed tall stems of firewood, with magenta flowers nodding and dancing on either side, some at least fifteen feet tall. Across the valley was a great swath of purple Oregon fleabane.

The distant chattering of a stream that flowed, white over boulders, along the edge of the narrow highway, became audible. Jak, who was leading the way as they neared the road, suddenly jumped to one side, gasping in shock as a sinuous garter snake weaved across the trail right under his feet.

"Likely wouldn't have harmed you," Finnegan said, laughing.

"Wasn't going t'find out," the boy retorted.

"IT'S AN OLD GAS STATION," J.B., who'd taken up the lead, called out. The rectangular building they'd seen from high above stood squatly on its own. Most of the windows were broken, and one corner of its flat roof had fallen in. The pumps stood undamaged, like robot sentinels on guard against intruders.

"No nuke damage," Ryan said, addressing the remark to Doc Tanner.

"This far north and west . . . it wasn't bombed so badly as other parts. Not many air bases or radar stations. Nothing like that up here in the mountains. Most of the missiles they used would have been low-yield. No point in dropping dirty heads here. Not 'nough people. Probably hit water and highways. Sever the communications, and the folks would have mostly moved out. Or died."

J.B. pulled out his miniaturized rad counter, checking in all directions. "Hot spot over to the east. And some action north. Nothing too dangerous. Doesn't rate even an orange."

"If'n that roof's safe, it could be a good place to spend the night. Only one door, at the front," Finn said.

Lori turned to Krysty. "This is like where I came for—I mean, came *from*. Caves and houses from old times that were used by bears to sleep and live."

"Best be careful then," Krysty said.

"We're always careful, aren't we, Finn?" Ryan asked.

The stocky mercenary winked. "Sure. Do bears shit in the fucking woods, huh?"

But there were no bears in the abandoned gas station.

It was a single-story building, two-thirds of it given over to a workshop, the rest an office. The sliding door to the work area was closed, but a smaller, half-glass door was open. Ryan approached it, while Finn and J.B. went around the outside. Only when they'd circled the building, reporting that it looked deserted and safe, did he risk entry.

The hinges creaked and broken glass crunched underfoot. Animals or humans had apparently stripped the place bare. A pile of windblown dried leaves from the aspens across the blacktop rested in one corner. There was an open cash register on a counter and an empty Coke tin against the far wall.

"Through here?" Finn said, pointing to the far door that probably opened into the workshop.

"Sure. Slow and easy," Ryan warned. "Krysty. You and Jak stay here and keep watch outside. Not a good place to get caught in."

In a narrow corridor there were two rest rooms marked Guys and Dolls in faded blue paint. Finn pushed each door open.

"Shouldn't you have knocked? Might have been someone in the ladies' room," J.B. said.

Finn shook his head. "Anyone still in there from the time of the long chill would have the worst case of shit-block in the history of the fucking world."

There was nobody there.

Nor in the workshop. In the dim half-light of the gathering dusk, they could see that all the tools had been removed from their places on long wooden racks. The floor was stained with long-dried pools of lube oil. The five of them stood for several long, silent moments.

"Shame it's empty," J.B. said.

"You were hoping for a mint-condition Cadillac with velvet upholstery, all greased and ready to drive away?" Ryan said, grinning. His grin spread when the Armorer threw him the finger.

"Let's go back now. This place smells deader'n a beaver hat," Ryan said. "Keep a single guard, tight perimeter outside."

"Sure," J.B. agreed. "Could do with a fire in here. Coupla broken window up high'll take out smoke."

From one of his sewn pockets, Jak removed some matches, dry-sealed. But there was precious little wood to burn. Outside there were some sizable branches that would go well once they had a fire blazing, but they needed some kind of kindling.

Lori pointed to an old calendar on the office wall, above the till. The years had bleached away its color, but it still showed the month of January 2001. "A small token of appreciation to Grannoch Pass Service Station from the suppliers of Xanthus Power Tools" was printed on it, beneath a sepia picture of the interior of a Victorian mansion. Doc stood in front of it, and Ryan joined him.

"Thinking how well that'd burn, Doc?"

To his surprise, he saw that the old man was weeping, silent tears coursing through the gray stubble on his lined cheeks.

"Hey, Doc, what's wrong?"

"What's up, Doc, is what you should say, Ryan. That was the old joke. Buggy the Bunny, he was called. Something like that. I'm sorry. You must forgive an old fool's streak of maudlin sentimentality. It's the picture."

"You mean like wanting old times back?"

"More than you know, my dear fellow. Oh, more than you know. That picture brings back such a flood of memories. Oh, the days and evenings with dear Emily."

"Who's Emily?"

They were alone. The others were scavenging around outside before darkness made it too dangerous to move in the open. Ryan looked up at the calendar, wondering what had triggered the old-timer off on one of his lack-brained trips into the past.

The calendar had a name on it. Currier and Ives. There was a large fireplace in the print, with logs blazing merrily in it, and there was a pine tree in a tub, decorated with ornamental candles in a way that seemed dangerous to Ryan. Pretty parcels were scattered around the bottom of the tree, each wrapped in bright paper and tied with ribbons of silk. The mantel was busy with vases and spelter statues of men on horseback, and over the mantel was a large painting. When Ryan peered more closely at the painting, he saw that it was a reproduction of the main picture—a fireplace with a tree in a tub. And over the mantel was a picture of a room with a fire and a tree and a picture over the mantel . . .

Doc Tanner was close at his elbow, looking at the way each painted image was reproduced and diminished, drawing the eye in and in and in through each miniature until the detail blurred.

"Who is Emily, Ryan?"

"Yeah. Heard you mention the name 'fore this, Doc. Someone you know?"

"I knew her, Ryan. A woman of excellent wit and beauty. One day I will tell you . . . But not now. It was this picture. I can hear those logs as they crackle and spit. Smell the freshness of the pine needles. Hear the excited laughter of young children as they wait to open the presents that jolly Saint Nicholas has sent them. The family parlor at Christmas. Damp moss and dry leaves. Belladonna, macassar oil and parsley. Peppermint oil and ipecac for those who had dined well but not wisely upon the turkey and the plum pudding.'' There were fresh tears again, glistening on his cheeks.

Embarrassed by this flood of memories, Ryan turned to look out the broken panes of glass to where the rest of the group was gathering wood to burn. And yet he was still deeply puzzled by the things Doc had said. Things that Ryan had never known. Things that seemed to him to come from such an antique past that it wasn't conceivable that Doc Tanner could recall them from personal memory.

It wasn't possible.

DESPITE ALL THEIR EFFORTS, the fire was proving stubborn to light. Most of the wood was damp and green, and nearly all the kindling they found was also wet. At Krysty's suggestion they tried the calendar, though Doc Tanner came close to objecting. But the card proved too thick to do more than lie there sullenly smoldering.

"How 'bout that?" Jak Lauren asked, pointing to the wood-framed counter that was built into the wall.

"Break it up, Whitey," Finnegan said. "Give it plenty of fucking boot and it might splinter dry."

The skinny little youth walked up and patted the solid structure, running his hands over it and testing the thickness of the wood and the amount of give when he leaned on it.

He took a couple of paces back, closing his pink eyes for a moment in concentration. The other six watched him closely. Ryan in particular was fascinated that such a frail body could harness such devastating power. It wasn't anything mystical, in the way that Krysty could fold her mind inward and draw on the force of the Earth Mother, Gaia. This was simply a great skill.

Jak gave a single, explosive grunt and lashed out with his foot, the whole front of the counter caved in, splitting lengthways as if a chainsaw had ripped through it. Without a pause, like a dancer, Jak wheeled on the other foot and kicked again. This time the entire left side fell away from the wall, leaving only one part still attached. A third kick demolished that.

"Fucking fan-fucking-tastic!" Finnegan whooped. "This'll burn real good."

"What's that?" Lori asked.

"Where?" J.B. said, moving to help Finn clear away the shattered splinters.

"There. The hole in the wall. It was hidden before by the wood."

The Armorer stepped over the wreckage of the counter and stooped where the girl was pointing. Then he spotted the shadowy hole that was no bigger than a couple of house bricks. "Something here."

"What?"

"Box. No, a tin, Ryan."

"Could be boobied, J.B. Watch it."

"Too well hid. Looks like it's been here since the big fires."

There was the scraping of metal on concrete as he eased the tin box from its hiding place and laid it on the floor near the shards of wood. They gathered around it, their need for a fire momentarily forgotten, even though the temperature had fallen so fast and so low that the gas station seemed filled with the mist of their warm breath.

"Got a lock," J.B. said.

"I'll blast the bastard apart. One round from the Beretta'll open it up like cracking an egg," Finnegan said eagerly.

"Why not just try and lift the lid first?" Ryan suggested.

It was open.

J.B. looked inside, then handed it to Jak. "Here, kid. You found it. You can have it." He winked over his shoulder at Ryan.

"I saw it," Lori said.

"I'll split it with you," the albino replied, carrying it to where the poor fire coughed and spluttered fitfully. It was the only light they had, apart from the pallid moon that sailed above them in a sky speckled by the remains of the chem-storm.

"What is it?" Finnegan asked.

It was a wad of paper. A couple of hundred small sheets, around five inches by three, with the rotted remains of an elastic band around them. Jak took them out, riffling them through his fingers. Dust flew off their edges, and they made a dry, flaking sound.

Ryan suddenly guessed what it was.

"Open them up," he said.

"Pictures," Lori said. "Pictures and numbers. I can do numbers. There's a ten and that's a hundred and a twenty and another ten."

"It's old jack," the boy said disgustedly. "Seen lots around West Lowellton. Left around. In wallets and pockets and bags. Dollars. Isn't that right?"

"Sure is, son," Doc Tanner said. "Must be a tidy nest egg there. Close on five thousand dollars. Cheating the tax department, I guess."

"Not worth shit now," Finnegan said.

"Wrong, Fats," Jak said, grinning. "Watch this." He took the handful of dry paper to the dying fire and poked it on, putting some of the broken wood of the old counter on top of it and adding a few of the smaller green branches.

He was right. The pile of money burned wonderfully well.

# Chapter Eight

RYAN WOKE DURING THE NIGHT and saw that the fire was dying. He rolled out from under his coat, tossed a couple more branches on the glowing ashes and watched as the dry wood began to burn. From out in the clutching darkness beyond the frail walls of the gas station came the keening wail of a hunting animal. Probably some sort of mountain lion was Ryan's guess. As he was sliding back to sleep, he heard a snuffling sound near the door, as if some large creature was moving there, having caught the scent of humans. Finnegan, who was on sentry watch, came in from the office area and saw that Ryan was awake. Moving to kneel beside him, he whispered, "Biggest fucking bear I ever seen out there. Must stand close to six feet at the shoulder. Only got to lean on us and this place's fold like a fucking pack of cards."

"Want me to get up, Finn?"

"No. I'll chill it if'n it starts to get too curious 'bout us." He stood up again. "Know what you call a three-thousand-pound mutie grizzly?"

"No?"

"Sir," he said, laughing quietly as he went back on watch.

THEY WERE UP AT FIRST LIGHT, bundling themselves into their furs and huddling against the bitter cold that frosted the ground outside. Thick slate-gray ice covered the puddles of water lying in the rutted mud. There was a fresh dusting of snow on the upper slopes of the mountains around them.

"Which way?" Doc Tanner asked, cupping his hands and blowing on them to try to get some warmth into his aged bones.

"North. Where that radio message came from. You never know what it could lead to," Ryan said.

The blacktop was cracked and showed signs of some major earth movements many years ago. Weeds peeked through the cracks and gaps, and the shoulders crumbled away into the earth around them. Every now and again they found places where mountain streams came rushing over sections of the two-lane highway, washing them out, and carrying debris toward the river at the bottom of the valley.

The road twisted and turned, gradually descending and revealing more and more of the long, wide lake to the right. They passed a sign, leaning drunkenly, pointing back the way they'd come. Klamath Falls 17, it read.

"Nice to know where we've been, lover," Krysty said to Ryan. "All we need to know now is where we're going."

Lori was leading them, striding at a moderate pace, her silver spurs tinkling brightly in the cool morning air. The chem-storms of the previous evening had disappeared, and the sky was again the unusual blue that Ryan remembered from the pictures in old magazines. At a hairpin curve to the left, Lori paused and stared intently into the valley.

"Ville there," she called out.

The others joined her to see where she was pointing. A large collection of buildings was scattered around a central road, with three or four side roads branching off it. The town, which seemed to run down to the edge of the lake, contained around two to three hundred houses. Part of it was obscured by the edge of a bluff, protruding on their right.

"One of the biggest villes I've seen for a while," J.B. said. "Can't recall seeing any big place on the old maps in these parts."

"Could be a new place," Ryan said. "Some sprung up where the old villes got chilled by the nukes. Best step light and find out who the baron is down there. Make sure we get a friendly welcome."

THEY ALL LOOKED at the sign: Ginnsburg Falls. Population 8,407. Alt. 4,950.

Printed neatly beneath that, in dark blue and gold paint in an elegant sans-serif type, were the words: Walk the Line and You'll Be Fine.

"Stout right-wing statement," Doc Tanner said, leaning on his sword stick. "Sets well with happiness being a warm gun and telling folks to either shape up or ship on out."

"That's a big population," Krysty said.

"Yeah. From higher up we couldn't see the whole ville. There's hundreds more houses on that strip development to the west, across from the lake. Laid out like a square grid."

"Got to be one of the biggest villes I've ever seen," Ryan said, agreeing with J.B. "But it doesn't look like it's military. No lec-fences. Nothing like that."

"Mebbe it's just left behind. Kind of shut away after the long winters and running all along on its fucking own-some. You figure?" Finnegan suggested.

"Let's go find out," Ryan answered.

"THIS BLACKTOP'S been swept clean," J.B. said, pausing when they were still a good half mile from the nearest building.

Krysty smiled uncertainly. "Yeah, it has. There's dried leaves lying all around, but the road's virtually clear of 'em. I never heard of a ville that's as clean as that."

"Neither have I," Ryan agreed. "Most villes…you can smell 'em before you see 'em."

"I hear something coming," Krysty warned. "Small wagon, gas power. Like one of the swamp bugs. Lighter sound to the engine."

The wind was blowing toward the ville, making it hard to hear anything from that direction. But within seconds they all heard the whining sound of a small, powerful engine approaching quickly. Each of them saw it at the same moment, breasting a rise in the road, a couple of hundred yards ahead. It was a small open wag, like a jeep, painted light blue. Four men were seated in it, all holding blasters.

"Easy," Ryan warned. "Nothing hasty or foolish. Could bring the whole ville down on us. Just keep ready."

"Winchester carbines," J.B. breathed. "Selective fire, M-2 models, thirty caliber. Look't the polish on them."

The guns glittered with a parade-ground patina, reflecting the dazzling sun. The jeep stopped in a squeal of brakes about fifty yards away. Three of the men leaped out, forming a skirmishing line across the center of the road. The driver moved to the back, swinging around a mounted machine gun. Ryan recognized the blaster. It was a M60E2. The 7.62 model.

The Trader had sometimes considered working on the principle that every stranger you encountered was an enemy and should be chilled before he had a chance to chill you. Nonetheless, it was equally true that most folks living throughout the Deathlands were reasonably honest and didn't have blood in their eyes and murder on their minds. So, you just stepped careful.

Ryan, too, was wondering whether they should have sent the newcomers off to buy the farm as soon as they had stopped their jeep. That way they wouldn't be in this standoff situation.

The men had the unmistakable look of a sec unit: Dark blue pants and thick jackets; cross-belts with brass buckles on them; knee-high leather boots; caps with shiny plastic peaks; dark glasses that hid the eyes.

"Fucking sec men, Ryan," Finnegan hissed nervously, fingering the butt of his HK54A2.

"Easy, Finn, easy," Ryan warned again.

The center man of the trio called out to them, voice neither harsh nor friendly. "You outworlders?"

It didn't sound like that difficult a question. But Ryan knew from previous experience that it was the sort of query that might have a lot behind it, the sort of question where the wrong answer could bring down a hail of lead to sweep a man away.

"Outworlders?"

"You have to ask, then that has to be the answer. You don't come from around here?"

"No."

"Where from?"

"Different places."

The man gestured with the muzzle of his carbine. "Got a lot of blasters. You mercies, or guns for one of the traders?"

"Neither. Just friends. Passing along."

"Where?"

"Where we want to go."

"You want to come into the ville of Ginnsburg Falls? That the idea?"

"Mebbe. How's that set with you?" The constant questions were beginning to grate with Ryan. He could feel a pulse beating at his temple, a sure sign, he knew, that there was a risk of his temper slipping out of control.

"You come in with us. Walk ahead."

"We got a choice?" J.B. asked.

"Sure." The man almost smiled. "Walk ahead or we chill you. All of you."

"Some fucking choice," Finnegan whispered.

# Chapter Nine

THE JEEP GROWLED along after them, keeping in low gear. One of the sec men kept position on the machine gun in the rear, covering the seven of them.

"Sure is a big ville," J.B. said.

Doc Tanner shook his head. "There is something about it that puts me unconscionably in mind of a trim little town in the Bible Belt before the war."

"In vids, you mean, Doc?" Finnegan asked.

"Yes, of course."

The leader of the patrol called out to them as they neared a barrier across the road: a single striped pole beside a small stone hut. Two sec men, carrying brightly polished carbines, marched briskly to and fro in front of the barrier. Ryan was struck again by the neatness and cleanliness of the whole operation.

"Hold it there."

They stopped. Ryan turned to face the jeep. "This going to take long? We're real tired and we could do with some food."

"You don't have any passes. Don't have any Ginnsburg Falls creds. No food slips. And you haven't seen Mayor Sissy."

"Who?" Ryan asked incredulously.

"Mayor Sissy. And I surely hope that isn't a smile I see on anyone's face. Best learn first off that rule number one isn't to find names funny. Believe me, an outworlder can get chilled faster than a fish down a fall. You'll meet Mayor Theodore Sissy before you reach your quarters. First, we got to get your names. Corp!''

The taller of the two guards on the barrier came smartly forward, giving a salute that involved patting his left shoulder with his gauntleted right fist. "Yes, Sec Commander?''

"Note of names.''

"Sir.''

The man in charge of the jeep came closer. "You're the leader here,'' he said, addressing Ryan Cawdor. "Watch your people and walk the line. You'll enjoy your time with us in Ginnsburg Falls. You'll do fine.''

"Have a nice day,'' Doc Tanner said, making the sec commander turn and look at him suspiciously, as though he suspected the old man was sending him up.

"You,'' the tall guard said, pointing at Ryan. "Name. Place.''

"You mean, where have I come from?''

"Yes. Place of habitation.''

"Name's Ryan Cawdor. I came from—'' he hesitated, wondering just where he did come from "—Front Royal out in the Shens.''

"Don't know it. That's outworld here.''

The Armorer answered next. "Name's J. B. Dix.''

The guard wrote it down on a large pad. "Another outworlder. What are the letters for?''

"What letters?''

"Your name? Your first name?''

Ryan's jaw dropped. He'd known the little Armorer for something approaching ten years, and he realized now that he'd never even known what the initials stood for. It had always been J.B., nothing else.

"First name's John.''

"What's the *B* for?"

"Barrymore, you double-stupe bastard! John Barrymore Dix. You got it?"

"Don't let anger lead you into dangerous pathways, my outworlder friend," the sec guard replied, calmly writing the name down.

"John Barrymore!" Ryan repeated unbelievingly. "No wonder you kept that closely guarded."

"Your mother must have had thespian interests," Doc Tanner said.

"She was as fucking norm as me, so watch that flapping lip of yours, Doc," J.B. warned, bristling like an enraged bantam cockerel.

"No, my dear friend. A thespian. A lover of the theatrical arts. There was a famous actor called John Barrymore many years ago."

"Oh," he said, slightly mollified. "I never knowed any of that, Doc."

"Oh, yes, indeed. A famous man. A wonderful, wonderful actor."

"Your name, old man?" the guard demanded.

"Dr. Theophilus Tanner, master of arts, doctor of philosophy and a citizen of the free world."

"Outworlder?"

"Yes."

"Thomas O'Flaherty Fingal Finnegan, born somewheres around the Windy City," Finn butted in.

"Where were you born, old man?" the sec guard asked, ignoring the fat man's exaggerated bow.

"South Strafford, a tiny hamlet close by White River Junction in the beautiful state of Vermont. In the year of Our Lord—" Suddenly he stopped, as if someone had jammed his tongue in a closing door. He coughed, glancing sideways, but only Ryan had been listening to him; the sec man wasn't interested in anyone's age.

"You, boy? By the crucified Savior! Your hair? And your eyes and skin. Are you the spawn of Beelzebub?"

"No, I'm Jak Lauren from West Lowellton."

The guard swallowed hard, then scribbled the name down.

J.B. raised a hand. "You never asked where I came from."

"Where?"

"Cripple Creek, in the Rockies."

It was all dutifully entered on the pad. The jeep still waited behind them, engine ticking over. Ryan watched the sec men and saw how sharp they seemed, constantly alert, never taking their eyes off the newcomers.

Particularly, he noticed, they were fascinated by the bizarre appearance of Jak Lauren, seeming almost frightened by the fourteen-year-old boy with the colorless skin.

"That's all," the sec commander said. "Head on in and we'll tell—"

"What about us?" Krysty Wroth interrupted.

"How's that?"

"You haven't taken our names down. My name's—"

"Shut it."

The command was flat and dismissive. Ryan felt Krysty stiffen in anger, and he put a cautious hand on her arm. But she shook him off and stepped up to face the man, staring into his hooded eyes.

"Don't talk to me like that."

Ignoring her, the sec officer said, "Outworlder Cawdor, tell her that in Ginnsburg Falls, it's only men that count."

"Don't understand," Ryan said.

The sec commander continued, speaking more slowly and distinctly, as if he were addressing a backward child. "Others don't function."

"What the...?" Krysty began, stopping when Ryan turned and glared at her.

"Unpersons here. Non-men. Just home-keep and breed. Or whores. Them two whores?" he asked, interested in both Krysty's striking red hair and Lori's long blond tresses.

"No. They're both...home-keeps. Can we go now?"

"Sure. Registration'll follow later. Go to corner of Fourth an' Sissy—that's the main street in the ville. Red building called Outworlders' Dorm. Don't leave there till you're told."

No OTHER OUTWORLDERS were in town just then, so they had the spotlessly clean building with eating hall and dormitories to themselves. Doc and Lori went into a small room with three beds, as did Ryan and Krysty. The others shared a room with six beds, overlooking Sissy Street.

An old man, apparently the janitor, seemed delighted to have seven visitors all at once. He wore a smart uniform of dark green, with silver piping around the lapels and down the sides of his pants. His gray hair was neatly combed, and he was clean-shaven.

"Lucky to be here in Ginnsburg Falls, folks," he said, speaking to the men but treating the two women as though they were invisible. "There's to be a stoning at dusk. Haven't had one o' them in weeks."

"What's a stoning?"

"Stoning, Mr. Cawdor, is what the name suggests. Those that crosses the laws here in the ville has to pay the price. Walk the line and you'll be fine."

"Stoned to death? Who by? What for?" Krysty Wroth asked.

The janitor ignored her. "Couple been caught in adultery tonight. Down the quarry. Follow Seventh to the edge of the lake and walk up the lane to the left. Mercy me! Why tell you that? Just follow the whole town and you'll see it for yourself." He hesitated. "Being outworlders, you won't know all the lines to walk, Mr. Cawdor. But homekeeps aren't allowed. Be trouble if they left here."

"Thank you," Ryan said. "We'll all take care to walk the line."

"Registers'll be here soon. Give you the cards and passes you'll need while here. Give you work allocations an' all."

"DOUBLE FUCKING WEIRD," Finnegan exploded after the old man brought them bowls of vegetable soup and fresh-baked cornbread. The old man paused for a moment when he saw Lori and Krysty sitting down with the men. Muttering something about stupe outies, he stamped off, leaving them alone with their meal.

"Yeah," J.B. agreed. "Never saw a ville the like of this one."

Doc Tanner spooned his soup, pausing and looking across at Ryan. "You know that this place is rife with evil, do you not, Mr. Cawdor?"

"How's that again, Doc?"

"Ginnsburg Falls. Mayor Sissy. A stoning. Nonpersons. Breeding. But not a speck of dirt to be seen. Neat guards with polished weapons. It appears to me to be a mutated and idealized version of some Midwestern fascist dream."

"Don't like this walk-line shit," Jak Lauren said quietly. The boy had been subdued ever since they'd been brought into the ville.

"See that sign at the entrance?" Krysty asked. "By the old man's cubicle? It said that any dropping of litter or dirtying meant a minimum of twenty hours ville labor. Never met such a tight hole. When do we go?"

Ryan sniffed. "Soon as we can. But I agree with Doc. We have to step careful. Walk the line, like they say. They got rules on top of rules. We make a mistake, and it could cost us. You two—" looking at Lori and Krysty "—have to be most careful. Women come way second in Ginnsburg Falls. Don't talk back, please. For all our sakes."

THE LIGHT WAS BEGINNING to fade when a pair of sec guards entered the building and motioned for the men to join them. "Outworlders come to the stoning," the one with two silver stripes on his sleeve said.

"Is that a request or an order?" Ryan asked, getting only a blank look for a reply. "Guess it's a little of both."

Leaving the two women behind, the men followed the guards out and down the scrubbed stone steps, turning left along the main street.

"Lot of folks," Doc Tanner commented.

"No," Ryan said. "Lots of *men*. No women at all."

It was true. The street was thronged with males of all ages, all neatly but plainly dressed, walking quietly along as if they were going to some sort of religious ritual. Several of them cast glances at the strangers, but nothing was said. None of them smiled or uttered a greeting. Just in front of them a boy about nine years old who had been eating some candy pushed the empty bag into his pocket. But in his haste it dropped out again and fell to the sidewalk.

"Jasper!" the father exclaimed in a voice taut with shock and anger.

"I'm sorry, only—"

The man swung a cracking roundhouse swing at his son, hitting the boy across the face. The slapping sound echoed all across the street, but only a few heads turned. The lad staggered sideways, hands flying to his mouth, blood flowing thick from a cut on his lip and oozing from his nose.

"Pick it up now," the man said, voice easing under control. "And don't ever . . ."

The boy picked up the crumpled piece of white paper and stuffed it in his pocket. Ryan and the other four watched in silence. The father caught them staring.

"Sorry, all. Please don't report us for . . . Wife's been ill and if reported we'd—" He stopped and looked more closely at them. "Outworlders! Didn't see at first. Oh, that's all right. Come on," he said to his son, dragging him by the arm along the street.

"Krysty's right, Ryan," Finnegan whispered. "Sooner we get out of this fucking ville the better."

"Yeah, Finn. With you there. Best get us some food and then mebbe hoist a wag and head on north."

They walked on in the thickening crowd. The calm of earlier had been replaced by a tenseness, an air of muted excitement. More and more eyes turned to look at the strangers, and again and again they heard the word "outworlder" repeated, plus the expression "first stone," or something that sounded like that.

The buildings were in excellent repair—far better than any ville Ryan, J.B. and Finn had ever seen. There were several stores, mostly selling plain clothes or food. Also for sale was a newspaper, the *Ginnsburg Falls Regulator*, whose proprietor, named on a trim board, was Isaac Sissy.

That name was obviously quite popular. There was also the Sissy Temperance Hotel and the Rachel Sissy Second Pentecostal Baptist Church of His Last Coming.

"This Sissy family sure has the ville sewn up tight," J.B. said.

"Don't like the feel at all," Ryan replied, keeping his voice quiet so that none of the men and boys surging around them would catch what was said.

"Me, neither," Jak said. "Dumb creepy mutie bastards, all of 'em. Why not go, Ryan?"

"Tomorrow," Ryan said.

There were lights coming on all around the township, with lamps on street corners glowing into golden life. Doc Tanner looked around in delight. "I swear that I have not encountered such a degree of civilization in…in many long years."

"Where's the power plant?" Ryan asked the sec guard, who still walked stolidly along beside them, the heels of his boots ringing on the stone sidewalk.

"West. On Salvation Avenue. Big generators."

"You got radio?"

"Yes. Just for us. No vids. Mayor says one day. Gotta get spares. Folks up north could help. So my father said to me. Said his father 'fore him heard the same."

"That must—" Finnegan began, stopping suddenly when Ryan surreptitiously angled a foot out to trip him. The stout gunman stumbled and nearly fell over. He looked at Ryan in sudden anger, then saw the warning shake of the head and calmed himself. Ryan didn't want the sec men of Ginnsburg Falls to know anything about the faint radio message they'd heard, and Finn nodded his understanding.

"Got vids or teevee?" Jak Lauren asked.

"Said not."

"Said no vids. How's 'bout teevee?"

"No." The word was flat and final.

Ryan was surprised they hadn't been ordered to remove their blasters and leave them with the sec men. All of them had chosen not to carry their heavier guns, relying on side arms. Most of the adult males of the ville wore pistols, many of which looked like remakes.

On some of the side streets small domestic wags were parked, and just beyond the Harold Sissy Memorial High School, close by the lake, there was a big old Kenworth rig with chromed exhaust.

They followed the throng off the main drag and up the narrow slope of Quarry Road.

Several of the older men were smoking pipes, and Ryan wrinkled his nostrils at the familiar smell. He looked sideways at J.B., seeing that the Armorer had also recognized the scent.

"Maryjane, huh?" he whispered.

"How's that sit with that temperance hotel back there?" J.B. wondered. "From the Mayor Sissy Cannabis Plant?"

"Watch the tongue, friend," Ryan warned.

"Fireblast!" exclaimed Ryan Cawdor when they arrived at the quarry. It was possible that more people had gathered here than he'd ever seen in one place. He did a quick count in the gathering gloom, estimating there were something like seven thousand men and boys present.

That meant there was something wrong. Something, somewhere, that was terribly wrong.

"Doc," he said, noting the villefolk had left a circle around the five outworlders as though they were suspected of being plaguies.

"What?"

"You're the man of science."

"Was, my dear boy, was."

"What did that sign say when we came into the ville? The population?"

"Eight thousand four hundred and . . . and seven. Real big town for these days."

"Do me a rough count on how many's here."

The old man was silent, lips moving as he let his eyes run around the natural arena, ticking off the figures on the different ledges in the quarry. Away to their left there was some sort of disturbance in the crowd, with a phalanx of sec men pushing through.

"Something between seventy-three hundred and seventy-four hundred. Difficult to count a shifting mob of chapped-hand yokels in poor light. I counted legs and divided by two."

Finnegan was listening to the exchange. "Wait a fucking minute," he began. "If there's a total—"

"Keep your voice down," J.B. snapped. "We get the picture, Ryan. Total population eight and a half thou. Man seven and a half thou. Take off some male babies. Can't leave more'n a few hundred women in the whole ville."

All four of them pondered that. The chatter around them had subsided, and the great granite bowl was silent, with only the whistling of the wind to break the stillness. As on the previous evening, it had become bitingly cold, and a chem-storm was raging away to the north, the crimson clouds torn apart with golden curtains of forked lightning.

There was a ramp that led to a raised podium near the middle of the quarry. The sec men were climbing it, with someone or something at their center. Jak Lauren had the keenest eyes.

"Cripple. They're wheeling."

Ryan saw him then: a tiny, frail man with a head, fringed with silvery hair, that looked too large for his body and a skin almost as pale as Jak's. They were only about fifty yards off, and Ryan could see the little hands, soft and pink, decorated with chunky rings and a golden bracelet. The legs trailed, wasted, in neat, highly polished shoes of black leather. The man wore a tailored suit of light cream cloth. As he was wheeled up to the platform, his head jiggled and rolled on his shoulders.

"Silence for Mayor Theodore Sissy," one of the sec men bellowed unnecessarily, since the crowd had fallen quiet the moment the leader of Ginnsburg Falls had appeared.

There was a microphone at the front of the stage, already adjusted to the height at which Mayor Sissy could speak into it comfortably from his chair. His voice was soft and trembling, like a nervous child.

"Bring them before us."

The stillness was broken by a murmur of sound that slithered around the quarry like some great rustling reptile.

A half-dozen sec men, including the leader of the patrol in the jeep, moved into the center of the quarry with two people in their midst.

"Let there be light," the cripple on the platform breathed. There was the sharp sound of a lever being thrown, and the whole place was flooded by arc lamps that stood on pylons circling the stone arena.

The stark glare made Jak's white hair stand out like spun magnesium. All round them the men and boys backed farther off, muttering and pointing. Fortunately they were distracted by the events at the middle of the quarry.

"Here stand Jolyon Manscomb and the whore. Taken in the act of adulterous lust. It is admitted that the whore lured him, as Eve lured Adam, with her cunt filled with honey. But both pay the price."

The woman was slightly built, with dull brown hair cropped raggedly at shoulder level. She was dressed in a short robe, like a shift, of some coarse material that looked as if it had been used as sacking. It was dyed a vivid, sickly yellow. The man, whose head was bowed and balding, was wearing a similar robe, colored flat ocher. Both of them were barefoot and both had their hands tied in front of them with a thick rope.

Ryan had noticed that he stood on uneven ground. It was covered with a thick layer of stones, ranging in size from pebbles to jagged chunks of granite as large as a man's fist. There were similar piles of stones all about the floor of the quarry, the nearest only a dozen paces from where he waited with J.B., Jak, Finn and Doc Tanner. He licked his lips, finding them suddenly dry as he realized what the stones were for.

"Outworlders, step forward," the little man in the wheelchair commanded, reading slowly from a creased piece of paper that one of the sec men had handed him. "Cawdor, Dix, Finnegan, Lauren and Tanner. All come to stand before me."

Conscious of every man's eyes upon them, the five stepped across the uneven ground, picking their way around the piles of stone. Ryan noticed that the woman in the sack robe watched them, but the man at her side remained with his head bowed, mumbling to himself, shoulders shaking as he wept.

"Welcome, outworlders, to Ginnsburg Falls." The little man had a face reminiscent of pictures Ryan had once seen in an old book of maps—chubby cheeks, pursed as though to blow a great wind across the quarry, eyes twinkling coldly in the flat light.

"Like a damnably evil cherub," Doc Tanner whispered.

That had been the word Ryan wanted. *Cherub*. But with a darker side of power and evil.

"When we have men in from beyond our borders, we allow them the privilege of aiding our rituals. You are blessed that you have an opportunity to prove your worth on your first night among us."

"Do he mean what I think he fucking means?" Finn said, looking around in disgust.

"Can the talk, Finn," Ryan hissed. "You'll get us all chilled."

Mayor Sissy had stopped, the merry glitter vanishing for a moment. When he resumed, the voice was a shade or two less amicable.

"The punishment of Jolyon Manscomb and the whore is now to begin. The shame is made worse by the help of the outworlders. By their actions shall they also be judged. Sec Commander?"

"Sir."

"Begin. Remember, all present, that you may share the stoning only when one full minute has passed on the counting of the sec commander here. To begin too early would disappoint me."

Ryan reached up and eased the patch over his left eye socket. He rubbed his cheek and found that he was sweating despite the cold.

"Are you ready, outworlders?"

Obviously an answer was required. Ryan coughed to clear his throat. "Yes. We're ready."

"Then begin."

Ryan didn't move. The others at his side tensed like hunting dogs. Without looking, he knew that fingers would be questing for the butts of blasters. He also knew that if they made one wrong move, death was a dozen heartbeats away.

"Begin, outworlders, or join the fool and the whore."

Bending slowly, Ryan reached down with his right hand and picked up a large, jagged stone, his fingers tightening around it.

# Chapter Ten

ALL FIVE OF THEM had picked up stones and were waiting.

"Now!" Mayor Sissy snapped.

"It were well done quickly," Doc Tanner said, surprisingly taking the lead. He threw his rock with a clumsy roundhouse motion, like a young girl attempting to pitch for the first time. The stone bounced yards short.

"Go closer," the cracking voice from the loudspeakers urged.

Ryan threw next, aiming at the man. The stone hissed through the chilled evening air, hitting Jolyon Manscomb high on the right side of his chest. He cried out, more in surprise than protest or pain, and staggered a little. His head remained bowed. The woman looked across at Ryan and his friends, shouting something flavored with disgust and anger.

J.B. and Finnegan threw together, both aiming at the man. Both their rocks struck home, one on the thigh, the other gashing Manscomb's cheek, sending blood flowing over his neck to dapple the yellow robe. In the brightness of the artificial light, the blood was almost black. There was a murmur of excitement from the watchers, like the sound Ryan had heard in gaudy houses when a pesthole slut was stripping, the moment when she would ease her satin skirt down over her hips, showing the dark vee of hair, revealing the spread lips of her sex.

The sound was the same—a tongue-smacking anticipation of what had been glimpsed, coupled with the knowledge there was much more to be seen.

Jak Lauren threw his stone underhand, like a child playing ducks and drakes on a town pool. It hit the woman on the forearm, just above the binding of the ropes. There was the clear, brittle crack of a bone snapping, and she screamed very loudly once, which brought a wave of laughter from the watchers.

"Mutie bastard," she cried at the boy.

"More," the little man insisted, leaning forward on the platform to see better. "More and faster and harder. It is not enough to cast only the first stones."

They threw a second volley of rocks, then another. Several of them were accurately aimed, one knocking the man clear off his feet. The whore was hit three times, one stone drawing blood from her leg, a hand's span below the right knee.

"Thirty seconds gone, thirty to go," the sec commander called out in a stentorian voice.

When they were felled, both of them struggled patiently to their feet, standing where they had before, waiting for more stones.

Above all, Ryan was a realist. He had sensed that the hunched figure in the wheelchair had been waiting for him to refuse, for one of them to refuse to take part in the obscene rites.

Now, all around the quarry, men and boys stooped, filling their hands with stones. Even the youngest lads picked up round pebbles, hopping from foot to foot in their eagerness to begin.

"Into Thy hands we commend their spirits," Doc Tanner said in a subdued, conversational voice.

One of them—Ryan thought it was probably Jak—hit the man in the lower belly, producing a shrill, womanish scream. The woman was knocked to her knees, but she rose again almost at once, her eyes locked on Ryan's face as if he were the sole aggressor.

"Fifteen seconds. Make ready."

Ryan took aim and threw. They were only about twenty-five feet from the yellow-clad victims, and it was hard to miss. Also, to miss accidentally might be spotted and treated as deliberate by the bright-eyed cripple above them. Out of the corner of his eye, Ryan noticed with a wave of revulsion that Sissy's stubby little fingers were busy in his lap, rubbing at a massive erection that distended the front of the tailored pants.

Since time was nearly up, he knew this could be the last rock he needed to throw. Then his part in the butchery could cease. He aimed at the woman's body, hoping only to strike her a glancing blow. But a clumsy throw from Doc Tanner came wheeling wildly in, hitting her on the foot at a second bounce. She fell to her knees at the very moment that Ryan released his own last rock.

Almost in slow motion he watched it wheeling toward the whore. His own lips began to shape the word *no*, as if it might change the flight of the missile.

The woman turned, dirt on her slender throat, hair streaked with mud. The bright lights made her eyes look glassy, as though she were blind. The sharp-edged hunk of granite, the quartz glittering like diamonds, hit her on the right side of her face between nose and ear. It found its target with such venomous precision that it cracked her cheekbone, smashing her right eye to a weeping pulp. Blood, mingling with the aqueous humors, poured over her face, soaking the shift she wore. The blow was so savage that it sent her spinning over, unable with hands bound to do anything to save herself.

The crowd whooped and cheered, and the thin little voice over the speakers congratulated him.

"Wonderful throw, Outworlder Cawdor. You will do well here in Ginnsburg Falls."

"Time," came the command from the sec man.

"YOU KILLED THEM!"

Ryan nodded. "No choice, lover. If we hadn't, we'd have been butchered. They were just waiting for it. And the man and woman would have died anyway. What the fuck would the point have been in that? Seven deaths instead of two. Five friends as well as two total strangers."

"There wasn't anything you could have done? You couldn't have argued?"

"With Mayor Theodore Sissy? I tell you, Krysty, if you'd been there..."

They were back at their dormitory. The men had been reluctant to talk about what they'd seen and done, but both Lori and Krysty were eager to hear about it. Both had been shocked into silence at first when they had heard the horrible story.

"Like raining," Jak said.

"I feared for our lives," Doc Tanner added. His face was lined with fatigue, and he sat slumped in a smart armchair.

"Fucking murderous. Only thing I figure is that they died fucking fast. I seen mebbe two hundred rocks hit 'em in the first ten seconds," Finnegan said.

J.B. nodded. "I guess so. Man's skull was soft when he hit the dirt. Like a bag of beans, so many breaks in it."

"What happened after it was over?" Lori asked, holding on to Doc's arm.

"Nothing. Sec men led us back here. Everyone was rolling high in the street. Talking and talking, like they'd been to a great show." Ryan shook his head in disgust. "I feel fucking dirty, I tell you. I killed me a lot of folks in my time, but never because some fucking gimp with a squeaking voice tells me to."

"You couldn't help it," Krysty said.

"Sure. But the way those sick bastards loved it! Nothing like a public killing. Surprised more barons don't liven their villes with 'em. I know some do, but never with fucking stones. Fireblast! I just want t'get to bed now."

But the day wasn't over quite yet.

Without knocking, the sec commander came marching into the long room, stopping in his tracks when he saw Krysty and Lori sitting on the beds with the rest of the group.

"Outworlder Cawdor. The home-keeps don't sleep or eat with men. Only whores. You said...?"

"No, they're not whores."

"Then they go."

"What?"

"You walk the line and you'll be fine. They can stay tonight. Past nonperson's curfew on street. They'd be in the quarry at dusk tomorrow if they were caught out now. This letter from the mayor tells you what's going to happen."

It was short and to the point, written in a neat, italic, sloping script on rough-edged handmade paper: "Outworlders report to me at nine in the forenoon. Then to militia induction. All passes and food creds will then be issued and accommodation arranged separately. Home-keeps to Arthur Sissy wing of workhouse for acceptance into general pool. First sight makes me reckon both could be whores if I decide suitable." It was signed "Theodore J. Sissy, Mayor."

There was also a postscript, obviously added as an afterthought: "Outworlder Lauren is a suss-mutie. He will be taken to the lake for rogation and nondesirable rating."

After the sec man had left, Ryan silently passed the note around. Finnegan read last. "Welcome to Ginnsburg Falls," he said. "Friendliest fucking little town in the West."

# Chapter Eleven

JAK SLIPPED AWAY at around three in the morning. They'd talked for a long while, deciding whether they should all break and run for it. The girls were both for leaving, but they were eventually overruled. Ryan had pointed out that if all seven of them escaped from the ville it was certain that the whole sec force would be turned out to hunt them into the mountains.

"Head out, kid," Ryan said finally. "Krysty 'n Lori, go where they tell you. We'll step careful, like walking on eggs. This ville is—"

"So fucking far out it's going to fucking meet itself coming back again," Finn said.

"Right," Ryan agreed. "I saw a big wag on the way to the stoning. Looked gassed up and ready to roll. We'll try to check it out sometime, if we get a chance. Get us some food and drink."

"I could find it in my heart to relish snuffing out a life or two," Doc Tanner said quietly. His deep, resonant voice was contemplative, his eyes staring out into some unseeable distance. "I've seldom met such bred-in-the-bone evil as in that gimpy dwarf."

"Main thing is to be away clear," J.B. said. "Won't be easy."

"Where to meet?" Jak asked.

"Depends on how many chase," Ryan replied. "We all agreed to track that radio message. The Kenworth truck's got a trans-receiver in the cab. Saw the whip aerial. Saw the only highway north, running along the side of the big lake. Past the quarry road. When you get clear of the ville, take that. Move fast and keep your eyes behind you."

The albino nodded. "Keep sec men out of m'ass. I'll hide up, 'round ten miles out. If'n there's fork, I'll leave marker which took. Watch for me."

Quickly they gathered around the open window of the dorm, which overlooked the sullen expanse of the lake at the rear of the long building, and watched Jak leave. Finn had crept down, making sure the elderly janitor was sleeping in his room in the basement near the roaring boiler.

"Keep warm," Krysty warned the boy.

"Sure. By time get safe away, light'll have come up. Find shelter. Got fire."

"Go," Ryan said, patting the skinny boy on the shoulder, feeling a pang of doubt and letting him slip away alone into the Oregon blackness.


"WELCOME TO GINNSBURG FALLS," Mayor Sissy said, his tiny frame perched behind a massive leather-topped desk with a polished oil lamp at either end. "I am touched with grief that your colleague, Outworlder Lauren, has run away."

His great head wobbled and shook on his scrawny neck, as though it might topple onto his desk at any moment. Behind him stood two stone-faced sec men, arms folded across their chests, carbines slung over their shoulders. Ryan stood with Doc, J.B. and Finn, facing him, trying to look calm and under control, knowing that a wrong word here could result in a collective icing.

"Nobody speaks to me? I think that this must be because of guilt."

Ryan shook his head. "Not so, Mayor Sissy. The boy joined us only hours before we met your sec patrol. We thought he might be a mutie, but we let him travel with us until we could be sure."

"If you'd been sure?"

"If we'd been sure the boy was a mutie, then I'd have chilled him myself."

"Or brought him here for trial and then execution."

"Yeah, of course."

"Now we must decide what to do with you. Your home-keeps are waiting for me to see them and decide if they are truly whores. What is your opinion, Outworlder Cawdor? Whores?"

Ryan shrugged, as though the question wasn't of the least concern to him. "What you decide will be right, Mayor Sissy."

He clapped his chubby little hands softly. "Well spoken, for an outworlder. You will all do well in our militia. But not the dotard," he said, pointing at Doc Tanner. "He can go to the Antigone Sissy Home for the Congenitally Senile and then be tested for removal to the Ronald W. Sissy Euthanasia Center."

"Senile! Euthanasia!" Doc roared, stamping the end of his sword stick hard on the floor and making both sec men reach for their blasters. "You posturing little . . . urrgh."

Ryan shut him up the only way he knew how, elbowing him so hard in the guts that Doc folded over like an eager courtier, dropping to his knees with a cracking of joints. His face turned the color of curdled milk, and he gasped for breath.

"See how he behaves," Mayor Sissy said. "So undignified for one so old."

"Old, maybe," Doc said quietly. "Not surfeit-swelled or profane."

"What are you babbling about, old man?"

"Just a thought came from nowheres, Mayor Sissy. Be glad to go and see this Home you talked about."

"Good, that's better. If you live in Ginnsburg Falls and you walk the line . . . what then?"

"You'll be fine," they said in chorus, receiving a beam of delight in reward.

"Excellent, outworlders." Sissy leaned back, ticking points off on his fingers. "The white-headed mutie will be hunted and destroyed. The old man to the home. That can wait until the morrow. The home-keeps for me to see . . . I shall leave that for tomorrow. I have to oversee an exposing."

"A what?" Ryan asked.

"An exposing, outworlder. All the nonperson babies born in the past three months will all be taken by the elders of the council and exposed on the slopes about the ville. It is one of the most important of all our rites to maintain the proper balance as our founders decided."

Ryan took a deep breath, trying to school his face to blankness. "I see, Mayor. Where is this done?"

"To the west, at the exposing place. The creatures of the wild gather for the ceremony."

At the back of Ryan's mind was still that peculiar radio message they'd received, promising help for anyone who went north.

"Not to the north?"

Sissy shook his head so violently that his tiny blue eyes rolled like marbles in lard. "Never north, you cretin! Even a stupe outworlder should know that. North is trouble and darkness and death. Any citizen of my ville that goes north is a dead man!"

"Should we go for the induction?" Ryan asked after the tiny mannikin had sat slumped in his wheelchair for several moments, seemingly exhausted by his vituperative outburst.

"Yes, go. No, wait. Wait. If there is to be the exposing today, many sec men will be busy. Let it wait. Go back to your dorms, or walk about the ville. Enjoy it. See what a pleasant life we lead here. Creds and passes will be issued. Don't ask what Ginnsburg Falls can do for you, ask what you can do for Ginnsburg Falls."

As they stepped out into the warm sunshine, Finn glanced around to make sure he couldn't be overheard. "Know what I don't understand? Why the fuck isn't it called Sissy Falls?"

None of them could come up with an answer.

THE WALK BACK THROUGH town heightened their feeling of alienation.

The ville was immaculate. There were no drink houses and no gaudies, except for the main one where most of the women were herded—kept in a form of purdah, locked away in seclusion and totally subservient to the whims of the males.

The clothes and the buildings seemed to conform to some sort of norm. Homes were neat frame houses, each with its own trim front garden and wire-fenced back garden. Ryan noticed that every house was painted white, and all of them looked as if they'd been decorated within the past few months.

"No blacks," Finnegan pointed out.

"All good, decent, red-neck WASPs," Doc Tanner said cryptically. None of the others knew what he meant by that, except that it sounded as if he were being ironic.

"No commies or Catholics or aidies," J.B. said, watching the good people of Ginnsburg Falls parading nervously past the outworlders.

"Some of these buildings go back better'n a hundred years," Doc Tanner observed. "And all the newer ones are built on precisely the same pattern. All got identical mailboxes and a box for the daily copy of the *Regulator*. Damnedest ville I ever did see. Can't wait to shake its dust off of my boots."

THEY ATE LUNCH TOGETHER, despite the disapproving glares and sniffs of the janitor. The food was reasonable, basic meat and vegetables. The meat was protosoya, flavored with fresh herbs, tarragon and nutmeg predominating. The vegetables were compressed blocks of spinach and shredded carrots with oversteamed artichokes. To complete the meal there were slabs of green gelatin, quivering gently on plastic dishes.

"Mayor says them got to go to the workhouse," the janitor said, offering them a malicious, gap-toothed grin.

"Tomorrow, he told us," Ryan said.

"New message. Today. Three in the afternoon, they go. Down the Arthur Sissy wing. Near the lake. By the wag park. Yeah, got to go, got to get an' go an' go and get gone they gotta go."

He went out, slamming the cream-painted door behind him. Doc Tanner shook his head. "Now there's a truly prime candidate for senility and euthanasia if ever I saw one. I'll slip him the mickey myself."

"We have to go?" Lori asked plaintively.

Krysty patted her hand. "Come on, lover," she said, to Ryan. "This has gone on better than long enough. This place is sicksville. Let's go after Jak."

"In daylight?" he replied. "Get some fucking sense in your brain, Krysty. They got old blasters, but there's mebbe seven thousand vigilantes all primed and ready. If you'd been in the quarry last night, you'd have seen what a swarm of mothers we'd have on our necks. When we go, it has to be night. Take a run north. Hope that the fact they're so shit-scared of up that way, they'll leave us be."

"So we go to this workhouse?"

"Sure. Keep your chrons hid. Check the time, and we'll aim to be there and spring you at a quarter after one in the morning."

"You better be there, Ryan," she warned. "If you're not, then Lori and me will be off and running so fast you won't even see our dust."

THE SEC COMMANDER CAME AROUND two to collect the women and escort them down the highway to the workhouse at the lake's edge. He also told Ryan something about the ville's militia.

"You two go and wait in the street," he said to Krysty and Lori, not even looking to make sure they obeyed his commands, grinning at the sound of their dragging steps.

"Mayor'll give them sluts something to walk heavy about if'n he goes to check 'em tonight."

"Mayor Sissy takes a real paternal interest in the whores, does he?" Ryan said.

"Damned right he does. The Sissy family took over Ginnsburg Falls a few years after the long winters ended. Up here we were lucky. Other places in Deathlands had it bad. All dead, or mutied. Sissy clan saved us from that. Now we take real good care which outlanders come in. You did good at the stoning, all of you. But the kid with the snow hair—we'll catch him, 'less he's gone north. And if he's gone north, then he'll die anyways."

"Why?" Doc Tanner asked.

"Bad things that way, old man. Hot spots. Heavy rad counts. Muties you wouldn't believe. They send out message to try and trap... Shouldn't talk like this. Mayor don't relish words about the north.''

"What messages?" J.B. asked.

"On radio. Loop tape. Forbidden to listen in. Tricks folks to follow it. Nobody never came back.''

"Like the sirens' song that so enchanted mighty Ulysses upon that wine-dark Aegean," Doc Tanner said, catching Ryan's eye.

"Don't know the name, old man," the sec man said. "But I just know for sure that anyone goes north goes up there to be killed and never comes back. I know that for sure.''

"Then we'll fucking keep away from there," Finnegan said, nodding.

The guard looked at him. "Blasphemy can earn you treadmill time here, Outworlder Finnegan. Mayor Sissy does not approve of swearing.''

"Sure, sir," Finn replied. "Don't want no trouble here, boss. Walking the line, boss." Ryan glared at him, fearing the chubby blaster would go way over the top and bring them all some trouble.

"Good," the sec man said. "Keep straight around the ville. Mayor'll see you on the morrow.''

"What 'bout the militia?" the Armorer asked, halting the man at the door.

"Men here all join militia. Good at it and you get to join sec unit. Not too hard. Part-time. Patrol for curfew breakers. Guard highways. Check out the wags and the gas supply.''

"You keep 'em gassed up an' ready?" J.B. asked casually.

"Sure. Haven't had a runner from Ginnsburg Falls for 'bout...a year now. Couple whores got men to break with them. Got caught. Good stoning, that one. Man kept dodging, even catching some of the stones. He played baseball for the ville.'' The sec man laughed at the reminiscence. ''Course the dumb stupe couldn't dodge 'em all.''

THEY SPLIT UP for the rest of the day.

Ryan suggested that Doc stay in the dorm, since his age made him vulnerable for removal to the senility and euthanasia center. Doc wanted to go down and see how Lori and Krysty were, but reluctantly he agreed to remain where he was.

Finnegan offered to recce the workhouse in preparation for their visit there later that night.

J.B. checked out the big rig they'd spotted, making sure it was filled up and ready to roll, and he talked to one of the locals, who was aggrieved he hadn't been able to go to the exposing outside the ville. The man told the Armorer that the Kenworth was the best wag in town, with a range of close to a hundred miles, even allowing for the aged engine and the deteriorated blacktops.

Ryan strolled around, trying to familiarize himself with the geography of the ville. It was a huge, sprawling place, laid out in a grid pattern, the streets crossing at right angles, the main roads running parallel to the big lake. One thing he noticed early was that Ginnsburg Falls had no dogs. In fact, not even a single domestic animal was evident—no cats, no birds in cages, no fish in tanks in the curtained windows. Intermittently Ryan spotted women peering at him through the white lace that covered most casements. Here and there boys played quietly in trim gardens, rode ramshackle old bikes or threw balls back and forth.

The exposing had cleared most of the population from the ville, so there were few civilians around to question him. There were plenty of sec men still on the streets, though. They marched in pairs, carbines slung across their shoulders.

The most exciting moment was when a young lad, who looked around twelve, came racing around a blind corner on an old bicycle much too big for him. The boy stood on the pedals, his face contorted with the effort. Ryan stepped aside, feeling the rush of wind, amused at the overreaction of terror and excitement he could sense in the boy. He heard a shrill voice, crying something that sounded like "Hiyo, Silver!" Then the sound faded into the restrained stillness of the afternoon ville.

DOC TANNER FELL ASLEEP around eleven, snoring a little, hands folded across his chest, stovepipe hat resting primly on the floor beside his bed. The other three talked quietly, mostly about the old times with the Trader, casual memories not worth forgetting.

"Remember that little mutie girl with the sweet smile and the broken arm?" Finnegan asked. "Old Fletch was carrying her, an' she reached up an' plucked his eye out just like picking a fucking grape."

"I recall the Trader with an old, old woman, near blind, who brought him a watch. Good make, but it was empty. No works. Just the case. Trader took it from her hand real gentle." J.B. paused. "Never forgot the look on his face. He picked up a dried soya box. Empty one. Figured he was going to give it to her as an exchange. He looked at the old woman, you know the way he had, and he—"

"We all heard it before, friend," Ryan interrupted the Armorer. "It's time to get ready. Weapon check."

Each man slipped into the private ritual of checking and rechecking his weapons. Doc Tanner awoke and agreed to stand by the door and keep watch for the janitor. Bolts clicked, and ammunition tinkled on the floor. Then bed sheets were torn into strips to clean and polish the guns.

It was fifteen minutes past midnight.

THEY WERE READY a half hour later. Finn led the way, surprisingly catfooted for such a bulky, clumsy-looking man, his HK54A2 with the drum mag and built-in silencer in his beefy hands. Doc came second, clutching the massive hand cannon of the Le Mat. Ryan prayed silently to himself that the old man didn't need to pull the trigger down on anyone with the ancient blaster. The noise would bring every man and boy in Ginnsburg Falls on the run, thinking their precious gas storage tanks had been blown.

J.B. was third, mini-Uzi braced at his hip, with Ryan, bringing up the rear of the group, holding the 9 mm SIG-Sauer pistol.

The building was quiet, with the occasional creak of settling wood and stone. Outside, through the clean windows facing north, the sky was alight with the distant pattern of lighting from a chem-storm.

They'd been watching the patrols from the dormitory, timing them and checking their frequency. Around eight in the evening, they'd heard wags come lumbering back into the ville, spilling out loads of excited men and tired young lads, exhausted from the day's ritual of exposing female infants. Since then, Ginnsburg Falls had become quiet. The pairs and triads of sec men had come down the main street, Sissy, making a left along Fourth in front of the dormitory. They had returned once every hour, at ten minutes to eleven, and again at ten to twelve.

"Clear," Finn whispered, trotting out of the main door and leaving it to Ryan to slide it quietly shut behind them. There was a sharp-edged section of moon sailing low across the mountains over the lake.

Ryan took the lead, moving quickly through the back-lots and yards of stores and large houses. It was a cold night, but not with the same dreadful bite that set cheek-bones aching with the sharpness. They passed a house with a row of laurels along its back border. From an open attic window came the unmistakable sound of a woman weeping. A man was shouting. Then there came a flat crack, like the palm of a hand across a face.

And then silence.

Doc Tanner paused. "If there was an amplitude of time, my friends, I vow that it would be a fine cleansing to burn this ville to the foundations. A place of more nugatory worth I never did see."

"I'd be happy to fucking chill it, Doc."

"No, Finn," Ryan warned. "What we want best is to get away quick and quiet and easy. If'n we need to ice some sec men, then we do it. J.B., I reckon it's time you went down and got the Kenworth ready. Start her up the moment you see us coming. We'll be moving fast and low."

"Sure. Shoot to kill, you guys," the Armorer said, grinning as he ran toward the wag park, his fedora at a jaunty angle on his head.

The other three kept on toward the oblong shape of the old workhouse.

RYAN SAW THE SEC MEN before they had a chance to see him in the darkness. He flattened himself against the chipped brick wall of a warehouse. There were two jeeps there, with a half-dozen men lounging around them. The way they stood made him suspect no officer was with them. They looked as if they didn't expect to be needed for some time.

Finn knelt down and peeked around the corner. "We can waste 'em all," he said.

"There's a back entrance," Ryan said. "Saw it this afternoon. Goes along the waterfront. There's an old pier. Runs the whole length and connects with another jetty. Cuts right in by where the wag's waiting for us."

The back door was open. Several low-watt bulbs were strung along the pale green corridor. A painted board directed visitors to the main entrance and reception areas, but a gilt arrow pointed to the Arthur Sissy wing, and Ryan and the others took this direction.

They passed many open doors to empty rooms that contained iron bedsteads. On each was a pile of gray blankets, folded with edges so sharp it looked as if they'd cut bread. The corridor turned left. The arrows led them up a short flight of stairs and through a pair of swinging doors along another corridor to a closed door on their right.

Ryan had seen old police vids where the heroes kicked open doors and leaped through. That often wasn't the way. Better to turn the handle and walk in slow and quiet, as if you had the right to be there, but with your finger on the trigger of your blaster.

He glanced at Finn and Doc. They nodded, the old man forcing a thin smile.

"Now," Ryan said.

There were five people in the room, which looked around twenty feet square. Two beds were pushed back against the far wall, and a window, barred and curtained, was on the left.

Standing just inside the door, a sec man glanced around as the three men casually entered.

Krysty Wroth sat on the nearest bed, face pale as death, eyes closed, lips pressed together. From the painful tension, Ryan spotted immediately that she was in the process of calling on her Earth Mother, Gaia, to give her the strange power and unnatural strength to perform some almost supernatural feat.

A second sec man was standing in the middle of the room, holding his carbine, its muzzle pressed against the back of Lori Quint's neck.

She was kneeling, hands supporting her on either side of her spread thighs. Her long yellow hair dangled around her face, hiding what she was doing. But the bobbing of her head made it unmistakable.

She was naked, with bruises across her shoulders and ribs.

Ryan heard the sharp intake of breath from Doc Tanner by his side.

The fifth person in the room was Mayor Theodore Sissy, sitting squatly in his wheelchair, eyes tightly shut, a sickly smile hugging his lips. From where Ryan stood, he could just see that the front of the cripple's trousers was unzipped. Lori's blond tresses brushed against the frail, dangling, stunted legs.

"Don't do it, Doc," Ryan said quickly, not wanting to have the building explode with the boom of the big Le Mat.

Finn didn't need telling what to do.

The Heckler & Koch was set on triple burst. He touched the light trigger just once, opening up the throat of the guard at the door. In the confined space, the silencer was surprisingly effective, no louder than fingers rapping on a table.

The man's body jerked back and hit the wall, sliding down and leaving a great smear of bright scarlet blood across the clean paint. The other guard turned, the barrel of his carbine jerking away from Lori's skull. His mouth dropped open in shock, eyes widening as he saw his death a pulse away.

Ryan took a chance, firing a single round from his pistol. At less than fifteen feet, the nine-millimeter bullet hit the sec man through the bridge of the nose. The impact lifted him off his feet, then his boots came clattering down, kicking and flailing for balance. The bullet exited out through the back of his head, slightly behind the right ear, taking a chunk of bone with it. Blood and brain splattered under pressure, dappling the whitewashed ceiling with a pink-gray mist.

"Close the door, Doc," Ryan ordered. "And keep watch. If we're lucky, the guards out front won't have heard anything. Too many doors and corridors between us. But listen for 'em." Turning to the women, he asked, "You all right, Lori, Krysty?"

"What the fuck are you outworlders doing? You are all fucking dead meat," Theodore Sissy squeaked, hands frantically trying to shove his fast-softening cock back inside his pants.

"You putrescent scum," Doc Tanner said, thumbing back the hammer of the Le Mat.

"The door, Doc."

Lori rose, her eyes locked on the seated man, her hands hanging loose at her sides, making no effort to cover her nakedness. Krysty shuddered, as if she'd just come from a deep, drugged sleep. She opened her eyes and looked across the room at Ryan, taking in the two blood-sodden corpses of the sec men.

"Hi, lover," she said. "You showed just in time. I was going to try and waste them myself. Just drawing on the power of Gaia."

"Get Lori dressed. Where are your blasters?"

"Under the bed in the corner. The sec men kicked them there out of the way, when the mayor arrived for his fucking sickness boost."

"If I scream, you're all dead. The whole fucking militia'll be here in seconds. There's nowhere to go. Nowhere you can run." The great soft face rippled as Mayor Sissy licked his thick pink lips.

"I'm all right," Lori said, shaking her head. "I'll get dressed. Won't take a moment."

Finnegan leaned on the back of the wheelchair, the warm muzzle of the submachine gun resting casually against Sissy's neck.

Krysty joined Ryan near the door. "The sec goons beat her when she refused to blow him. She gave in. I was going t'be next. He'd decided to get a guard to ass-fuck me while I sucked him. That was when I was going to kill him and try for the other two. The carbine wouldn't have stopped me."

In his wheelchair the diminutive mayor of the ville was wriggling from side to side, looking around at the dead guards. He turned to Ryan Cawdor and asked, "You hope to use me to get you safe away?"

"No."

"You hope I'll spare you?"

"No."

Lori was almost dressed. She pulled her soft leather boots up over her muscular thighs, the spurs jingling with a cold, frosty sound, then stood up from the bed and buckled on the belt and holster for her pearl-handled Walther PPK .22. Brushing her hair away from her face, she moved to stand in front of Sissy.

"Not a lot of time," Ryan said. "Got to pick up the wag. J.B.'ll be wondering where the fuck we are."

"Won't take long, this won't," the girl replied, her voice flat and hard.

Doc stuck his head back into the room. "All quiet out here." Seeing Lori looking at the crippled Sissy, he said, "Let me, honey."

"No," the girl replied.

"Let me go and I'll let you all go free," the mayor pleaded. His face jerked and twitched. He gripped the wheels of the chair, trying to roll away from the icy stare of the tall blond girl. She jammed one foot hard between his legs, making him squeal in pain, her heel holding him still.

"You fuck. You miserable little fuckhead bastard. Making me... Open your mouth, Mayor." Sissy opened his lips as wide as he could, and she drew her pistol, ramming the barrel into his mouth and breaking off one of his front teeth so that blood trickled over his chin and down his elegant suit.

Ryan lurched forward, but Krysty restrained him, shaking her head. "Let her," she said.

"Suck on this, Mayor," Lori said, blowing a kiss to the helpless man. Her own lips peeled back off her strong white teeth in a feral grin as she added, "Suck it good."

The small-caliber pistol jerked in her hand, the noise almost completely muffled in the the man's mouth. Sissy's head snapped back, his whole body convulsing. Lori kicked the chair, sending it spinning into the wall to one side of the window. It tipped over, spilling the dying man on the floor, where he thrashed, arms trembling violently. Blood spilled from his open mouth and his nose. His eyes stared blankly at the ceiling.

"The fucker ate it good, didn't he?" Lori said, holstering the blaster.

"Sure did," Ryan said. "Now let's get out of here."

A MILE OUT OF TOWN Krysty wanted to stop at another of the population markers. ''Want to go and knock one off for the late Mayor Sissy,'' she said.

''Late and unlamented,'' Doc Tanner added.

''Best keep moving,'' Ryan said.

J.B. hugged the wheel of the big Kenworth truck, gunning the motor, pedal to the metal, twin lights blazing a path along the old blacktop. About ten miles out of town they picked up the bedraggled figure of Jak Lauren.

For the rest of the night, the seven drove on, away from Ginnsburg Falls, following the northward trail, tugged on by the radio message.

With its mysterious words of hope.

Of hope?

# Chapter Twelve

IN THE PALE LIGHT of dawn, they passed a bullet-riddled sign, leaning drunkenly to one side, telling them they were on State Highway 62.

J.B. had found a creased and taped map of the district in the glove compartment of the big truck. He opened it carefully, knowing from previous experience how delicate very old documents could be. The light in the crowded cab was a faint, flickering, uncovered light bulb, and he angled the map beneath it, trying to hold it steady against the lurching of the big vehicle.

"Watch the damned bumps," he snarled at Finnegan, who was at the wheel.

"What the fucking bumps yourself!" The Kenworth hadn't taken kindly to being pushed along at a speed beyond what its age could handle. In the first hour a couple of the forward gears had stopped functioning, and the shift was becoming uncomfortably hot to touch.

"See where we're heading, J.B.?" Ryan Cawdor asked, blinking his good eye at the hills that towered up on either side of the blacktop. "There's a big mountain, called Mazama. Old volcano, with a round lake in its crater."

"Crater Lake," Doc Tanner said, yawning, trying to stretch himself awake and finding that there wasn't enough room for his spindly legs with Lori asleep in his arms.

"Know anything about that?" Ryan asked, hoping that the old man's precarious memory might be triggered off to give them some useful information.

"Some."

"Yeah? Go on."

Doc shook his head, his stringy hair dangling across his shoulders. "Cerberus and the other projects were intensely secret. But there were others. I was not privy to many of them."

Everyone in the party, except the albino boy, was awake. Krysty was puzzled. "What does 'privy' mean, Doc?"

"At one time, dear lady, it had the meaning of a place for one's bowel movements and bladder evacuations."

"What is that?" Lori asked, opening her eyes.

"Means where you piss and shit," Ryan said. "Don't it?"

The old man nodded, the pearly light from the east illuminating his oddly perfect teeth. "But in this case, my dear Ryan, it means there were doors closed to me. I was allowed certain knowledge on a need-to-know basis. I do recall that Crater Lake was...what was it?"

Finn applied the brakes and cursed his way down through the gears, fighting the truck to a slowing halt. "Road's blocked," he said, pulling the hand brake on with a hiss of compressed air.

Ryan ignored him, concentrating on clinging to Doc's elusive memory. "Crater Lake was what?"

"In truth it was. A man might trudge along, noting every passing phenomenon..." He hesitated, savoring the word, rolling it around his mouth as if he were trying to identify an exotic herb on his tongue. "Phenomenon. Truly said, my boy. It was that and more."

It was too late.

The frail highways that linked brain and memory had fallen asunder again. Gradually, Ryan thought, Doctor Theophilus Tanner was returning to some kind of normal.

"Is someone going to get off their ass and move that fucking pile of wood?" Finn said, winding down the window of the truck and spitting out into the freezing morning. Though the engine was beat-up, at least the heater worked. Outside, the temperature was way down past freezing. Ryan almost expected to hear Finnegan's spittle turn to ice in the air and tinkle on the road.

Ryan peered through the windshield. Ahead he could see the blacktop rolling higher between the banks of dark conifers. Above them, to the left, there'd been an earthslide, bringing down a jumble of debris, including the snapped branches and fallen trunks of pines. By the look of it, the blockage had been there for a while, confirming their suspicion that the good folk of Ginnsburg Falls didn't travel north very often.

The driving easterly wind blew a flurry of snow against the glass, blinding him for a moment. As it cleared, Ryan thought he spotted movement among the stunted young trees at the side of the highway. But when he stared, there was nothing to see.

"Come on," he said. "Let the kid sleep. Rest of you out and start shifting that mess."

He was glad they'd all equipped themselves with warm coats. The gale was like a whetted knife, making his eye water, the ice particles it carried ripping at the tender flesh of his cheeks. He huddled into the collar of his trusty suede coat, happy to have a moment to admire Krysty's looks. Her fiery hair whisked about her shoulders as she stood tall in her knee-length black fur, its hue so dark it seemed almost blue in the strengthening light.

There was a dusting of snow on the road, and it swirled around his boots. The truck stood tall, its crimson flanks streaked with mud. The long exhaust had retained its original chrome and now reflected the pink glow of the distant sun. Ryan looked at the hubcaps and saw the stunted, distorted image of himself and the others. Then the memory of the flicker of movement in the scrub gave him pause.

"J.B., watch our backs."

"You smell muties, Ryan?"

"No. Thought I saw something out there."

The Armorer nodded. Ryan didn't need to explain any more than that. In the Deathlands, if you thought you saw something, then that was enough. The man who waited to be sure he'd seen something would eventually end up feeding the maggots.

It was even colder here than it had been up in the far north, in the part of the land once known as Alaska. Here it was a bitter, dry cold, a chill so intense that Ryan felt the hairs beginning to freeze in his nostrils. His skin felt a size too small, and if he opened his mouth it made the gaps in his teeth sing with the icy shock.

Finnegan kept the engine of the Kenworth ticking over, occasionally gunning it when it began to falter. He knew, as they all did, that if the truck failed them here, their chances would be a whole lot less than good. The smoke from the exhaust hung blue in the morning until the wind snapped at it and dragged it back along the valley.

The road was blocked for about twenty feet, and Ryan considered asking Finn to gun the engine and drive the rig slowly forward hoping to shift the tangled mess. That might be a whole lot easier than trying to move it by hand. If it didn't work, then it was a long walk to Ginnsburg

Falls, and they certainly wouldn't get the red carpet treatment if they went back there.

"Let's get it done," he told the others.

IT WASN'T THAT HARD. The wood was bone-dry, snapping easily as they pulled and wrenched at it, clearing a path wide enough for the Kenworth. As they toiled, the snow grew thicker, blinding them, settling on their coats, covering the tangled branches and making it difficult to see what they were doing. It took them about fifteen minutes, working together, the sweat steaming off them.

"That'll do it," Ryan called, waving to Finn, who had the side window partly down so that he could see what was happening.

The throaty sound of the powerful engine deepened, and Ryan heard the gears grinding as Finn fought his way up through the box. The wheels began to turn slowly, and the rig eased forward, crunching the remains of the debris into the icy road.

"Climb on!" Ryan called to the others, watching as Lori jumped up, pushed from behind by Doc Tanner, who used the opportunity to snatch a quick feel, his gloved hands sliding between the girl's thighs before he climbed into the Kenworth himself.

"Go on, Krysty," J.B. said, walking along the side of the rig, eyes flicking to the dark shadows in the undergrowth at the edges of the blacktop.

She scrambled up and was pulled into the cab by the pale hands of Jak Lauren, now fully awake, his white foxy face peering into the ghost-dancing snow. Ryan motioned for the Armorer to go next, readying himself to swing up off the highway.

With one hand on the pull bar, his body half on, half off the rig, Ryan called out to Finn to gun the engine. He was looking directly into Krysty's green eyes when he saw them open wide in shock and her mouth begin to form a warning.

The impact knocked him clean off the truck, and he hit the rutted snow with rib-creaking force.

He'd left the G-12 caseless in the cab, his SIG-Sauer pistol holstered at his hip. But the long coat hampered him, tangling as he fell. His ears were filled with a ferocious snarling, his nostrils overwhelmed with the rank stench of the creature that had attacked him.

For a few moments Ryan couldn't even see what it was. He did know that it was large and coarse-haired, and that it had curved canine teeth that snapped at his throat. Part of his brain guessed it was a big timber wolf, but most of his attention was wonderfully concentrated on fighting off the murderous bastard.

He managed to get a forearm across the beast's neck, keeping its clashing teeth a few inches from his own face. Then it kicked, its sharp claws ripping at him, trying to spill his guts steaming into the snow. The Kenworth had gone, probably stopped some way down the slope, the others tumbling from it in a bid to rescue him. But the snow had thickened to a blizzard, dropping visibility to only a couple of yards. If he didn't save himself, the others would be too late.

"Fireblast, you fucker!" he grunted, managing a clumsy punch that made the creature whine in pain and back off for a moment, where it crouched on its haunches, eyes glowing like living rubies.

It was a wolf—one of the biggest Ryan Cawdor had ever seen.

There were burrs matted in its brindled coat, and bloody froth dripped from its reeking jaws. It stood close to four feet tall at the shoulder. Keeping his eye fixed on it, Ryan reached for his blaster, but the torn strip of leather from his coat was still tangled about the butt of the gun. He dropped his hand to the cold hilt of the eighteen-inch panga on the other hip and drew the blade in a whisper of steel.

"Come on then," he called out, blinking in the driving snow.

The world had shrunk to a shifting circle of whiteness, barely two paces across, containing Ryan and the mutie wolf.

Ryan dropped instinctively into the classic knife-fighter's crouch, the blade in his right hand pointed up, feet a bit apart, shuffling in at the wolf, keeping his balance, breathing lightly.

The animal continued to snarl at him, belly down in the snow, inching closer.

Ryan feinted a low cut at the wolf's muzzle, making the beast hiss defiantly as it held its place. The ice was slippery, and Ryan edged closer carefully, watching the monster's eyes. It was one of the things his dead brother had taught him when he was only a callow boy.

He heard Morgan's calm, gentle voice in his head. "The eyes, little one. Always watch the eyes."

The great timber wolf blinked at the human that dared to face it down. Then Ryan saw the signal, deep in the glowing crimson coals.

Now.

He sidestepped the baying charge, hacking at the creature's shoulder as it brushed past him. The blade of the panga bit deep, and he felt the jar as it cracked into bone. Blood sprayed, steaming in the cold, patterning the snow around them. The wolf howled, a tearing, unearthly banshee wail that froze the blood. Then it whirled around, snapping at its own wound, and charged again.

This time Ryan stood his ground.

Meeting the rush head-on, he swung the foot and a half of blood-slick steel with all his power, as if he were trying to fell a great oak with a single blow.

The blade hit the leaping wolf's frothing muzzle and sliced through the flesh of the animal's upper jaw, snapping off oversized teeth and burying itself finally in the side of the creature's skull, just below its crazed eye. The weight of the wolf pulled the panga's hilt out of Ryan's hands, and rolling over in the snow, the beast kicked itself to its feet again, the steel dangling from its narrow head.

"Tough mother, huh?" Ryan said to himself, carefully freeing the pistol from his coat. The animal was panting, blood flowing freely over its grizzled pelt and soaking the earth around its forepaws. Despite the crippling wound, the wolf wasn't finished yet.

The P-226 9 mm blaster was in Ryan's right fist, its twenty-five and a half ounces of weight feeling as familiar to him as his own face in a mirror. The barrel was more than four inches long, and it held fifteen rounds of ammunition. One bullet in the right place would kick a man over on his back, leaving him looking blank-eyed at the sky.

It was enough even for the mutie wolf.

The animal lurched toward Ryan again, hackles up, snow hanging in the folds of muscle around its throat. The gun barked, the flat sound muffled by the storm. The bullet hit precisely where Ryan had aimed it, between the kill-mad eyes.

The wolf howled, the long drawn-out scream of pain and frustrated rage echoing and fading off the trees. The high-velocity round exited from the back of the beast's skull, a fine spray of brains and blood hanging in the air for a moment. A great splinter of bone, inches across, pulped into the snow. The body was knocked sideways, the legs kicking frantically. Ryan heard the mutie beast's claws scrape through the ice at the road gravel beneath.

"Where are you, Ryan?"

It was Krysty, stumbling over the slippery ruts of ice, her Heckler & Koch pistol in her hand. Ryan saw her looming through the wraiths of wind-torn snow. She stopped when she saw the twitching corpse of the timber wolf. "By Gaia! That's a big bastard. You all right, lover? I just saw it come out of the shadows at you, but I couldn't be sure what it was."

The Kenworth had finally ground to a halt just around the next bend in the road, its exhaust vomiting smoke. To Ryan's educated hearing, it was obvious that the truck's engine was beginning to fail. There was a much rougher note than when they'd left the town, and he could actually catch the taste in the air of burning oil as the engine overheated. His guess was that they'd covered around fifty miles from Ginnsburg Falls, moving slowly along the treacherous highway. They'd been told that the range of the Kenworth was only around one hundred miles. If that was right, they'd soon have to consider returning and trying to get to the gateway through the town.

Or going on and risking being totally stranded in the desert of rocks and snow.

ONCE THEY WERE ALL SAFELY in the cluttered, cramped cab of the rig, they discussed what they should do.

"There's a big fucking ridge ahead," Finnegan said. "Saw it 'fore this fucking snow came down. It's only 'bout five, six miles ahead. Sky seemed clearer north."

"This wag won't run much longer," J.B. commented, taking off his glasses and polishing them clean of the smears of snow. "I doubt we'd make it back to the ville."

Ryan nodded his agreement. "Could be best to go on, I guess."

Jak stared moodily out of one of the high side windows and picked his nose. "The trans message was this way? Came for that. Go on."

Krysty shook her head. "If we stop now, then we should make the gateway. Try somewhere else. Farther we go on, the farther we've got to come back. Mebbe on foot. It's a bleak land."

Doc Tanner coughed to clear his throat. "We blunder across the Deathlands, like children, lost in a maze, like the players of some celestial game where we know neither the object nor the rules."

"What's your point, Doc?" Ryan asked.

"The point, my dear and somewhat brutal Mr. Cawdor, is that we could have here a chance, rare as Vatican charity, to improve our tiny store of knowledge."

"The message, you mean?"

"Indeed, I do. I, for one, am set that we should continue across this darkling plain, blighted by the long-dead ignorant armies."

"But we don't know where we're heading," J.B. said. "Got no radios with us."

"Ah, Mr. Dix," the old man said, grinning. "That is where you are wrong. Show the nice gentleman the pretty toy you found on the floor of this rumbling behemoth, dear child."

Lori smiled at him and reached inside her gray fur coat, pulling out a small black plastic box with a dial and several buttons.

Finn glanced sideways at it. "Fucking ace, lady. Nice little radio-trans. Where didja find it, Lori?"

"Under the seat when I get in."

"Got in," Doc Tanner corrected gently.

"It work?" Jak asked.

"Sure does, son," the old man replied. "You found that recorded message on the dial last time, Finn, did you not?"

"Yeah."

"Can you do it on this?"

"Sure. Strength of the signal should tell us if'n we're heading in the right fucking direction. Someone else can drive this crumbling shit heap a spell."

J.B. took over, muttering to himself in a bad-tempered monotone at the way the steering was becoming loose. Finn changed seats and took the little radio from the girl, peering at it in the light from the east of the valley.

"I think it was..." he began.

There was a faint crackling of static and hissing. Ryan had read in an old book, from before the Apocalypse, that in the golden age it was possible to spin the dial on a radio-trans and pick up hundreds of different stations, all broadcasting at once. Now you were very lucky to pick up even a single station.

"Mebbe we've gone wrong," Krysty suggested.

"Mebbe we—"

The voice was deafeningly loud, booming out in the cab of the Kenworth, repeating the same message they'd heard before.

"Stay tuned to this frequency. North of Ginnsburg Falls where the old Highway 62 reaches the trail to Crater Lake. Go there and wait. You will be contacted."

There was a brief pause and then the loop-tape message began again.

"Anyone receiving this message who requires any assistance in any matter of science or the study of past technical developments will be aided. Bring all your information

and follow this signal where you will be given help. Stay
tuned to this frequency. North of—''

Finn switched the machine off.

''How far?'' Jak said, breaking the sudden silence in the
cab.

J.B. was still wrestling with the steering of the ailing
Kenworth, taking some time to answer. ''Can't be more
than a few miles. That signal's nearly on top of us, isn't it,
Finn?''

''Guess so. Little fucking toy like this trans here… Can't
have a range more'n five, mebbe ten miles tops.''

''Straight ahead, up those hills?'' Ryan asked, rubbing
at the windshield with his glove, trying to see out through
the swirls of light snow.

The Armorer nodded. ''If this bitching wag can make it
that far.''

His concern was well placed.

About eight miles farther along the old blacktop, just as
the bright sun of late afternoon was breaking through, the
engine coughed and then seized up with a grinding, metal-
lic sound that had a dreadful finality about it.

Everyone got out of the rig.

# Chapter Thirteen

"BY GOD, BUT THIS was such a good country once," Doc said, voice low, hushed by the staggering natural beauty of the sight ahead of them.

By Ryan's calculations they'd walked around three miles, having left that ruined wag standing like a slaughtered behemoth at the side of the snow-covered road. The blizzard had faded away behind them, with skies to the south that were like frozen lead. It was still bitingly cold, but the driving wind was also gone. The sun shone through a dome of blue, laced with high fluffy white clouds. The air tasted clean and dry, with none of the acrid toxics caused by the lowering chem-clouds in other parts of Deathlands.

Suddenly, over the rim of the trail, they'd come across what Ryan had recognized immediately as the Crater Lake they'd been talking about—a bowl of jagged rocks surrounding a massive lake of the bluest water he'd ever seen in his life. Now, gazing with awe at the tranquil scene, they all sat on small boulders that bordered what could once have been a parking lot for domestic wags.

"Hell of a fine country," the old man mused. "Must have been like this most everywhere before we came trampling all over it in nailed jackboots, despoiling the earth."

Krysty nodded agreement. "I saw pictures in old books back in Harmony. Pictures of what the old ones called paradise. I guess as a young girl I always thought that their paradise must have been something like this.''

Rare in the wastes of Deathlands, there was a profusion of natural life, with no visible evidence of any mutations from radiation.

Ryan was no expert, but he recognized great stands of hemlock, fir and pine around the rim of the huge crater. Guessing, he figured the lake must be close to five miles across, with a circumference of thirty miles. A couple of islands broke the surface of the lake. One, on the far side, was small and shaped like a ship. The other was closer and larger, with a miniature volcanic cone at its center. Ryan thought for a moment he saw some isolated movement on that island.

''Look. Big fire,'' Lori said, pointing away to the west. A distant forest was divided by a great swath of blackened stumps where a lightning strike had triggered a fire that had raced across half the face of one of the surrounding peaks.

It was hard to believe the evidence of their own eyes at the living creatures that moved around them, seemingly oblivious to the presence of humans.

Marmots lolled in the clearings, bellies splashed yellow. Their brave indifference to Ryan and his friends was a clear sign that this wasn't an area where man was a hunter.

In the high branches of the trees that shaded them, squirrels chattered at one another. Ryan saw a badger snuffle for roots as it lumbered across a sun-splashed glade. A bobcat, lean and tawny, padded by within twenty paces of them, not even bothering to turn its head in their direction.

Bright jays darted and scolded in the bushes that grew thickly from the top of the slope down to the dark water.

Jak pointed above them, his keen eyes spotting a golden eagle circling majestically on a thermal over the lake.

It was unlike anyplace any of them had ever known; it seemed close to a mythic idyll of peace and serene happiness. Krysty lay on her back, one foot crossed over the other, staring around her, relaxing on a soft couch of deep green moss.

"What you said, Doc, about how it used to be... Was it really like this?"

"Oh, indeed, it was, my dear lady. I swear it was like this. Of course there were cities. Great wens that soured the land and skies around themselves, blighting the environment. That was the buzz word. Environment. But there were limitless billions of acres of unspoiled wilderness."

They were silent for a moment, locked into their own thoughts. Ryan lay next to Krysty, and he felt her hand rest on his, warm and loving.

"Why keep moving, lover?"

"What?"

They kept their voices quiet, private.

"Why keep on moving all the time, Ryan? Why not stop? Stop here?"

Ryan breathed in, deep and slow, trying to find words that would be an answer, not coming up with anything that sounded right or tasted good.

"I guess...I don't know," he said finally.

"Up here the air's like...like nectar. I recall that from an old vid I once saw. Like nectar. Means sweet and fresh. There's valleys all round here," she said, indicating them with a sweep of her hand. "Fresh water and good timber. We could build us a home."

"Us? Who's that, Krysty?"

"You. Me," she said, hesitating. "All of us. We get on well. Got the skills. We could settle, like they used to on the old frontier. Mebbe try and farm some. Run the ridges of this green land, Ryan. Raise us a family one day.''

It was out, the words lying in the air between them. Words that both of them had thought about ever since they'd first met. Words that neither of them had said before, not even whispered during their lovemaking, or after.

"One day, Krysty," Ryan said finally.

"One day, lover?"

"Yeah, one day."

But not yet.

THEY CAMPED FOR THE NIGHT on the rim and built themselves a small fire from the abundance of fallen branches, lighting it with a pyrotab from J.B.'s capacious pockets. As the light faded, they watched small brown deer come cautiously from the woods to feed, their hooves crunching delicately on the loose pumice that lay everywhere along the slopes, a legacy from the original eruption of Mount Mazama, seven thousand years ago.

It had been agreed that at dawn they'd split into two groups, one going east around the narrow perimeter trail, the other west. Finnegan was convinced the radio message that had drawn them on from Ginnsburg Falls must have come from very close to the lake.

"We'll walk easy and take care."

J.B. had asked about guards. The Trader had instilled into them that you always posted sentries—it was universal practice.

"Even here?" Finnegan asked.

Ryan was torn. All his senses told him that even in paradise there might be poisonous serpents. But the temptation to succumb to the beauty and peace of the place was overwhelming.

"Let's let it go a night. Nobody can come up without waking one of us. Not over that loose stone."

"Be real good to have a fucking night without having to get up and fucking walk around on guard," Finnegan said, grinning from ear to ear.

RYAN WOKE ONCE, disturbed by the charred end of one of the branches falling into the gleaming ruby embers of the fire. Through the lattice of the branches of the pines around him, he could see the bland face of the moon shining serenely down. He got up to take a leak at the edge of the clearing, his urine steaming in the cold.

His mind was filled with Krysty's words about settling down and raising a family. And he remembered Doc's words.

"Must have been a hell of a good land," he whispered to himself before rejoining the others and enjoying the best sleep he'd had in ages.

They woke to find themselves prisoners.

# Chapter Fourteen

Jak Lauren woke first, disturbed by the faint crunching of boots over the rough pumice. He blinked his eyes open, looked quickly around the clearing where they all slept and saw that it was still night, with only the cloud-fringed moon casting a pale silver light. The fire had died away to a pile of gray ashes.

"We got company, friends," he said in a normal conversational voice, taking the greatest care not to make any hasty movements.

Ryan woke next, his one good eye opening. He too looked around while keeping very still.

"Fourteen," he said to himself. And if he could see that many, then he was almost certain that there were more in the trees around the camp.

Lori woke next, sitting up, her hands going to her mouth in shock when she saw the ring of silent figures in identical uniforms of black plastic that reflected the silver moonlight.

J.B. reacted like Jak and Ryan, simply opening his eyes, taking in what was happening, not taking any risks on getting shot. Squinting in the darkness, his eyes locked on the intruders' weapons. Their blasters were stubby, like machine pistols, with a narrow barrel above the firing muzzle. They probably had some kind of laser-controlled firing system, he thought, but the magazine seemed to hold ammunition unlike anything the Armorer had ever seen.

Krysty, awake now too, looked calmly at the silent enemy. Her long, brilliantly red hair curled softly and defensively around the nape of her neck, the tendrils brushing her skin. She found it unnerving that it wasn't possible to see the faces of their antagonists, or even determine their sex.

Apart from the gleaming black uniforms, they wore long boots with flat heels made of the same plastic material, and their domed helmets had visors that totally concealed their eyes.

Finnegan was snoring on his back, but Jak's voice finally penetrated. His first reaction was to reach for his blaster, but at his movement, every one of the strange weapons veered in his direction. He shrugged his shoulders at the inevitability of it and grinned at the nearest person. "No problem, brother. No fucking problem. Am I right, or am I fucking right?"

There was no reply.

Dr. Theophilus Tanner was the last one in the group to fumble his way back to consciousness, and only when Lori shoved his shoulder.

"Too early for Communion, Emily, my dear," he muttered as he gathered some shreds of control and sat up. Then, rubbing the sleep from his rheumy eyes, he looked at the silent circle around them. "By the three Kennedys! We are attacked by Death Vader." He glanced at his puzzled companions. "A famous character from the popular fictions of... I disremember me when it was."

The nearest of the encircling group, with a small crimson flash on the carapace of its helmet, finally spoke. The voice was flat and unaccented, lacking any kind of emotion, or humanity. Each word was measured and weighed before being delivered. Each word stood on its own and seemed more the product of a machine than a man.

"Come with us. Hostile reactions will be met with ultimate force."

Finnegan looked across at Ryan. "Ultimate force? Do that mean what I think it mean?"

"It do," Ryan replied. "Let's go."

The sec guards herded their six prisoners into a tight circle, allowing them to pick up all their arms and possessions, which greatly surprised Ryan. He walked with Krysty, looking at the curious creatures that had captured them.

"What d'you figure?" he whispered.

"Andies?"

Ryan shook his head. He'd seen androids, and read about them, but he knew that nobody around the Deathlands had the skill to make humanoid robots that truly worked.

"Could be adapted muties."

"Retards?"

"Mebbe, lover, with some kinda electronic voice activators."

The figure with the red stripe on its helmet turned, its blank visor angled toward Ryan and the girl. "Do not speak with no permission to speak."

At first they walked parallel to the crumbling blacktop that circled Crater Lake, then they were led down an increasingly steep slope toward the water. The path was extremely treacherous and slippery, but the guards picked their way at high speed, without a single slip.

"Ultrascope enhancers in the visors," J.B. whispered to Ryan.

The moon was hidden by the surrounding trees as they drew nearer to the lake, and several times one or another of Ryan's group stumbled and slipped. Each time it happened the sec patrol stopped and watched. It was a singular and creepy experience, since they all stopped at precisely the same millisecond.

Eventually they had all picked their way between the trees and boulders to the water's edge, where five dark green inflatable boats waited. It struck Ryan as a further oddity that not one of the guards had been left behind with the boats. It showed an amazing confidence in their control over the area. Whatever had sent out the patrol clearly ruled the region with total power. Ryan wondered what kind of baron could run a ville like that.

The boats had small, compact engines that pushed them through the water at an incredible rate in total silence. Apart from the bubbling of the water as it churned under their bows, they could hear nothing.

"Heading for island," Jak said, his white hair almost luminous in the fading moonlight.

A fanciful person might have been tempted to pinch himself to see if he was dreaming this bizarre experience. Ryan trusted himself and his own reflexes. However strange and new things seemed, he knew they had to have an explanation. His main concern was to watch and learn as much as he could. As far as he could judge, they were not being threatened, just so long as they did what they were told. The fact that they'd been allowed to keep their weapons was a reassuring sign.

They landed with a faint jarring sound, and several of the guards climbed out and waited for their captives. Their movements were peculiar. Neither fluid nor clumsy, yet not quite human either. The moon had edged behind a bank of scudding cloud, and it was very dark. Ryan could make out a concrete slope that rose thirty yards to a large doorway concealed beneath an overhang of jagged rock. He guessed that it would be difficult to spot even in daylight. One of the green inflatables was hauled up out of the water, and he noticed to his surprise that it had wheels slung beneath it, making it also usable as a road vehicle.

"Follow yellow lines strip to skin leave clothes weapons check all fresh clothes will be issued. Do you read?"

Ryan nodded. "Yes, we read you." He turned to the others. "We got coldcocked by these mutie bastards back there. No point in trying to break for it. Do what they say and try and keep your eyes and ears on overdrive."

"Second warning unspeak. Third offense leads to termination."

Against the threat of such overwhelming force, they really had no choice but to obey. There was a line seared into the stone, glittering golden, and Ryan led the way along it. A small door within the large doorway swung open with a hiss of hydraulics, and they passed through it, accompanied by the sec guards.

Doc Tanner trembled like a willow in a stiff breeze, and Lori had to take his arm to steady him. His eyes rolled, and his teeth chattered. *"Lasciate ogni speranza, voi ch'entrate,"* he said.

Apart from the local dialect gabble of muties, Ryan had never heard much talk that wasn't in American. "How's that again, Doc?" he whispered.

The sec patrol had fallen a few paces behind them, content to shadow and keep the six covered with their strange weapons.

"Means abandon all hope, all ye who enter this place," the old man replied.

"Fucking cheerful, Doc," Finnegan sneered.

"Don't mock, my portly companion. Oh, mock not, ye of little knowledge. Strip off your clothing. Follow the yellow lines. Not yellow stars. Lines. Follow them. Through the door. Into the bunkers. Poison gas showers for all. Line up to be freed of lice. Into the chambers.

Close and bolt the doors. Marks of nails, gouged in the stone. Screams. Blood and excrement. The stench.''

Ryan was worried that Doc Tanner had finally lost what was often a fragile hold on sanity and reality. As they walked, the old man began to chant names in time with their steps. A litany of names. People? Places? Foreign words with harsh syllables. None of them sounding like any names that Ryan had ever heard.

"Belsen...Treblinka...Mauthausen...Ravens-bruck...Vught...Sobibor...Dachau...Theresien-stadt...Auschwitz."

There was something inherently ugly and unpleasant about the pattern of their names, something that echoed the clicking heels of their captors.

"Death camps. Bastard Nazis."

One of the sec guards moved in closer, and Lori tugged warningly at Doc's arm, shutting him up. Ahead loomed the door of what looked like some kind of elevator.

"Place is like a redoubt," Ryan said to Krysty. "Can't be any normal kind of ville."

She shook her head as a command from the sec leader brought them to a halt. "I can feel some real bad chills from this place, lover. By Gaia, but the air's filled with the cold, flat taste of death! We must step careful."

The heavy mesh gates slid across, and they walked into a massive elevator. "Big enough for a dozen war wags," he said.

"Look." Jak pointed at a tiny notice, less than three inches across, pinned to the far wall.

J.B. was nearest, and he stepped closer, peering at it through narrowed eyes. He took off his rimless glasses and polished them on the sleeve of his coat, then put them back on his bony nose and read the notice.

"What's it say?" Ryan asked.

"Welcome to Wizard Island."

They descended in the elevator, with only eight of the visored guards keeping them company. With its walls and ceiling of dulled steel, it wasn't possible to judge how far down they went, but Ryan counted eighty-five seconds before they stopped moving. At that reasonably fast speed, it meant they were way below the surface of Crater Lake. Once again he wondered what kind of complex they'd allowed themselves to be lured into.

The door slid back to reveal another dozen or more identical sec men. They all seemed much the same height, and Ryan wondered again whether it was possible that someone in the Deathlands had mastered the arcane skill of creating working androids.

"Go into doors numbered five through ten. Take off all weapons and clothes. Wash and put on fresh clothes. Wait there for orders."

The lack of any human inflection was disquieting. So was the idea of giving up all their weapons. Several of them, notably J.B. and Jak, had blades and even some residual pieces of plas-ex hidden in their coats.

"Why can't we keep our own clothes?" the Armorer asked, addressing himself to the apparent leader of the sec patrol, who stood as though locked in silent communion with himself, the strip lights along the ceiling reflected in his visor. Ryan noticed the many small remote vid cameras that were set high in corners of the corridor and over doorways, constantly blinking on and off, moving ceaselessly, like some hydra-headed techno-beast.

"I asked why—" J.B. began again, but the guard replied.

"Interdict."

"What?"

"Negative request refused. Comply now."

As though a single brain were controlling them all, the sec guards raised the muzzles of their unusual blasters.

"Fine," Ryan said. "We're doing it. What do we do after the shower and change of clothes?"

The mirrored plastic turned in his direction. Once more there was the curious delay, and Ryan imagined he could hear minute cogs and wheels whirring and connecting somewhere inside the helmet.

"Compliance positive then wait in numbered rooms for further orders."

"Let's do it, people," Ryan said, leading the way toward the door marked with a neat black 5. He could feel his body tense as he thought about what might lie behind it.

In the neat cubicle, the omnipresent vid focused on him as he laid his range of weapons on a square white table: the H&K G-12, the SIG-Sauer pistol, the steel panga with the gleaming eighteen-inch blade, and finally, a small dagger. His coat held plastic explosive, primers and detonators, but he laid it on the table with everything else.

"Concealment of any weapon will be regarded as treason against the Wizard Island Complex for Scientific Advancement and a mandatory termination will result."

The clicks at the beginning and end of the message indicated to Ryan that it was probably a recording. He began to strip, placing his boots, socks, pants and shirt on a bench that ran down one side of the eight-foot-long cubicle. But he kept his white scarf to one side.

Very casually he put the scarf on top of a pile of dark blue coveralls, which had the monogram WICSA sewn on the left breast.

On the wall the vid camera watched him with a blank, glassy stare. There was no comment from the tiny speaker below it, so Ryan guessed that keeping his scarf might work.

"Go through the sliding door into the sanitary and hygiene facility, which is completely private. After your shower, please pass through the body scanner built into the doorway. You are warned not to attempt to conceal any item in mouth, armpit, ears, vagina or rectal orifice."

Ryan tried to think of some snappy reply, but decided silence was probably safest.

He pushed open the door and found himself in a shower stall, four feet across, with a chrome drain set in the floor. There was a circular control for the power and temperature of the water and a vent in the ceiling. He remembered the ravings of Doc Tanner and peered up at the meshed hole, wondering if some toxic gas would be pumped through to asphyxiate him.

"They'd have chilled us with their blasters," he said to himself. "They wouldn't have bothered with this devious scheme." He reached out and turned the handle, wincing at the power of the steaming water that gushed out, and had one of the best washes he'd had in a long time.

The supply of water was endless, controlled to the most subtle degree by the metal handle. A trim rectangular dish held two kinds of soap, each with the rich scent of summer flowers. When he finally came out, Ryan saw a pair of fluffy linen towels draped over the table where his weapons had been. His clothes were also gone.

But the long white scarf remained on top of the newly supplied coveralls, apparently left by an oversight. It was the first scintilla of hope that the baron who ran this ultrasophisticated ville might be fallible and have a weakness after all.

"WHAT'S HAPPENED TO OUR BLASTERS and clothes and all that fucking stuff?" Finnegan asked the leader of the sec patrol, waving an angry finger at the sheen of the visitor.

"All stored main entrance gate. Will be returned if... when you leave complex.'

Krysty turned to Ryan at the long delay between "if" and "when," but he simply raised an eyebrow and shook his head.

"When do we get to meet the people who run this institution?" Doc Tanner asked, his damp gray hair pasted flat to his long skull, making him look like an unusually intelligent goat.

"Induction from Human Resources Section Wizard Island. Soon," the sec guard told him.

The seven of them, in their snug-fitting coveralls and white sneakers, were led along more corridors and past more prying vid cameras. Ryan had tucked his scarf carefully into the neck of the coveralls so that it didn't show.

"Them fucking blasters can sting you," Finnegan whispered, raising his sleeve to reveal a nasty burn, like a red zigzag, across his forearm. "Just tried to keep a fucking blade behind, and one of 'em saw it. Said it was a warning and next time'd be for keeps."

"That the worst they can set them on?" J.B. asked.

"No. Looked at that dial on the butt. Bastard had it set at two. Scale goes up to twenty."

As they continued walking, Ryan got the impression that the building rambled over a vast area beneath the surface of Crater Lake. It was decidedly functional in design, with raw concrete, weeping a little from the damp, lining all the walls.

"Stop here," the sec leader commanded suddenly.

Ryan noticed another body scanner was built into the trim doorway ahead. He reached up casually and tucked his hands inside his coveralls, as if they were chilly, then grabbed the metal weights at each end of the silk scarf and folded his fingers around them, hoping that it might just be enough to mask them from the detectors.

"Induction will follow food. Through this door is non-sec area. Go in peace." There was a pause. "And have a nice day."

None of the guards followed them through. The door swung gently shut behind them, and they stood, gasping, finding themselves in a totally different world from the harsh cubism of the concrete. Here there were pastel wall hangings and soft carpets of nonstatic acrylics. Music played from concealed speakers in gentle swaying cadences that lacked any distinctive tune.

The lighting was muted, with pink and cream shades over the naked bulbs. Several doors, all closed, were covered in teak veneer. And the voice that came floating to their ears was totally different from the artificial speech of the mutie guards.

It lisped softly. "Welcome, outworlders, to Wizard Island. Induction will follow shortly after you have been fed in the eatery in room 18 to your left. For now, welcome from everyone here on Wizard island. All of your questions will be answered just as we hope you will cooperate with our own interrogation."

Ryan wasn't sure he liked the sound of the word "interrogation." He'd been interrogated before and had never found it much of a pleasure. It was always associated in his mind with broken fingernails, drilled teeth and electric terminals attached to genitals.

"Come on," Finnegan said, attracted by the sound of the words "fed in the eatery." He moved briskly along, checking the numbers of the rooms. Doc and Lori followed, then J.B., while Jak walked with Ryan and Krysty at the rear.

"Don't like it," the boy hissed. "Bad taste. Bad air."

"Seems fine," Ryan said.

But Krysty disagreed. "No, lover. The kid's right. If ever I met somewhere to take care, it's here. Gives me the creeping."

"Here's eighteen!" Finn yelled.

"Enjoy your nourishment. Here on Wizard Island it is always the present. But we are also our own past. And we shall soon be the future."

Ryan thought the voice sounded like an extremely reasonable and balanced lunatic.

# Chapter Fifteen

KRYSTY WROTH PULLED A FACE, spit the first mouthful of food back on the cream plastic plate and dropped the cream plastic spoon alongside it.

"By Gaia!" She shook her head in disgust. "That's the worst food I've ever tasted. Grade alpha mutie dreck. It's…" Words failed her, and she sat in silence, looking at the small pile of light brown goo that rested smugly in the center of the plate.

"It even *looks* like shit," J.B. said, pushing his plate away from him.

Jak Lauren, on the other hand, savored the food. "Had worse. Ate a cottonmouth once. Been dead weeks. Melted in mouth. Like jelly. Bits like rice." He paused as everyone waited for the explanation of the bits that seemed like rice. "Maggots," he explained as he grinned and took another spoonful of the soft mix on his plate.

Doc Tanner cautiously dipped the end of his spoon into the substance. Raising it to his lips, his tongue flicking like a sun-warmed lizard's, he said, "I swear that it puts me in mind of…of what? Ah, I believe I have it." He sucked in his lined cheeks like a wine taster. "Yes, the pap they used to serve on airliners. Bland, and yet with an awful, lingering aftertaste. Loaded with vitamins and preservatives."

"I *like* the flavor of some addies," Finnegan said, taking another large mouthful. "There's some in this fucking stuff I've never tried."

Doc Tanner laid down his spoon. "Anyone who has two bites of this must be a glutton, my dear Finnegan. When they first began to mix chems in with good food to try to maintain it longer, they found one odd side effect."

"What was that, Doc?" Ryan, who still hadn't tried the food, asked.

"Didn't just keep food longer. It also made human corpses last longer without decomposing. Morticians were the great beneficiaries of it."

"Horrid," Lori said, following Krysty's example and spitting her mouthful back on the plate.

"How 'bout you, Ryan?" J.B. asked.

Ryan sniffed at the food, trying to decide what might be in it. One thing was certain: there was nothing in the mixture that had ever lived, nothing that was either animal or vegetable. But there was a whole lot that was mineral in it. In some places in the Deathlands, the main source of food was chemicals, processed, colored and flavored to make them smell like normal food.

He spooned up a little, transferring it to his mouth and rolling it around his palate. The others were right. It was dreadful—a horrid mingling of dull and sharp flavors overlaid with a bitter aftertaste.

"I guess the folks that run this ville must eat this as well," Ryan said finally. "They seem to do fine on it. Guess we ought to try and finish it up."

Finnegan was the only one who seemed to actually relish the pallid sludge as he wiped his plate, and slurped from the plastic beaker of water.

"Hey! Least the drink's fucking good. Clean and fresh as Sierra meltwater."

"Probably what it is," Ryan commented.

Then the loudspeaker clicked on. "Now that nourishment has taken place, you will be taken to induction. Do not attempt to move within the complex here without orders. Security operatives are waiting outside the door to escort you. Go now."

Finnegan eased himself sideways on the bench and let out a rasping fart, making Jak giggle in a high-pitched voice. "My fucking guts aren't used to such rich food," the blaster said, grinning.

When they got outside the room, they found eighteen black-uniformed sec guards, each one holding a gun at the hip. The helmets were still in place, the visors locked down over their eyes. Ryan began to wonder whether these muties actually had normal eyes, or whether they'd been surgically replaced with comp-vid scanners. He'd once heard of it being done with guard dogs. And if it could be done with hounds, then why not with muties?

"Induction with complex leader is now. All follow. Talk is allowed here."

It was either the same sec man with the scarlet flash on the helmet, or another man, absolutely identical. Ryan studied them, watching their peculiar halting gait. Six walked at the front in three columns of two, with six more at the rear. The other six kept pace with the prisoners, three on each side.

Ryan came up beside Doc Tanner, gesturing for Lori to walk with Krysty. It was strange that they had been in the huge building for well over an hour and still hadn't seen an actual person.

"You sure this isn't a redoubt, like some of the others, Doc?"

"Still functioning? After nearly a hundred years, Ryan? You've visited a mess of these places, have you not? Ever seen any that showed life?"

"Sure. One up in the Rockies had a nest of stickies in it. But I know what you're getting at. So who runs this?"

"Some big-wheel baron. To hold this together for a century means a kind of power I didn't believe could have existed."

"There was an immortal comic hero called Superman, wasn't there?"

"Clark Kent—lived in Gotham City. Or was it Metropolis? I remember him. A fighter for justice." The old man grinned. "You think that Superman still lives and runs this place? We shall soon see, Ryan. For, unless I miss my guess, I believe I can make out a sign on yonder door that reads Induction, does it not?"

"It does, Doc. It does."


"SIT DOWN, one to each desk, and wait. The complex leader will be here soon. Stand in the presence of the complex leader."

All the guards had waited outside, stopping and standing quite still, like children's toys discarded suddenly in midgame. The room they were in was stepped like a theater. It contained at least a hundred desks, each with a pen and a notepad. Ryan and his six companions took the entire front row.

"Stand now for the leader," boomed the speaker, which was situated above a pale green light screen.

"Here comes Superman," Doc Tanner whispered.

The speaker coughed and whistled. Lights dimmed, then flickered and flared brighter. Music came from the corners of the large room, hesitantly at first, then swelling to a rather tremulous mezzo-soprano.

"Oh, say, can you see, by the . . . by the . . . by the . . . by the . . . by the—"

It was switched off.

A door began to slowly open, and Ryan signaled to the others to stand, pushing back his chair, the legs scraping along the floor.

"The leader of the Wizard Island Complex for Scientific Advancement!"

"Holy fuck!" Finnegan breathed, two places along from Ryan.

The leader was barely four feet tall. A pudgy, dumpy little woman, she had pink jowls of fat, like the dewlaps on a bloodhound, dangling on her shoulders. She was wearing a fawn-colored lab coat buttoned up to her throat. Immensely thick spectacles turned her tiny eyes into great goggling orbs of blue and white. Her hair was so thin that her scalp gleamed through the screwed-back mousy locks. She had an enormous bosom, which was out of proportion with the rest of her body, and forced her to lean back as she strutted in on stumpy legs like miniature tree trunks. One arm, the left, hung withered at her side, while the other fiddled with a hearing aid pinned to her lapel. She stopped at the desk at the front of the room and heaved herself slowly onto a box so that she could see the seven strangers who were staring openmouthed at her.

"Assume the seated mode," she said. Though she looked to be about fifty years old, her voice had the soft lisp of an eight-year-old girl.

Ryan sat down, followed by the others. He leaned forward and stared intently through his one good eye at the woman. If she ran a place of this size, then her appearance had to be deceptive.

"My name is Doctor Ethel Tardy," she said. "I function as leader of this complex. You are our first guests for a considerable temporal period. Why did you come here, journeywise?"

"We picked up a message on a trans," Ryan replied. "We're a group of friends, traveling this way. We were visiting Ginnsburg Falls."

"We monitor all communications. You closed the life window of their leader."

Ryan was shaken that they knew about the killing. He nodded. "Yes. It was—"

Dr. Ethel Tardy held up her right hand. "It means nothing, concernwise. Since your arrival in the complex you have all been measured and checked in all ways. All are healthy, though one has an incipient carcinoma, which may result in closure some years future."

Doc Tanner raised a hand. "May I ask a question, Doctor?"

"Indeed, Dr. Tanner, you may."

Ryan could feel ground slipping away beneath his feet. What in the long chill was going on here? How could they know all this? Names, illnesses?

"This has nothing to do with Project Cerberus, does it?"

The answer was some time coming. "Not precisely, Dr. Tanner. Project Cerberus was limited on a need-to-know Grades Delta and up only. We are the descendants of the initiators of Project Eurydice, the project from which there shall never be a looking-back situation."

Doc Tanner sat down again, eyes flicking toward Ryan, who thought that he'd never seen the old man look so worried.

"Interruptionwise, we are in a negative situation. I shall relate all you need to know before aligning you with us."

It was another of the "when, not if" situations, the kind that made Ryan feel uneasy.

For the next hour Dr. Ethel Tardy, in her silly little girl's voice, squeaked and lisped her way through a concise account of the utterly extraordinary history of Project Eurydice, a tale so incredible that the seven friends sat in amazed silence.

Afterward, Ryan tried to recall everything that she'd told them but found he could remember only the bare bones of the story.

During the mid 1990s, when war fever took over the land, a great number of secret missions were set up in what was then the United States. Protest was useless, and even national parks were taken over and used. Though Crater Lake was one of the most beautiful places on the continent, experts pronounced it suitable for deep excavation beneath the cone of Wizard Island near the center of the deep lake. A huge and intricate complex was set up there and staffed by some of the top military scientists. According to the doctor, by the end of the century the only scientists who received any funding were those involved in pure military research.

Bigger weapons.

Better weapons.

Then came 2001, and civilization, as it had been known, disappeared forever. The population wasn't just decimated. It was decimated again and again until only a tiny fraction survived. Among those survivors were the scientists who ran the Wizard Island Complex for Scientific Advancement.

"In the summer of that year, rosterwise," the doctor told them, "there were seventeen hundred personnel here. Security was not a predicated condition."

To the astonishment of Ryan and his friends, the diminutive woman described what followed the nuclear Armageddon that blasted the world. Sealed in concrete and steel, the scientists were spared. Their air was filtered, the food self-produced from limitless supplies of time-safe chemicals. They were totally self-sufficient.

And all they needed to do was proceed with their work. With their research.

"Which we did, ladies and gentlemen. We received no instructions to alter our program schedulewise."

Doc Tanner again raised a hand. "But you are aware that the society that originally funded and ordered your project is long gone? Dust these hundred years?"

"Of course, Doctor. We are not fools here. But we have been reared here. We are born here. Genetically we breed and we die. But always the generations carry on."

"What of fresh blood?" Ryan asked her.

She smiled a gentle, dimpled smile at his question. "What need is there?"

"You breed within the complex and never go out?" Krysty asked.

"Of course. Negative dispersal, socialwise. Nobody ever leaves the complex, except in death."

"How many are there of you scientists now?" Doc Tanner asked, casting a meaningful look across the room at Ryan.

"Sixty-one approved personnel."

"Sixty-one," Jak squeaked. "Then . . . you said seventeen hundred?"

"Affirmative, young white head. There *were* that many. Now we are sixty-one working operatives, sciencewise."

Doc mouthed something at Ryan, but it took the one-eyed man three attempts to understand it. The old man was trying to pass him the word "inbreeding." That had to be it! Ryan had seen enough closed communities to know what happened when the genes never got a chance to get rejuvenated by new, outside blood—there were mutations and still births.

And the ville eventually died away.

From seventeen hundred of what must have been the top scientific brains in the land down to sixty-one of...of people like Dr. Ethel Tardy.

Suddenly, like a thunderbolt, a question came to Ryan's lips. But he quickly suppressed it. The woman knew the name of Doc Tanner. But evidently she didn't know the names of the rest of them. How did she know the Doc?

She went on, in her sweet little girl way, telling them how the original sec guards had died away when some had tried to go outside. Rads had gotten them. And she told them how the scientists had needed menial servants. "Slaves," Krysty whispered.

They had taken some retard muties and given them voice box activators that were controlled from within the complex. They had also made some implants in the cortex to render the creatures totally obedient to the will of the scientists.

"Fucking slaves," Finnegan hissed.

"How many?" J.B. asked, leaning back in his seat, the brim of his fedora tugged low over his face, making it hard to see his eyes.

"Query sec total? Forty. That balance is now maintained, by culling."

The story was becoming more and more incredible. The picture of this sealed palace, with its generations of super-brains locked away from the horrors of the world outside for a century, breeding and interbreeding, with slaves to work for them, chilled the blood of Ryan and his compatriots.

Ryan's immediate guess was that in another twenty years or so the place would wither and die out altogether.

The doctor was remarkably open and frank with the strangers, something else that planted another seed of worry in Ryan's mind. A place like this would contain enough to keep someone like the Trader in business for life. Any bandit would give his right arm for such a prize. And here was Dr. Tardy telling them all of the secrets and details of how the complex operated. Would she do this if there was any risk of their ever getting out? Locked away, thousands of feet below the surface of Crater Lake, the chances of escape weren't very good, Ryan knew.

"There. That's all I can tell you about us," the doctor finally said. Now that she was finished her talk, the tiny woman seemed more at ease, having dropped some of the parroted jargon that had dotted her speech earlier. "Later we'll get to know more about you all, factwise, apart from Dr. Tanner, of course."

She ventured a nervous, trilling laugh that made her cheeks wobble, then climbed down off her box, just as the door started to ease open. Before she could leave, Doc Tanner held up his clawlike hand yet again.

"Yes?" the fat little doctor asked, a smile pasted solidly in place.

"I have another query, Dr. Tardy."

"Indeed?"

"Throughout your most interesting dissertation, you spoke much of the past, even a little of the present, but nothing of the future. Why is that?"

"The future is a chalice held in all our hands, Doctor."

"And what does that cup contain?"

"It contains hope."

"And?"

"Hope of an end to suffering."

Doc pressed her. "Through peace? Through an end to disease?"

"No. Not that way. That is not the path on which we must tread."

"What frightful fiend doth tread behind you?" he asked, voice low, almost as if he were speaking to himself.

"I don't read. We are not interfacing, communicationswise, Dr. Tanner. Let us terminate on that."

She bustled out, cheeks flushed, eyes averted from her audience. It was screamingly obvious that, quite deliberately, Doc had touched her on the rawest of raw nerves. What the scientists were actually doing in the complex under Wizard Island was something they wished to keep secret.

The seven of them sat there, at their lecture desks, each one with much to think about while they waited for the speaker to crackle into life and give them further orders.

Where they should go.

And what they should do.

# Chapter Sixteen

THERE WERE NO CLOCKS in the Wizard Island Complex for Scientific Advancement, not clocks that showed any sort of real time, just circular chrons, divided into three equal parts, red, amber and green, each subdivided into five equal portions lettered from *A* to *E*. Ryan and his companions quickly came to realize that the scientists operated a simple three-shift day of eight hours each. But they didn't use hours and minutes in allocating time. They would talk of eating at Red *C* or of using one of the deeply buried bathing pools at Amber *B*.

Ryan Cawdor's body clock was infallible, and he knew that when they were taken to have their second meal of the day, it was close to noon in the Oregon mountains far, far above them.

It was identical in every way to the first meal, except that it was possibly a more yellowish shade of brown than the first plate of sludge. It was difficult to detect any change in the taste.

Having escorted them to the visitors' quarters, the visored sec guards left them to stand patiently and silently in the corridor outside the only door. But the roving vid cameras still blinked and rocked their serpentine necks back and forth.

Apart from certain specific research areas, they had been told they'd have unlimited access to anywhere they wanted to go. The section of the complex that contained the main elevators was also out of bounds to them. After they'd eaten, a voice over the speakers had urged them to go and explore. It added that the computer maps were, unfortunately, malfunctioning.

Within seconds Ryan had combined with Finn, Jak and J.B. to work out if there were any areas in their rooms that the cameras couldn't see.

There were.

Several. Angles behind furniture, or tucked at the rear of open doors. And surprisingly, behind the door marked Hygiene Facility, there was a sizable area where they could converse unseen.

To avoid arousing suspicion, Ryan used yet another of the old tricks taught him by the Trader. With people that you trusted, you passed messages on, one person at a time. That way, there was never a great bunch sitting around, heads together.

He went into the toilets first, and Jak followed. While they stood together, Ryan talked quietly out of the corner of his mouth. Behind them he'd turned on a noisy faucet, drowning out their whispered conversation.

"Don't like it. Might not let us go. Eyes and ears open. Spread out. Report back like this. Soon as we find out what's happening we'll try and make a move. Until then it's step light."

The boy nodded. "Long as bastard sec men don't try push me around. Can't take that, Ryan."

The older man patted him on the arm. Then he zipped up the front of his trousers and went out, motioning for Finnegan to follow him and receive the message from the albino boy. And so on, down the line. Doc went last but one, ready to explain the orders to his beloved Lori, whose own very limited vocabulary meant she always had to be last in the line of message passing.

During the afternoon, around $D$ on amber, they set off to explore the Wizard Island complex. Doc went with Lori, Finnegan with J.B., and Jak and Krysty with Ryan. To leave their quarters they had to stand beneath a vid camera and request permission to have the main door opened. After a delay of several minutes, the request was granted.

They found very quickly that the promise of more or less free access was a myth. They were allowed to wander where they wanted through the main living areas, where they met and talked to more of the scientists. But when they tried to move into areas marked with black circles split with yellow triangles, there were always guards to prevent them, warning them off with the laser weapons, harsh, flat voices croaking threats.

"Any attempt to enter research sections topmost negative prevention deterrent force."

As far as they could judge, it seemed as if most regions of the vast building had been given over to research. During the introductory speech from Dr. Ethel Tardy, she had made it clear that the complex existed as it always had—for scientific work into military possibilities. The scientists worked as their fathers and mothers had worked, and their fathers and mothers, back to their fathers and mothers before the long chill had begun. Each generation had trained the next, handing on the torch.

Several times Tardy had mentioned a mythical government that had given birth to Wizard Island, and was still somewhere out there, waiting, gathering strength, like a wounded beast that would one day be whole again. She had referred to this as "Central," using the word with the same kind of awe that a primitive native would reserve for his most feared deity.

One thing that Ryan immediately found odd was the complete lack of anything from before the terminal war of

2001. In fact, there seemed nothing in the whole complex that was older than a year or so. He asked the first of the coated scientists that they saw that afternoon.

"Nothing old? Define your terms, stranger."

"Nothing more than a few years old."

The man was stooped with only a few tendrils of pale hair pasted across a skull that showed the scars of surgery. Ryan noticed that the man's ears were reversed so that they faced backward.

"A few. What is a few?"

"Five," Ryan said, seeing that this absurd game of chopped logic could go on forever.

"Is there anything here older than five years? Yes, I can answer without hesitation that there is."

"Any books?" Krysty asked.

"Books? Define your terms. What precisely is a book, young woman?"

"Something you read."

"Ah." A wintry smile flitted for a moment across the sallow face. "The tag here that bears my name. Dr. Darren Canting. Can you read that, stranger?"

"Course I can."

"Then the question does not compute. You ask if there is anything you can read. You say you can read my identification pass. Ergo, you can read something that is here."

"Thanks, Doctor," Ryan said. "We'll be on our way." He led the other two along a lateral corridor and up a gentle slope.

"He's fucking crazy." Jak was about to spit his disgust on the spotless floor, then changed his mind. "Like fucking swampy with head blown off. They all like him?"

As the day wore on, it became increasingly obvious that the Wizard Island complex was filled with some of the strangest men and women Ryan and his friends had ever seen.

Dr. Tardy had said there were sixty-one of the descendants of the original scientists left. What she hadn't mentioned was that hardly a single person could qualify for the word *normal*.

They didn't seem like the muties who haunted the hotter parts of Deathlands, but they showed all manner of physical oddities.

There were dwarfs of both sexes, one of whom pulled himself along in a spidery frame, powered by one of the silent motors that ran the inflatable boats. His head shaking, he smiled at them so radiantly that the room seemed to light up.

A giant, at least eight feet tall, with the lumpy features of acromegaly, was assisted past them, almost being carried by a pair of sec guards. A young woman, face and skull totally devoid of hair, saw them watch him. "Dr. Vayr is our most brilliant astrophysicist. His intelligence quotient is below eighteen in all other matters."

Ryan nodded his understanding. "It's often the way, isn't it? I knew a man couldn't fart his way out of a wet paper bag, yet he could flick ear wax into a plastic cup at twenty paces. Every time. Never missed."

The woman smiled blandly and went on her way.

"Why did you say that? To the woman with no hair?" Krysty asked when the woman was out of sight.

Ryan shook his head. "Because I wanted to see just what sort of zombies we're dealing with. Fireblast! There's every kind of freak under the sun. It's like giving little kids a bag of stun grens to play with. Are they really just carrying on with their fucking research, like they say? There's got to be more, lover."

Jak's interest rose when they met two girls. Both were about eighteen, with long hair the color of prairie wheat and eyes as blue as the Kansas sky. Both wore lab coats of pale cerise, belted around their trim waists. Behind them there stood the enigmatic figure of one of the sec men, carrying several items of clothes over its arm and a mop and pail with the other arm.

"You are the strangers everyone speaks of?" the taller of the two girls asked.

"Your hair is white as paper," the other said, reaching out tentative fingers to touch Jak's mane.

"You never go out?" the boy asked.

"Out?"

"In fresh air. Up top. Above lake. Don't you ever go?"

They both shuddered dramatically, giggling, then clung to each other. "Externalizing quadruple negative, stranger," the first girl sniggered.

"We work. Research for Central. That's all."

"What's your specialty?" Krysty asked.

"I'm Dr. Louella Hall," the shorter of the two told him. "I work on neural destruction from airborne alkaloid disseminators."

"And I'm Dr. Angie Pflaug. My work is research into neural-directed laser personalized missiles for low-intensity termination of selected targets."

"I'm Jak Lauren, and I fuck pigs," the boy said with a low bow.

His words set them on another dreadful fit of giggles, piercing shrieks of laughter that grew louder and increasingly shrill. They held on to each other for support, eyes squeezed shut, tears flowing over their smooth cheeks. At the first meeting, Ryan had thought these two might have been the only normal scientists in the complex, but as the laughter went on, scraping at his ears, he realized they were just as weird as the others.

"What's that smell of...?" Krysty began, her nose wrinkling in disgust. "Oh, Gaia!"

Ryan looked where she was staring and exhaled a sigh of revulsion. The laughter had affected the two young women to such an extent that both had lost all control of bladder and bowels. Their legs were streaked with the vivid evidence of their joint failure. Without another word, they tottered away down the corridor, leaving the mute sec men to put the clothes down and mop methodically at the mess they'd left behind.

Ryan, Krysty and Jak waited a while, then moved away in a different direction.

Later, when they met up for their last meal of the day, they all had similar tales of the complex's strange menagerie of scientists. The clocks showed that it was around *C* in the green. The food was identical with the middle meal, but there seemed to be less of it.

Finnegan tucked into it with such eagerness that he managed to snap the bowl off his plastic spoon, leaving a jagged end. He held it up silently for the others to examine. Ryan shook his head.

"Too weak, Finn, I guess."

"Better'n fucking nothing," the portly blaster replied.

"Give it here." Finn passed Ryan the broken spoon. "Look."

He drove the broken end into his own arm, against the soft material of the coveralls. The plastic was so brittle that it splintered again, doing no damage at all.

"Anyone lend me their fucking spoon when they've finished eating?" Finnegan said, grinning.

JUST BEFORE GREEN *D*, the door of their quarters hissed open and in toddled Dr. Ethel Tardy, accompanied by a limping man with an artificial plas-limb where his right arm should have been. They were accompanied by four mutie sec men, holding their laser guns at the high port.

"May Central be with you," the diminutive woman scientist said.

"Hi, there," Ryan said, staying seated on his narrow bed.

"You have seen what you wished, visitwise?" she asked. "Monitoring reveals you have."

"We've been allowed to see what you wanted us to see. Not anything else."

Doc backed up Ryan. "Why can we not have unlimited access to all aspects of Project Eurydice? What is there for you to hide?"

The cherubic smile vanished, and the woman frowned. "Visiting personnel take care. Imperative cooperation with us or—" The sentence dangled between them unfinished, the threat as clear as a knife blade.

"What do you want, Dr. Tardy?" Krysty Wroth asked, trying to ease over the difficult moment.

"It is time for questioning. To find out about the rest of you."

"Why do you say 'the rest of us'? What *do* you know?" Ryan asked.

The smile came flickering back, hanging on the soft little cheeks, never reaching the pale eyes. "We know about Dr. Tanner. He is someone…but that is not for you. Only Grades Delta and above. But we wish to know more about the rest of you. Him first." She pointed a stubby finger at Jak. "He will come with us."

"What for?" Ryan asked, finally standing. He noticed the way the muzzles of the laser blasters swung toward him.

"We make decisions, stranger." The smile had gone again, fast as the dew off a summer lawn. "There are all blood tests. Encephs. Bone marrow scrapings. Sight and hearing. The usual for strangers on Wizard Island."

"Don't like the sound of that," the albino said, poised on the balls of his feet, hands hanging loose, his body relaxed, ready for action.

"Me, neither," J.B. said, rising.

"Resistance is negatived. The blasters are set on level two. Scorch flesh only. If put up to twenty, instant death." She smiled. "Ugly termination."

It was a tense moment. Ryan was aware that every one of his six companions was razor-ready, needing only the flicker of a signal for him to attack, regardless of the opposition.

"I'll go with 'em," Jak said, quietly stepping forward. "No point in getting chilled now. Wait chance, eh?"

"Sure, kid," Ryan said.

"Take care, Jak," Lori said.

Finn gave him the thumbs-up signal, getting a nod from the young boy.

Ryan realized how young and slight Jak was, seeing him as he moved to stand next to one of the sec guards. In the coveralls and sneakers he seemed to be about ten years old. The jagged scar at the corner of the lad's cheek tugged up the corner of his mouth, making it look as though he were giving them a wry grin. His white hair floated like a mist around the nape of his neck.

"Wise, decisionwise," Dr. Tardy said. "Come, Dr. Avian."

The other man hadn't spoken, had merely observed what was happening. Once he lifted the false arm to scratch at the tip of his nose with a creaking finger. Now he reached out with it and tugged Jak by the sleeve.

The albino jerked away automatically, knocking into the nearest of the mutie guards. He retaliated by swinging his gun toward Jak and squeezing the flat black trigger. There was a brief burst of blue light, dazzling and intense. Jak yelped in pain, grabbing at the side of his ribs where a small strip of cloth was scorched and smoldering.

"Fucking bastard!" he shouted, pushing the crippled scientist away so that the man staggered and fell, bringing Dr. Tardy down on top of him. There was instant chaos in the living quarters.

A mutie sec man raked a line across the plastic floor in front of Ryan and the others, leaving a burned strip as a warning against interfering in the fight.

Helpless, they could do nothing but watch the fourteen-year-old take on the other three sec guards, without benefit of a weapon.

The blasters gave only the faintest hum and crackle when fired. From the floor, Dr. Tardy squeaked an order to the muties not to use their weapons. With so many people crowded together, she knew there was a good chance "innocents," such as herself, might get injured.

"Minimum force! Subdue the stranger!"

But the stranger wasn't about to let himself be subdued.

Over the years, Ryan Cawdor had seen men and women who had lethal skills in hand-to-hand fighting, but he'd never seen anyone quite as good as Jak Lauren.

The boy dropped to the floor, pushing out with his fingers, kicking at the knees of the nearest guard. There was the clear crack of bone snapping, and the mutie toppled sideways, landing with a crash on the plastic tiles. The guard's helmet rolled off, revealing, for the first time, the face of one of the scientist's sec men.

It was the face of a slobbering idiot—rolling eyes behind the glittering visor, and a mouth that opened and closed like a landed fish. Only the faintest mewing sound could be heard.

The creature came up on one knee, hands snatching at the broken joint, spittle trailing across his chest. Jak glanced sideways, measured the distance and kicked once more, his foot striking the base of the mutie's broad nose. Cartilage split and bone splintered. Jagged shards were driven deep into the front of what passed for brains in the sec man.

The guard flopped back, legs kicking and flailing, blood trickling from his open mouth where the rictus of dying agony had made him bite through his own blubbery tongue.

Jak wasn't interested in the man behind him. He jabbed with a clenched fist at the solar plexus of the second sec guard, doubling him over like a fawning courtier. The breath whooshed from the mutie's lungs, and he fell to his knees, gagging. A thread of yellow-green bile wormed from under the rim of his helmet. As he bent over, he exposed the nape of his neck for several seconds.

Jak needed only a couple of those seconds.

Using the board-hard cutting edge of his left hand, the white-haired boy chopped down at the helpless creature. Doc Tanner winced at the sickening sound of vertebrae cracking. The mutie's voice box gave a shriek of electronic feedback as he fell, mortally wounded, to join his partner on the blood-smeared floor.

The third guard backed away, waving the laser blaster helplessly, head turning back and forth, waiting for orders. Dr. Tardy had gotten to her feet, ignoring her companion who was having problems with his prosthetic arm. She chattered into a tiny lapel mike, too quietly for Ryan to hear what she was saying. It didn't need a giant intellect to guess she was calling up reinforcements to take the boy.

"Hit the mutie fucker, kid," Finnegan yelled, hands opening and closing as if he imagined himself squeezing the throat of the sec guard covering them.

"Set on twenty!" the little woman screeched, fists clenched in impotent rage.

"Watch him, Jak!" Ryan warned, seeing the third sec man fiddle with the dial control on the side of his weapon, then push the slide from two up to twenty.

From scorch to destroy.

But Jak was too quick. He came in like a dancer, perfectly balanced, red eyes glowing ferociously. As the mutie clumsily leveled the blaster, Jak batted it aside with one hand. There was a brief crackle from the gun, but no stream of luminous death. The force of the blow was enough to send the stubby weapon spinning into the air. It landed with a hiss, and a microsecond stream of deep blue light spat from the muzzle. The beam hit the wall to the left of Krysty's bed, blasting a smoking hole in the concrete. Fortunately for everyone, after that single brief pulse of laser power, the gun lay still.

Standing with legs slightly apart, the guard turned to watch the flight of his blaster. That gave Jak all the chance he needed. With dazzling streetfighter speed, he kicked hard, his foot crunching between the sec man's thighs, pulping the scrotal sac against the sharp edge of the pubic bone.

"Malfunction has ensued malfunction has ensued malf—"

The voice box was activated. The tone was calm and measured, at odds with the figure rolling helplessly at the feet of the white-haired boy, hands clutching his groin.

For a few fluttering heartbeats, it looked as if Jak was going to do it. The guard covering the others hesitated, head turning, blind-visored, seeking orders. Dr. Tardy stood away from the door, face pale as death at the sight of two of her precious sec men down and dying and a third crippled.

Then the backup force arrived.

Through the door came a dozen or more black-uniformed muties, all holding blasters at the ready. They fanned out and covered the single skinny young boy.

Ryan sucked at his teeth, knowing the cord of Jak's life was a heartbeat away from being severed forever. One word from the woman...

"Negative termination," she said, panting as if she'd run a hard race over a plowed field.

The cripple was finally on his feet, wiping sweat from his high forehead with his normal hand. He leaned forward in a curiously reptilian manner, studying the albino boy.

"He is m-m-m-m-most interesting, Dr. T-T-T-Tardy," he stammered.

"Indeed he is, Dr. Avian. I have never seen or heard of such skill and control, lethalwise."

Ryan relaxed. They weren't going to have the kid turned into steaming spray and spilled guts, after all.

"You will go to Control, boy," she lisped to Jak.

"You're going to chill him?" Ryan asked. If the answer turned out to be yes, he would let them take Jak and watch for a chance to go after them and save the kid.

"I don't read you."

"Kill him. Waste him. Send him to buy the farm. Terminate him?"

Jak stood, watching, his chest hardly moving more than normal, despite having put down three armed men, two of them for keeps. The other sec men kept their blasters on full power, covering Ryan and the rest.

The only sound was a bubbling little giggle, like that of a tiny girl seeing her first fireworks, an obscene, crazed noise in that room of death.

"Negative termination. We must examine him carefully and cherish him. A mutie beyond all muties, this one. No. Remainder of you can sleep peacefully. He comes." The voice hardened. "No more resistance, or megacull. You understand, strangers?"

Ryan nodded. "Yeah. We understand, Doctor. Jak, you take care now. We'll be in to see you in the morning."

In their supertech world, it was obvious the scientists had never come across anyone with the raw power and ruthless skill to off armed men with hands and feet only. Ryan's guess was that that should be enough to keep the kid alive for a while.

That was his hope.

The sec men wheeled clumsily around, circling the young boy. Jak brushed back his snowy mane of hair, pale face schooled into stillness. The crippled scientist went haltingly out first, followed by the patrol.

"Hold your fucking head up, Whitey!" Finnegan shouted.

"Sure, Fats. I'll do that," the boy replied.

Dr. Tardy was last out, pausing in the doorway to turn and rake the six of them with her pebbled eyes. "Strange company for a man such as you, Dr. Tanner. We shall examine and test all of this. But it must wait. Central will become impatient if we do not proceed. And we are so nearly ready. So very nearly."

The door hissed shut, and Ryan and his companions were left alone.

Later, on his narrow bed, under the subdued lighting of the dormitory, Ryan found sleep difficult. The room still tasted of death, though the corpses had been removed and the floor cleaned.

There were too many rules he couldn't understand. Too many pieces missing from the puzzle.

"Fireblast!" he whispered to himself. He didn't even know what the game was called.

# Chapter Seventeen

THE SIGN ABOVE the door said: Information Storage and Retrieval.

To Ryan's surprise they had been encouraged to visit Jak after they'd taken their first meal of the pallid sludge. The boy was safe and well, though in a closed security unit under a heavy guard of visored sec men.

Later, they'd again split up, to explore the Wizard Island complex, Ryan and Krysty wandering far into an isolated wing, descending in a smaller elevator, finding themselves in a region that seemed totally unused.

There were tiny heaps of dust in the corners of the corridors. All of the doors were locked, and few carried any sort of sign. It seemed as though it was a part of the complex that had drifted into disuse, possibly as the population decreased so rapidly.

J.B. and Finnegan had gone in search of ways of getting through to the main entrance and exit elevators, checking out the levels of security coverage. Lori hadn't been feeling well, but she and Doc were going again toward the closed research areas, in the hope that Doc's name might find them a way through.

"It's what they used to call a library," Krysty said, hands on hips, looking down at where her sneakers had become dirtied.

"I've seen 'em before. Lots of redoubts had them. Books and vids an' mags. Micros and fiches. All old stuff. Most so far gone it's useless."

"Shall we go in?"

"Sure. Probably locked like the ... No, it isn't."

The door was stiff, the bronze handle reluctant to move at all. As it opened, they felt the faintest draft of stale air, which made the girl's vivid hair coil and shift.

"Tastes like a well-kept grave," Krysty said.

"Been long years since this was opened up. I know that smell from other places, other times."

Hand in hand, like children, they walked in, their shoes squeaking on the dull floor.

AFTER AN HOUR or more of wandering the endless rows of files, Ryan called out to Krysty, "This is madness, lover. There's all the history of the fucking world here. Everything, right up to January 2001. All from outside. But you scan anything after the bombs fell, and it's from Wizard Island."

"Yeah. Post the nukes, it's all inbred stuff. Like the world outside stopped dead. Which it nearly did. But they didn't record anything after that. Like nobody ever left here."

"That's what that poisonous scientist dwarf said. Nobody ever leaves Wizard Island. Not until us."

Krysty stared around her, shaking her head. "There must be plans in here of how the redoubt was built. If'n we knew that, we could maybe find how to get out. Or how to wreck it."

"Take forever."

"I guess so. But I feel that—" She looked down at her feet.

"What is it?"

Krysty grinned. "You know there's a kind of mutie streak in me, lover. I can feel some vibrations from in here."

"What? Somebody in here? Can't be. We been clear round it, and there's only the one entrance."

"No. Not that. Ryan?"

"Yeah?"

"Stay here, by this microviewer. Keep quiet. Don't move or speak."

Ryan did as she asked. He already knew that Krysty had some strange powers—exceptional sight and hearing, as well as a doomie's sensitivity. He watched her, stepping light as a cat, eyes almost closed, head raised as if she were scenting the dulled air. She vanished behind a row of shelves, and he waited, patient, unmoving.

He heard a wheeled ladder being moved, rusted casters squeaking, cabinets opening, drawers slamming shut. Once he heard her coughing as though dust had gotten into her throat.

"This one."

She held out a flat disk in a laser-scan envelope. There was a seal across it, with a tiny pattern of microcircuits dappled over the top. On the front were the letters: TT/ CJ/Ce.

"Why?"

"That's the one we have to view. I don't know why, lover. Just try it in the player."

He took it and broke the seal, sliding the disk into the machine. The red light on the front remained steady, but the screen was stubbornly blank.

"Malfunctioned?" Krysty asked.

"I don't ... Ah, here she comes."

The screen glowed a pallid green, and finally lettering appeared.

*Access denied. Refer to subcode CJ, all secs. Go to mainframe on limit/inject. Enter code now for reading. Repeat NOW.*

Nothing more happened. The words disappeared off the screen, leaving it blank again. Ryan and Krysty looked at each other.

"Don't like this," Ryan said.

"Me, neither."

Then the screen came to life again. *Warning. If access reading code not entered in fifteen seconds from message end then all sec services will be notified. Warning ends. Fifteen-second delay begins now. Fifteen. Fourteen. Thirteen...*

"Time to move on out," Krysty said.

"Never get beyond the door," Ryan said. "Looks like this is the time the piss floods the tubes."

*Ten seconds. Warning repeats. Security caution in ten seconds. Nine. Eight. Seven...*

"It's *E*, then *M* and finally *Y*," a quiet voice behind them said.

Without even looking around, Ryan punched in the three letters.

*Three. Two... Access open. Sec warning deleted. Proceed.*

"Thanks, Doc," Ryan said, finally swiveling in the seat to see the old man leaning up against the wall, looking indescribably ancient and bone-weary.

"Pleasure. Didn't want those faceless goons on top of us."

"Where's Lori?" Krysty asked.

"Back in the dormitory. Wasn't feeling at all up to scratch. So I came wandering. I confess I had a most peculiar feeling I would find you in this place."

"But what's...?" Ryan began. "And how did...?"

"Just key it in," Doc said quietly.

Krysty leaned over Ryan's shoulder, her hair brushing against his cheek in a subtle, caressing gesture. She pressed the button marked Run with her index finger.

The code had opened up the secret file, and now the screen glowed once more. *Subject. Tanner, Theophilus Algernon. Doctor of Science, Harvard. Doctor of Philosophy, Oxford University, England.* There followed a whole string of further qualifications, degrees and honors, many from Europe. The screen scrolled through some forty lines of them.

"Fucking impressive, Doc," Ryan said. "But there haven't been any of these college places for a hundred years now. How d'you fake all this?"

Ryan laughed, but Doc Tanner didn't. He simply leaned against the wall and watched the screen with blank resignation.

*Birth date and location. South Strafford, Vermont. February 14, 1868.*

Ryan laughed again. "There's a lot of things in this complex cracking up. 1868." He stopped. "But it's wrong all ways. Can't be 1968. Nor 2068. So...?"

Krysty pressed Query and Repeat.

*February 14, 1868.*

"Got to be a mistake," Krysty said doubtfully. "I'll punch up the portrait."

It was unmistakably Doc Tanner.

The long, thin face with bright eyes. The oddly excellent set of strong teeth. The picture on the screen was a man dressed in more or less the same kind of old-fashioned clothes Doc had been wearing when Ryan and Krysty had first met up with him.

Ryan pressed the Amplify key, using the cursor to underline the date of birth.

*Date confirmed. Day known as feast day of Christian saint called Valentine, in year of 1868 during the period in the history of the United States of America known as "Reconstruction," after the Civil War.*

"That was when they fought over slaves, wasn't it?" Krysty asked.

"Slaves and much more, dear child," Doc said softly. "Oh, much more."

Ryan ignored them. His mind racing, he frantically moved the tape on fast forward, pausing now and again to try to absorb the mass of information about the old man who stood behind him.

An old man who was, if the machine was to be believed, some two hundred and thirty years old.

*Married June 17, 1891. Wife Emily Louise, née Chandler, deceased. Children, two. Rachel, deceased at age three in 1896. Jolyon, deceased at age one in 1896.*

"Fireblast!" Ryan breathed, shaking his head in disbelief. "He was married with a coupla kids. But two hundred years ago. How...?"

He caught the faintest of sounds behind him, like a quickly muffled sob, then feet moving fast on the dusty floor and the door opening and closing.

He and Krysty were alone again.

The record raced by, and Ryan was able to absorb only the highlights of it. Doctor Theophilus Tanner had been a truly eminent scientist, tipped for greatness, doing research at both Harvard and Princeton.

*First located and targeted by TT.*

"What's that?" Krysty asked.

Ryan queried it. The answer came up on the screen that the initials stood for an exercise called "Time-Trawl." It seemed that scientist working at the very end of the twentieth century had been dabbling with temporal travel, and had been searching the Victorian times for a possible victim, or specimen, to be trawled forward.

There was no explanation on the disk of precisely how this would be done, not even the vaguest of hints, except for a cross-reference that was a jumble of letters and numerals.

"Chron-jumps," Ryan said. "Old doc's mentioned that a few times. Just a broken word or two. Thought he was raving, like he...you know."

"Sure," Krysty whispered. "We all did, lover, we all did."

Now a pattern of order began to make sense out of the chaos of jumbled ideas and half memories from the confused old man.

As the disk wound on, Ryan and Krysty sat, openmouthed, hardly able to believe the evidence flashing up on the screen in front of them. Doctor Theophilus Tanner had been trawled in a time experiment operation in November 1896. Krysty pointed out that this was the year both of Doc's children had died and wondered if there could be any connection.

At one point Ryan noticed there was a passing reference to some other failed experiments in time-trawling, including a judge on the United States Supreme Court named Crater, a name that Ryan recalled had seemed to mean something to Doc Tanner when they'd first mentioned this lake.

It seemed as though Judge Crater had been lifted successfully, but had never arrived safely in 1998. The word used was "incomplete," which conjured up a horrific picture.

Doc Tanner's lift appeared to have been the only one that could reasonably have been called successful. He was trawled forward to only three years before the long winters began. Physically it seemed he had been in fair shape, but his mind had been tainted by the shattering experience.

*Subject's refusal to become reconciled to temporal correction proved difficult. Several abortive attempts to bribe or cheat his way into the chron-chambers were undeniable evidence of his overwhelming desire to travel back to his own time and rejoin his wife.*

One thing puzzled Ryan. "Krysty? What the chill would have happened if they'd returned him to his own time, but a day before they trawled him?"

"You mean, if he'd met himself?"

"Yeah."

She paused the disk, then entered a query concerning potential temporal anomalies. "It's the old one about going back in time and killing your own father before you were born. You wouldn't exist. So, you couldn't go back in time and kill your own father. So you would exist. So... and so on."

The machine whirred and clicked before it began to print an answer. In that dusty mausoleum, filled with the useless knowledge of an entire civilization, Ryan found himself sweating. He wiped at his forehead, but the salty liquid trickled down behind the patch over his left eye, making the puckered, raw socket sting. He eased the patch off and wiped at it with the end of the weighted silk scarf around his neck.

*Temporal anomalies are not clearly understood, nor easily explained. Evidence is limited as experiments have not proceeded far or fast. Most experts hypothesize that time is multistranded. There is at any one second millions upon millions of time possibilities—an infinite choice of parallel futures, any or all of which will persist. Thus, it is believed that the classic example of a person traveling back*

*into the past to alter his own present is false. He will alter
only one of the parallel streams, but his own present will
not change. He could be killed in the past, but his own
time stream will not be sullied by the disturbance. But in
one universe, he will cease to exist. This is all that is
known.*

"Thanks for fucking nothing," Ryan muttered.

"Move the disk on, or someone's going to get very suspicious about where we've gone and what we're doing.
There'll be a sec patrol along here any time now."

Ryan took her advice and pushed the fast-scan control,
reading the screen as the information poured out.

*Subject's constant attempts to rejoin "Beloved Emily"
and his own century became a considerable irritant. Doctor
Tanner was taken by the appropriate responsible authori-
ties and placed under restricted access and egress.*

"Means he was a bastard prisoner," Ryan said.

Together they read through several more pages until
Krysty paused the info disk. "So the old man became too
damned difficult for them to control. Surprised they didn't
just lose him out of a copter off the coast. But they found
a better way."

Ryan shook his head. "The poor, mind-blown old . . .
The cold-hearted icers sent him forward. Used a gateway
in Virginia. End December, in the year 2000. Couple of
weeks before the big one and the end of all that. Send him
onward."

"To Mocsin and Jordan Teague and Kurt Strasser. And
then on to join us."

Krysty walked away from the viewing console, burying
her head in her hands as she leaned against a wall of the
library.

Ryan also stood. "Nothing more on the disk. Stops with
the information that they pushed him forward. Ends up

saying there were no contingency plans for further trawling or return of subject.''

''It hardly mentions that he worked for a time on Project Cerberus, and it doesn't mention this Project Eurydice anywhere.''

It was true. There were passing references to redoubts and gateways. It looked as if all research into chron-jumps had more or less ended when they had pushed Doc Tanner forward into the unguessable future. One anomaly that still puzzled Ryan was whether they could have brought him back from the future. Would the old man have had knowledge of the nuclear holocaust that was to destroy most of the planet? Would they have believed him? Would he have changed things? Not if you credited the theory about there being parallel universes.

''But he worked on the chron projects, so he does know something about how to make the gateways function for time jumps as well as just for mat-trans.'' Krysty whistled between her teeth. ''This is . . . If we found a redoubt still sealed and with its gateway functioning for chron-jumps, then we aren't just limited to going anyplace, are we, Ryan?''

''Nope. We can go anywhen as well.''

Doc Tanner was waiting for them when they finally emerged from the echoing vault of the library. They closed the door carefully behind them, hearing tumblers click into place, locking it tight.

''You read it all?'' the old man asked. His eyes were red and swollen, sore from weeping.

''Sure. Why didn't you tell us about it?'' Ryan replied. ''It can't hurt to tell someone.''

''No. I suppose you are correct in that assumption. But I am so alone, my dear Ryan. A speck of infinity, two centuries old, with my wife and children long dead. Yet, in their world, they are all alive. I still cherish the hope that one day—''

"But these parallel streams? Doesn't that mean you can't return to that world ever again?''

Tanner sniffed. "It's a theory, that's all. It may be right. Until we test it, we shall never know. Traveling with you gives me that tender shoot of hope. One day, in the right gateway, it might . . .''

His voice faded away once more.

Later that evening, somewhere between $B$ and $C$ in Green, Doc came to Ryan, who was lying on his bed alone.

"Will you tell the others, Mr. Cawdor?''

"About where you come from?''

"Yes.''

"You mind if'n I do?''

The old man smiled weakly. "Tell you the honest truth, Ryan, and nothing but the truth, I'm relieved it's all out in the open. Load off my mind.''

He reached out and shook Ryan firmly by the hand, then went to rejoin Lori.

# Chapter Eighteen

"FUCKING LIAR!"

"It's true."

"You're a fucking liar, Ryan Cawdor."

"It's true, Finn."

"You too, Krysty. Couple of fucking liars. You think I'm still wet behind the balls, huh?"

"I said he wouldn't believe it," Krysty sighed.

Ryan tried one last time. "Doc Tanner is over two hundred years old."

"And I'm a swampy's foreskin. Come on, friend. Just forget it, will you?"

They had better luck with J.B.

"Over two hundred years old?"

"That's right, J.B., that's right."

The Armorer took off his glasses and polished them on the sleeve of his overalls, then squinted up at the ceiling lights through the gleaming lens. "Trawled and then sent on forward to our time? That's what you're trying to tell me, Ryan?"

As he spoke, one of the strip lights flickered and went out. Since they'd been in Wizard Island, they'd noticed how much of the technology seemed on the point of failing, or had simply failed. Ryan guessed it was because the scientists, much diminished in numbers, probably lacked the time to deal with such mundane matters. They were too deeply embroiled in Project Eurydice, whatever that was.

"Yeah. Born over two hundred years ago."

"If he was trawled when he was only around thirty—that's what you said?—then he spent only a few years in the time before the long chill. How come he looks around seventy?"

Ryan had wondered that. Krysty had pressed for more information when they'd watched the story scrolling on the computer screen in the library.

The answer had been vague and incomplete. *On the most limited data, it appears that chron-jumps can result in speeding or slowing of metabolism, resulting in aging either faster or slower than usual. This was observed in the specimen, Tanner.*

J.B nodded as Ryan tried to explain this to him. "So he's older than the real body time, but a damned sight younger than true elapsed time. I get it. And you figure he might know how to use some gateways for chron as well as mat-trans? Be good."

They couldn't tell Jak about Doc's age until the next morning. The old man told Lori himself. Ryan asked him how it went.

"The child is a caution, Ryan. She smiled as though I was joshing her. Kissed me on the cheek and said it didn't matter to her if I was one million years old. She is such a sweet dove."

THEY HAD NO FURTHER VISITS from Dr. Tardy or any of the other scientists. Finn and J.B. had failed to reach the main elevators and the sole exit from the complex, but the Armorer figured it could be done.

"Mean spilling a lot of blood. If'n we can get past a half-dozen sec men, then we can get at where they're keeping our clothes and blasters. Once we did that, we could clean out the whole place."

Finnegan had managed to persuade one of the scientists to take him to where the sec men exercised and practiced shooting their stubby blasters.

"Down another level. Lots of blaster stores. Locked tight. I see them shooting at comp targets. Nearly every fucking time they put them dials up to twenty, the fuckers misfired. I reckon it…ablind mutie could do better 'gainst them than those blasters. Odds must be hundred to one they won't work."

"Sounds like good odds," Ryan said.

AFTER THEY'D PLOWED their way through the stodge that served as food in the Wizard Island Complex for Scientific Advancement, Ryan and Krysty retired to their section of the dormitory. With something of a struggle, they'd managed to move one of the single beds off its mounting, snapping the rusting screws and pushing it alongside Ryan's bed to make it possible for them to sleep together.

Though it wasn't just sleep that was on Ryan's mind at the moment.

He lay pressed tightly against her, his erection poking into the warmth of her buttocks, his arms enfolding her. Pushing back against him, Krysty reached around to caress his penis, squeezing her fingers hard around the shaft and making him moan softly.

"That's nice, lover," she whispered.

The lights had failed in his section of the big dormitory. Since the vid cameras weren't infrascanners, he was fairly confident their lovemaking wasn't being witnessed and recorded.

His right hand cupped her breast, the nipple wriggling into hardness against his palm. Ryan nibbled at the back of Krysty's neck, nipping with his front teeth. The girl drew in a slow breath, pushing harder against him. Her sentient red hair shifted against Ryan's face, touching his skin with an electrifying arousal.

Knowing what she most liked, Ryan slid slowly down the bed, until his cheek was pressed against the muscular curve of her hip. He reached over with his hand and touched the coils of hair between her thighs. She opened to him, warm and moist, as his fingers found the trigger to her own deep arousal.

By shifting a little he was able to bring his penis against her ankles. Krysty felt him, laughed very quietly, then took him between her feet, rubbing him gently.

He probed at her with two and then three fingers, readying her. The girl tangled her own strong fingers in the long hair at the back of his head, pulling insistently at him, making him know what she wanted.

What she needed.

Her thighs clamped on either side of his face, drawing him into her body, and his tongue flicked out, tasting her, lapping at her softness. Krysty locked her heels together between her lover's shoulder blades, keeping him in place, pumping her hips against his lips and tongue. She felt the familiar, delicious fluttering of her stomach muscles as her orgasm rushed forward.

Ryan could judge how far she'd gone along the road, licking and sucking at her, centering on the core of her love, feeling her finally gasp and shudder, her thighs so tight around him he could hardly breathe.

At last she relaxed, and he was free.

"One day I'll break your neck doing that, lover," she sighed.

"I can't think of a better way to go," he replied, grinning up at her in the darkness.

"Your turn," she said, sliding down the bed, kneeling over him, her hair brushing now over his groin and lower stomach. The fiery tendrils actually curled around his cock, bringing him instantly to the edge of losing control.

"No," he managed to gasp. "Be too fucking quick."

"Can't have that," she teased.

Her head lowered over him, and he felt himself swallowed, sucked into her mouth. Krysty was the best Ryan Cawdor had ever known. He'd once, many years back, spent too much jack on a gaudy whore out Missouri way. She'd had ways with ice and with a length of knotted, waxed twine that had made his head spin.

But Krysty was undeniably the very, very best ever.

After she'd brought him moaning to the edge of a shattering orgasm, she withdrew her mouth, knelt astride him and lowered herself on the thrusting erection. Ryan pushed up to meet her, his eyes tightly shut, mouth sagging open. The gaudy whore used to promise two ups for every down, but it hadn't been like this.

When he came, he felt as though his entire body were gushing out through his penis. His back arched, and he cried out, pulling her down on him, his fingers digging so hard into her shoulders that they left vivid bruises for days. Krysty collapsed on him, kissing him tenderly around the face, her lips brushing him with the softness of a moth's wings.

"That was good, lover," she whispered.

"Yeah," Ryan said. "It was."

They made love twice more during that long night. They did it the second time with infinite slowness during the quiet hours of early morning when normally the blood flows at its most sluggish and the elderly and ailing are nearest to death.

The third time was around D in the red. Ryan woke, nestled against Krysty, and he was immediately possessed of a desperate need for her body. He rolled on her and took her quickly, almost brutally, while she was still barely awake.

Afterward, they held each other tightly, slipping back into sleep until they'd had their fill of sleep and were ready for another day.

RYAN WENT ALONE to visit Jak Lauren.

The corridors were patrolled by the helmeted sec men, marching in clumsy unison in pairs, none of them even turning to watch the stranger walk by. Ryan tucked his scarf into the neck of his coveralls, pausing at a corner with an attack of painful gas from the turgid food they'd been given. There had been no word from any of the scientists on what they should do that day.

"Go where you can and find out what you can," he'd told the others.

The security units were at the end of one of the corridors farthest away from the center of the Wizard Island complex. Once upon a time they might have been considered unbreakable, but now some of the comp bolts and locks had ceased to work, and there were ordinary bolts rusting on a couple of the doors. One single guard stood outside the main cell where the albino was being kept.

Ryan stopped in front of the sec mutie. "Can I go on through?"

The vid camera above their heads turned and whirred. After a delay of several seconds, Ryan heard a human voice answering him.

"Permission granted, visitwise."

But the sec man didn't move. He stood foursquare, blocking the doorway. Ryan looked up at the camera again, hoping for intervention, but nothing happened. He took a half step forward, and the sec man's blaster shifted, its narrow muzzle centering on his stomach.

"Fireblast! Move out of the fucking way, you stupe bastard!"

The speaker crackled again. "Regret signals not being received. Please go away and return in one-half letter. May the peace of Central go with you."

"Thanks," Ryan muttered.

When he returned, he found Dr. Ethel Tardy waiting for him, pacing up and down the narrow passage outside the security section.

"Apologies for delay," she snapped. "We are most busy and normal operational repairs have been put on the back burners for too many years. Soon, it will all change. You and your companions may work with us, involvement-wise, and share Central's rewards."

"Sure. Can I see the kid?"

The tiny woman nodded, waving her withered arm in a sort of salute. The sec man had disappeared, and all Ryan had to do was slide the bolt at the top and bottom of the door and pull it open. Jak was sitting on a narrow bunk bed. As the door opened, he stood up, his body tensing, but he relaxed as soon as he saw Ryan.

"Hi," he said.

Ryan glanced around and saw Dr. Tardy waddling off. But the dark figure of the sec man had mysteriously reappeared and now stood with his back to them. Ryan pushed the door closed and glanced around the cell. Then he looked closely at the boy's face for any sign of ill treatment. But Jak looked just as he always did—a narrow foxy face devoid of color, the eyes like distant rubies in sockets of wind-scoured bone, the familiar scar across the left cheek that tugged the mouth up into a simulacrum of a smile.

"How ya doing?" he asked.

"Not good. Not bad. Food's terrible. Bread and milk'd be better. How the others?"

"All fine. We found out the truth about Doc Tanner. Where he came from. How old he is. That kind of stuff."

"Yeah. How come?"

Ryan told him quickly, knowing it didn't matter much if the room was bugged. What they knew was already known to the scientists anyway.

Jak sat silent, occasionally asking a question. He wanted to know whether the date of Doc's trawling was linked with the date of the deaths of his two children and was puzzled about Doc's real age. But he never questioned the truthfulness of the story.

"So we could go time traveling? Yeah?"

Ryan nodded. "That's the theory, kid. All we have to do is find a redoubt with the right controls. And find someone who knows how to operate it."

"How 'bout Doc?"

"Who knows?"

They talked for another half hour or so. Jak told Ryan he'd been visited by a couple of scientists who had been interested in his highly developed fighting skills.

"Didn't care I chilled two sec men. Just wanted to know why did it. Not even how. Mostly why."

"After their generations of inbreeding, they must find the idea of slaughtering with your bare hands really weird."

"But minds weren't on it. Worried about research. Told me Central'd be pleased. Nearly got Eurydice done. Any day now."

"Any way now," Ryan muttered, vaguely aware he'd quoted from some old song one of the drivers on War Wag One used to sing all the time.

"How 'bout getting me out?"

"They talk about doing any experiments on you?"

Jak nodded. "Sure. Fuckers wanted neural readings. Synaptic reflex results. Motor speed. Muscle response. Plus lotta brain scans and bone samples. Not facing that, Ryan. You read me?"

"Sure. But not yet, you figure?"

"Not yet. Not until got their experiments done. Won't be long, Ryan."

"No. See you later. Any news, tell us. Any real problem, then get out and run for it. Best advice I can give you, kid."

"When you going to move?" he whispered, head very near to Ryan's.

"Soon." Ryan held up three fingers, showing not today, not tomorrow, but maybe the day after.

As he closed the door and walked past the sec man, Ryan realized how much was was coming to dislike the Wizard Island Complex for Scientific Advancement.

LORI STAYED IN THE DORMITORY all day, nursing her stomach illness. Krysty stayed with her for some of the time. At one point, though, she went back to the library on her own, but this time the sec door was securely closed. J.B. completed his working plan of the redoubt, putting in all the blind corners and potential danger spots, marking elevators and filling in where he knew. But when he showed his completed plan to Ryan that evening, there were huge blank areas he'd marked only as "Research?"

"What do they do there?" he asked. "I just can't figure it out. They got what I guess is around seven-eights of the place out of our sight. If they're doing weapons research, then they could be building missiles to the sun for all we know."

DR. TARDY APPEARED around early *B* in green. Her whole diminutive body reflected her anger.

"Your colleague and leader, Dr. Tanner, has caused disgrace here."

"How? What's he done?"

Lori heard this and came running out. She was on the edge of tears. "Where is he? How is he? Is he all right? Tell me."

"Terminate noise," the scientist snapped. "For the first occasion in seventy years there has been an incident of a person being drunk here."

"Doc? Drunk!" Ryan exclaimed.

"Yes. And with poor Dr. Avian, who is diminished, healthwise."

"How come?"

"He is being brought here now. His stomach has been pumped in the medic wing, and he will recover."

"Sorry 'bout that," Ryan said.

Finnegan, who'd spent most of the day sleeping on his bunk, appeared bleary-eyed in the doorway, grinning as he caught on to what had happened.

"Fucking good for the old man," he said, laughing as he punched his right fist into his left palm with a loud smack.

"Unamused," Dr. Tardy barked. "Our projects here are finely balanced, near to fruition. In the next six or seven daily periods, we shall be ready to test several of our..." She stopped, as if she wanted to say more but couldn't. "That's enough. Our efforts for the peace of the world are nearly done. Soon we can go up to the place beyond to claim our reward in the world we will have reshaped for Central."

Behind the thick lenses of her glasses her eyes glittered and danced. A film of frothy spittle dangled from her coarse lips, running over her chin among the warts.

Behind her, off down the main corridor from the center of Wizard Island, they suddenly heard the raucous sound of someone singing.

"See 'er on the bridge at midnight,
Throwin' snowballs at the moon,
She said, 'Jack, I've never—'"

The song broke off, and they all clearly heard the noise of someone throwing up violently.

"In Central's name, shut him up," the little woman whined. "He will ruin our concentration, and as for poor Dr. Avian..."

She spun on her heel and waddled away from them, passing Doc Tanner at the corner of the passage. He was being supported by two stumbling sec men, his long arms drooped over their shoulders as if he were a dying scarecrow. His long jaw fell, and his eyes squinted at the scientist.

"Good morrow to you, Mistress Whateveryourfuckingname. *Pax vobiscum*. May you... Greetings, Master Cawdor. My dear, dear friends. Mistress Lori, my felicitations to you, above all."

Ryan and Finn took him from the two sec muties, who stood there, staring blankly, as if their orders hadn't gone any farther. They were still there when J.B. shut the door on them.

"Get me to bed," Doc said. "Had a little drink 'bout an hour... Gone right to..." He locked his bony fingers in the top of Ryan's coveralls, pulling the one-eyed man's head down. There was the smell of vomit and the stench of raw alcohol. But when Ryan looked, Doc's eyes were as clear as limpid pools, and his whisper showed no signs of inebriation.

"Ryan. Know all 'bout Project Eurydice. I mean *all* 'bout it.''

"Yeah?"

"Think of your worst nightmare, and it's a hundred times worse. By the three Kennedys, but it is truly, truly dreadful!''

# Chapter Nineteen

HOISTED UP BY FINNEGAN, J.B. found it easy to short out the vid camera and sound mikes in half of the dormitory. There were so many pieces of equipment malfunctioning in the Wizard Island Complex that there seemed little risk of any of the scientists becoming at all suspicious. And it gave Doc Tanner the chance to tell them all what he'd found during the day.

"I encountered that halting fellow with the plas-steel fingers, the one who can hardly stammer through his voice box."

"Avian," Krysty said.

"Yeah. Got friendly. One scientist to another. He showed me part of his lab. Near shitting his breeches in case any of the others found out. Had him some pure alcohol. Showed him how to dilute it then mix it with some of that good spring water they've got here. We... Phew, but I fear I have imbibed a little too... I must..."

He pushed them aside and tottered off into the washroom, where they heard him retch. Lori went to follow him, but Ryan shook his head.

"Leave him be, girl. Best thing when you feel like that, with your mouth like a sticky's crotch."

Doc reappeared, looking rather more jaunty, singing some old chant about being born in a dead man's town. The rest became inaudible as he bent double with a coughing fit. His cheeks were almost purple as he fought for breath. Eventually he managed to straighten.

"Upon my soul, I am getting too old for this sort of taradiddle. I shall eschew all alcohol. I swear it."

"Tell us what you found, Doc," Ryan urged.

"Indeed, I will. Dr. Avian and I shared a beverage or two. His capacity was markedly less than my own. After a beaker or two—or three or four, I disremember me how many—well, he stammered out the whole filthy, despicable tale of Wizard's Island. Should be called Devil's Island. How it started. How it's gone on. What they do. What they'd done. And what they will be doing within the next week. We have arrived at what Dr. Avian called a 'nodal point' in the life of the complex. The past hundred years have been research and rehearsal for the next week. And we, ladies and gentlemen, are here. And we must stop it." He coughed again, then looked around at each of them. "There can be no argument. We *must* stop it."

For a century, Doc Tanner told them, the scientists had stuck to their chosen path with a crazed, religious fervor. As a generation died, the flame burned more brightly. As they bred and interbred, the streak of genetic madness grew broader until all sanity was lost forever.

All that mattered to them was research for Central. And now Doc had found out just where that research was being aimed.

Very simple. Bigger and better methods of total genocide. Ways of wiping the last pitiful survivors of the planet from their fingernail hold on a form of life. As though the slaughter of the long chilling of 2001 hadn't been enough, the scientists of WICSA wanted more.

Doc spoke for a long while, his voice pitched low, drawing the others into the nightmare world he'd accidentally stumbled upon. Once he asked Finn to bring him a glass of water for his dry throat. The rest of the time he just talked.

The scientist operated largely by committee. With their ranks thinning, and with any sense of balance gone forever, they had decided some months ago to test-launch all their new babies into the unknown world beyond the lake. And their arsenal contained all manner of horrific weapons.

Some old-fashioned and conventional.

Some chemical, some biological and some postnuclear in design.

Doc told them that the scientists had perfected a particle beam missile, linked to a rail-gun employing kinetic energy bullets, a missile system, fully integrated, using pulsed laser beam riding and a multifunctional infrared-coherent optical scanner.

The complex was protected from the results of its own toys. Even a high-power electromagnetic pulse that would knock out all conventional electronics and computers wouldn't touch the deeply buried Wizard Island complex.

The scientists were also producing grossly malignant strains of germ culture that could be disseminated by low-yield missiles and used on a fire-and-forget premise. Doc talked about the old Russian-initiated chemical agents, how the scientists had taken them and made them more foul. Particularly there had been research, led by Dr. Tardy, in the uses of tabun and thickened soman.

"The 'dirty' missiles were specifically designed to produce the most fatalities and the highest incidence of terminal cancer in survivors—hundreds of milli-Sieverts pouring out across the ravaged Deathlands.

"I'm not surprised they've developed a successful rail gun," Doc said. "Parallel conducting rails, linked to a direct current. Sliding armature between them that completes the circuit. Plasma-arc materials were always best. Current on. Down one rail and through the armature up the other rail. Acceleration is produced by the Lorentz force. Put the projectile in front of the armature, and it goes with it.''

"How fast?" J.B. asked.

"Between fifty and one hundred kilometers per second," Doc replied.

The Armorer laughed at that. "Come on, Doc. That's around three hundred and fifty thousand kilometers an hour. Nothing goes that fast."

"Rail gun does," Doc said simply.

He also told them what Dr. Avian had stammered out to him about some of their germ and drug research. Most of their testing had been on their own breeding stock of muties. One drug, based on an animal anesthetic, had made the victims begin to devour their own bodies. They'd start with their fingers, then pluck their own eyes from the sockets and tear strips of flesh from their own chests and stomachs.

Ryan asked Doc why he wasn't surprised about the success of the scientists with projects like the rail gun.

"They've built on foundations before the long chill. Way back over a hundred years ago, round 1986, the people hereabouts spent a hundred million dollars on rail guns."

The catalog of megadeath and horror went on, voiced in Doc's calm, well-rounded tones. Things that would travel in the air. Some in the water. Some that would come with fire and noise. Some that would come with silent invisibility to coat the skins and eyes of sleeping innocents. The products of one hundred years of the most concentrated work by the scientists—for their beloved Project

Eurydice, for the Central they worshipped, blind to the fact that it no longer existed.

"And they aim to release all this? Soon?" Krysty asked when Doc Tanner finished his recital and lay back on his bed with a sigh of exhaustion.

"Next week. That is their plan."

"We'll stop them, won't we, Doc?" Lori asked.

"Indeed we will, light of my life, fire of my loins, sweetness of my heart."

Lori smiled and blushed.

"Just how the fuck do we stop 'em, Doc?" Finn asked, standing up and stretching, moaning as his muscles locked from kneeling on the floor by the old man's bunk bed for too long.

Doc Tanner opened his eyes again. "Kindly allow me to make myself quite clear, ladies and gentlemen. From the drunken mumblings of poor Dr. Avian, who is madder than the craziest of hatters, I have no doubt whatsoever that within the week Dr. Tardy and her comrades will have put their toys out to play. The result will be the end, within less than six months, of all life, not only in Deathlands but throughout the planet."

"You mean people, Doc?" J.B. asked.

"I mean life. Animal and vegetable. There will not even be a speck of bacteria. Earth will be utterly, eternally barren. And that must not happen, even if our own poor lives are pawns in the great game."

"Talk's cheap," Ryan said thoughtfully.

"I am aware of that, my friend. I am also aware that the saying goes on about the price of action being quite colossal."

Ryan glanced at the Armorer. "What d'you think, J.B.? Can we take this place out? It's the strongest redoubt I ever saw."

"May just be the weakest as well," J.B. replied, his glasses reflecting the dim light from the far end of the room.

"How, when and where?" Ryan asked. "That's what the Trader used to say about making a war plan. Not much else matters."

"When is the easiest. Has to be in the next couple of days. We have to spring the kid first."

Ryan nodded his agreement. "Sure, J.B., sure. And where couldn't be simpler. Here. Problem linked to that is how the flying fuck we get out of here after we've done it."

"Got to blow her up," Doc said. The old man looked exhausted, blinking away his tiredness. "Set charges and get out. Way that stammering sot put it, there's enough stuff down here to blow the planet in half. Most's fission, so we won't trigger it in a fire or explosion."

"This place's fucking deep enough to bury anything, isn't it?" Finnegan asked.

"Sure. Only problem is..." Doc Tanner hesitated. "You know this used to be an old volcano. Mount Mazama? When it went up, it left Crater Lake. These *scientists*—how I hate that word now!—they've dug so deep they must be damnably close to tapping into the old magma chamber under the caldera. Big bang down here and the force hasn't anywhere to go. Except down, mebbe."

"Mountain might go bang," Lori said.

"As usual, my dearest child, in your simple way you have placed your cunning digit upon the core of the question. It might indeed, 'go bang,' as you put it."

Doc fell asleep shortly afterward, with Lori at his side. The other four went to another part of the dormitory to formulate a plan that would enable them to overcome forty or so heavily armed mutie guards and destroy the most sophisticated weapons complex in the history of civilization.

It took them all of twenty minutes.

Finnegan was the most confident. "Those fucking toy blasters they have. Blasters! Couldn't blast their way through a gaudy house blanket."

J.B. was more cautious. "They must work some of the time, Finn."

"One in a fucking hundred, that's all. You won't get better fucking odds in any firefight, I tell you. Easy as hitting a fucking war wag with a Sharps fifty."

Ryan laughed. "Hope you're right. You're too big a target, Finn. That's your trouble." He glanced at the big chron on the wall. "Look. It'll soon be in the red. Let's get some sleep. Big day tomorrow."

# Chapter Twenty

JAK LAUREN HAD SLEPT WELL.

He often dreamed of the old days of childhood, back in the humid swamps of Louisiana. His night phantoms were mutie alligators or swampies with blind eyes that floated over the sucking mud, webbed fingers grasping for him as he danced from them with an elusive ease. The albino always relished such dreams, never dreading the demons that rose in them.

This night it had been different.

A couple of times Jak's father had taken him, as a child, into the outskirts of the ruined urban spread that had once been the proud city of New Orleans. It had become a featureless waste, with an occasional spire of twisted metal where a water tower or aerial had stood. There had been great fires, Jak's father had heard from his father's grandfather. Fires that had ravaged anything that had remained after the nuking. Fires that had gone on burning for years, drawing on gases and liquids far beneath the crust of the earth.

The dream had been a little like that.

He had been walking briskly along what was left of an old blacktop highway, its surface cracked and seamed with ridges like waves where the shocks of the missiles had turned stone into a corrugated ribbon. Plants burst in profusion through the ravaged road, but they weren't from Louisiana, though the dream somehow seemed set there.

There was alpine fireweed, stonecrop, bog orchids and purple asters, goldenrod and brown-eyed Susan, all flourishing and bright in a landscape that was predominantly gray and leprous white.

Near Lafayette Jak had known of an age-old cemetery, with angels and graceful ministers of moss-stained stone weeping mournful tears in the damp air.

There they were, all about him, his feet sinking silently into long, cropped turf. Graves, each with its own memorial tablet, bore witness to the name and dates and virtues of the persons who lay buried there. Jak paused to stoop and peer at the nearest stone.

"Jak Lauren," it read. "He died in agony and sleeps forever waking."

The next grave said the same.

And the next.

Next.

A pallid sun cast watery shadows among the tombs, but Jak himself threw no shadow at all. There was a mist weaving about some stunted yew trees, their boles and knobbed branches draped in long fronds of Spanish moss. It was impossible to see more than twenty or thirty yards in any direction, and Jak began to feel he was not alone.

He began to walk faster, picking his way among the graves. Now he was in an older part of the cemetery, where some of the stones had fallen, their jagged edges ready to trip the unwary.

The ground rose and fell, making it difficult to maintain a steady pace. Jak paused several times, staring into the roiling banks of fog seeping all around him. He laid his head to one side, straining to catch any noise. There was a faint rumbling, like a well-laden wag laboring up an incline. And water. The sullen sound of water dropping over cold rock from a great height.

The graves disappeared, and he was on an open hill-side, among heather. Tough, wiry roots gripped him by the ankles, and he fell several times. He heard laughter some-where below him.

Or was it from above?

The air was thin and cold, searing his lungs as he fought for breath. Once, as he fell, he laid his hand upon a nest of tiny, wriggling maggots that squirmed away from him at enormous speed, vanishing into the earth.

A lake became visible through the shifting cushion of fog. A shingled beach, with round, smooth pebbles that rolled under his bare feet, clattering and echoing. The echo carried on even when he stopped running, sounding closer, as though whoever pursued him was gaining.

Or whatever pursued him.

Then, half turning, Jak saw it. Saw *them*. Tall, lumber-ing creatures in glittering black armor, with masks made from dull mirrors. As the boy stared at them, he recog-nized myriad reflections of himself, white hair drifting about his crimson eyes, menacing him from every helmet.

He ran again, now at the edge of the lake, stumbling into it, the water burning him with its fiery chill. It splashed about his naked body, leaving a livid blotch for every drop that touched him. Jak's left eye hurt him, and he lifted a hesitant hand, feeling a black patch that sealed off his sight, as though it were grafted to his own living skin.

They were gaining on him. He didn't dare to turn now, so close were they, their clawing fingers straining to peel the flesh from his back. He knew that the masks were gone and that they grinned at him with charnel faces, the skin dripping off in wedges from the scabrous bone.

Someone was calling to him out near the middle of the vast lake, calling him by name. Jak struck out, seeing a piece of rotting wood in his way. He pushed at it, but it bobbed up and down, blocking his way past. There was carving on it, the letters etched deep in the soft surface, some of them almost obliterated by a gray-green fungus. But he could make out the last part.

*... died in agony and sleeps forever waking.*

Something immeasurably huge moved, swirling far below him in the water. The voice still called him, but it was moving away, becoming more faint. Treading water, Jak tried to make out something that appeared for a second through the fog. It was in a small boat, and it had a great nodding, spongelike head that was, mercifully, turned away from him.

At that moment he woke up, still in the clean, antiseptic cell of the security section of the Wizard Island Complex for Scientific Advancement.

It was hard to reckon how long the dream had lasted, but he felt refreshed, as though the rest of the night had passed peacefully. Still, the images continued to haunt him as he sat on the narrow bunk and waited for the mutie sec guard to bring breakfast. By squinting through the barred slot in the door, the boy was able to see the corner of a clock.

It was around the middle of $E$ in the red. The first plate of pallid, tepid stodge normally arrived just as the pointer shaded from red into amber.

The sec man moved across his line of sight. Jak was tempted to call out to him, but he knew from previous attempts that it would be futile. The speaker on the wall would respond to him, but only to ask what his request was. His keen hearing caught the sound of someone walking in the corridor beyond the outer door. The sec man also heard the noise and stood up to block the entrance, blaster at the ready.

Jak guessed it was Ryan Cawdor even before he heard his voice.

"Hi. Can I come through to see my friend?"

There was the usual delay, but this time Ryan didn't have to repeat what he'd said. The speaker came on almost instantly. "Greetings, stranger. The experimental sample can be seen. But work will be done on him during this three-color period. After that all access will be withdrawn."

Jak didn't much like the sound of that. Maybe it was getting time to move on out. He'd talk to Ryan first, though.

The rusty bolts slid open, and Ryan walked in. His long white silk scarf was wrapped around his throat and tucked into the neck of his coveralls. Jak grinned crookedly at the older man, who smiled back, brushing his mouth with the index finger of his right hand—the signal they all knew for caution.

"You all right?"

"Sure."

"Doc got piss-ant drunk last night."

"In this place?"

Ryan laughed, moving in closer to the boy. "Yeah. Even in here. Got to talking with one of the scientists. Found out how interesting the work is."

Jak was puzzled. He didn't see where the conversation was leading.

Ryan sat down on the bed. "Fact is, we could all go like Baron Tourment. You remember him?"

Jak could hardly forget the evil genius who'd run the ville where he'd first lived, nor could he forget how the baron had ended up. "I get the meaning, Ryan."

"Best we got things moving real fast, kid. Real fucking fast."

Ryan jerked his thumb toward the half-open door in an unmistakable gesture, running his hand across the front of his own throat as if he were slicing it with a sharp blade. Jak shrugged his shoulders, showing open palms. How were they going to make the break from the security section without weapons?

"Glad it's all good." Ryan stood up.

"It's good."

"Guess I'll have to go. The scientists are going to start their experiments on you today. So we might not meet up again."

"I heard that," Jak replied, also standing.

"Well. Best go, kid. Take care now, you hear. Everyone sends their best to you."

They shook hands, Ryan managing a wink with his right eye as he pulled the door open and called to the sentry outside. "All right if I leave?"

The blank-visored face turned incuriously toward him. The mutie stood quite still, waiting for instructions from his scientist masters.

"I asked if I could go," Ryan repeated.

"Egress permission affirmative," the corner loudspeaker squawked.

The guard turned away from the two men in the cell and gazed down the corridor.

Ryan clenched his fists together and swung a dreadful clubbing blow at the creature's back, striking it with crushing force a little to the right of the small of the back over the kidneys. The sec man gave a choked cry of pain and shock, forced out past the voice activator, hardly louder than a whisper. Jak darted in like a hunting animal and snatched the laser blaster as it dropped from nerveless fingers.

As the guard dropped to his knees, almost paralyzed by the awesome power of the double punch, Ryan flicked off his heavy helmet. The face turned up toward him, eyes rolling in agony, the mouth drooped open, showing yellowed gums. The hair was cropped to the scalp, one ear completely lacking.

Despite all, it was unmistakably the face of a woman, pleading silently for mercy.

Ryan didn't hesitate, chopping with the edge of his hand across the front of the throat and crushing the delicate electronic implant. His hand also pulped the thyroid cartilage and crushed the laryngeal branch of the vital vagus nerve.

The sec guard was dying, sliding forward on the floor of the corridor on her face, arms and legs moving spasmodically, gloved fingers scraping feebly.

Ryan glanced around to make sure the killing had been done out of sight of the watchful vid cameras. Jak turned the power control dial of the gun all the way around to the upper limit of twenty.

"Finn swears those blasters don't work ninety-nine times out of a hundred," Ryan said. "So watch yourself."

"Why we moving?" the boy asked.

Ryan quickly explained everything Doc Tanner had found out the previous evening, adding that they now knew the scientists were intending to start their physiological experiments on the white-haired boy that very day.

"And we don't think the bastards intended you to be up and walking after they've done. Termination mode for you, kid."

"So we blow 'em?"

Ryan grinned wolfishly. "Clean out the nest, Jak. What we're good at."

IT WAS CLOSE to $B$ in amber when Ryan and Jak finally arrived safely back at the dormitory. One good thing about the vast research sections of the complex being sealed off from them was that the scientists seemed to rarely move anywhere else, having most of their living and eating quarters near their precious work.

Twice they'd seen sec patrols, but they'd been absurdly easy to dodge. More and more Ryan had come to realize that the Wizard Island complex was like a security sieve. When it had first been established, it had probably been the last word in tightness, but over the years it had fallen apart. The research had taken priority, and there had never been any threats to the scientists from outside.

Everyone in the dormitory was ready and primed. Doc had recovered from the alcoholic excesses of the night before and looked chipper. The first priority was to get hold of some weapons, and the blaster Jak and Ryan had won was a start. J.B. had made the suggestion at their battle meeting that they should try to get their clothes and weapons back. That way they would fight better and be ready to make a swift run for it. At no time during their brief discussions had anyone suggested the possibility they might fail.

If you succeeded, it wouldn't arise.

And if you didn't, then it wasn't going to matter much.

"When shall we start?" Krysty asked now, sitting cross-legged on her bed, doing slow-breathing exercises to ready herself for the coming combat.

"Now's good as any time. Who wants to take this laser blaster?"

Finn grinned at Ryan's question. "Have to be me. I'm the man with blasters. Don't have many skills, but I fucking know 'bout blasters. Gimme, Ryan."

He caught the short, vicious gun, then dropped into a fighter's crouch, pretending to spray the room with the lethal blue beam. In the laughter, none of them heard the warning sound of the main door hissing open.

"M-m-m-m-my suspicions were in affirmative m-m-m-m-mode," Dr. Avian said. He stood there, a malevolent smile of triumph on his face.

He was flanked by four armed sec men.

# Chapter Twenty-One

"CAREFUL, FINN," Ryan Cawdor said quietly, not wanting to provoke the rotund man into any action that might leave them dead within seconds. Whatever Finnegan might say about the fallibility of the laser rifles, it figured they had to work sometime. With four of the sec men, it was too long a shot.

"I trust you have recovered from the peculiar illness of last night," Doc Tanner said, offering a half bow to the limping scientist.

"Poison, Dr. Tanner. Poison." With an obvious effort, the man was controlling his stammer, speaking slowly and with great care.

"Poison, sir? That is an aspersion upon my honor! By the three Kennedys, my seconds shall be calling upon you."

Ryan had no idea at all what Doc Tanner was rambling about. Neither, obviously, did Dr. Avian. The scientist waved a threatening plas-hand at them all.

"You t-t-t-try to betray us all."

"What're you going to do 'bout it?" J.B. asked. "Take us in?"

Dr. Avian looked bewildered, as though he hadn't actually thought the confrontation through. Without any sign from Ryan, the others had spread slowly into a half circle, leaving a scattered target for the blasters, each one waiting for a sign from Ryan to make a move.

Only at that moment did the crippled scientist notice Finnegan was holding one of the sec guard's blasters.

"Where d-d-d-did you... And the white head is free from the..."

In any firefight there is a crucial moment when the situation goes beyond words. If the moment is recognized, then there is a chance of staying alive. Missing it kills a man deader than chicken-fried steak.

Ryan knew the moment had come.

"Chill the gimp," he told Finnegan in an ordinary kind of tone, the way you'd ask someone to open a window for you.

Finn aimed the blaster and squeezed the trigger. The weapon spluttered and fired a brief burst of blue-green light. The scientist squealed and staggered back, the front of his coat scorched and smoldering. Finnegan threw the useless gun on the floor.

"What a fucker!" he spat.

Already, Ryan and the others were moving in on the sec men. During the brief stay on Wizard Island, Ryan had come to suspect that the guards operated with virtually no free will at all, performing their patrols and chores by a simple programmed rote. Anything above and beyond that had to come from a specific order from one of the scientists.

That was a key factor in his risking an attack.

Unlike the unreliable blasters, it worked.

Not one of the mutie guards tried to defend themselves against the attack. While Dr. Avian rolled around on the floor, stammering cries for assistance, the sec men went down like helpless tenpins. Ryan broke the neck of the nearest. J.B. kicked the next one in the crotch, felling him, then did a jump and knee drop on the center of his chest. The crack of snapping ribs was obscenely loud in the silence of the fight. None of the sec men even cried out as they went down one after the other.

Jak chopped the legs from the third sec man, leaving Krysty to straddle the creature, her long, strong fingers tightening around the exposed neck. The helmet rolled away, and the idiot face goggled up at her, eyes rolling, mouth opening. The hand made a feeble effort to move the woman, but Krysty was too strong and too experienced. Her strangling fingers clamped around the windpipe. The eyes protruded even more, and the tongue, blackening, burst from the bloody froth that filled the mouth.

Finnegan hit the fourth and last sec man, taking out his anger and frustration at the failure of the laser gun. He was about as tall as the black-uniformed figure, but outweighed him by around sixty pounds. He sent the creature crashing back into the edge of the door with a spine-jarring impact. The guard's gun went flying one way, his helmet spinning the other. As the mutie began to topple, Finn hooked two fingers into his brutish nostrils, jerking the sec man off-balance even more. With amazing lightness for a big man, he pivoted sideways and struck with his forearm across the front of the mutie's neck. Unable to breathe, the guard slumped to his knees, face purpling, waving his hands helplessly in the air. Finnegan, with contemptuous ease, stepped behind the sec man and locked his hands under the creature's chin. Bracing himself like someone pulling a cork from an enormous bottle, inhaling mightily with the effort, he snapped the sec man's neck like a dry branch.

"Four down and done," J.B. said, picking up one of the laser blasters and examining the dubious firing mechanism.

"T-t-t-t-t-termination with utter p-p-p-prejudice," Dr. Avian gasped, reaching for the tiny trans-speak that hung from the top pocket of his long coat.

"Not us, Doc, you," Ryan said, stooping to snatch the tiny transmitter and crush it under his heel.

"You wouldn't kill a man of science? It is b-b-b-beyond logic."

"Chill him, Ryan," Doc Tanner said, face cold as sierra granite.

"You are a colleague," Dr. Avian whimpered, still lying on his back and waving his artificial hand.

"Colleague," Doc Tanner hissed. "I would as soon claim kinship with a diseased timber wolf. A scientist should labor only for betterment and for peace and for life. For the positive things. No man knows that as well as I do. You and your crawling, loathsome colleagues are working only for the powers of darkness. For the black lords of chaos. No, Dr. Avian, you should be crushed like a poisonous worm. Kill him, Ryan. Quickly, so that we can get on with our cleansing business."

Ryan had never seen the old man so angered. He seemed to grow in stature, his eyes blazing with a menacing fire, his fists clenched at his side.

"I'll ice him, Doc," Finnegan said, glancing at Ryan for confirmation.

"Do it," Ryan said.

It was so simple for an experienced killer like Finnegan to take out the frail scientist. In the brief struggle, the false hand became detached and began to make its own laborious way across the floor, trailing wires and a green circuit board behind it. As it neared the door, Lori followed it and set her foot on top of it. There was the tiny crackling sound of shorting circuits, and the hand was still.

J.B. broke the sudden silence. "These guns are totally U.S. All of 'em."

Lori turned to the Armorer. "What is that meaning?"

"Unserviceable," J.B. replied, dropping the blaster on the bed. "For once Finnegan's right. Odds must be hundred to one on them working. They're fine at low power but fucking useless if you push the dial around."

"What now?" Jak Lauren asked.

"We go get our own weapons," Ryan replied. "And our clothes."

"And if we meet trouble?" Krysty asked, shifting her stance to avoid the spreading pool of blood that oozed stickily from the open mouth of one of the dead sec men.

"We've taken four. We can take the rest."


THE CORRIDORS WERE EMPTY when they made their move.

Now that they were irreversibly committed to a course of bloody action, there was no point in concealment. No point in anything except speed.

"Place they stored our stuff's around the next corner," J.B. called, holding his handmade map of the complex.

In his other hand he held one of the blasters; he, Ryan, Finn, Jak and Krysty had each taken one. Despite Finnegan's lack of confidence in the weapons, and the evidence of their own eyes, they were better than nothing. At the suggestion of the Armorer they set the illuminated pointer on ten rather than maximum power.

"Take a look, kid," J.B. said, motioning for Jak to sneak ahead of them.

The boy flattened himself against the wall of the corridor, brushing his mane of snowy hair away from his eyes. He cautiously edged his face around the corner, then pulled back sharply.

"Nobody," he said, grinning.

The storage room door was sturdier than many others around the complex, but it yielded to a succession of crushing kicks from Finnegan's right foot. The hinges squealed and finally split, and the door burst open, revealing shelves and lockers.

"Let's get ready, people," J.B. said, leading them inside.

Jak waited in the corridor, keeping watch for sec patrols while the others quickly found their own clothes, tore off their coveralls and changed. They also found their own weapons—a far more important discovery.

"Let's fucking go take 'em," Finnegan said, waving his HK54A2 submachine gun. The big butcher's cleaver in its leather sheath dangled menacingly at his left hip, balanced by the 9 mm Beretta pistol on his right hip.

Jak carefully checked his satin-finish .357 Magnum, peering along the six-inch barrel at one of the overhead lights. Slowly he reloaded it, not taking any chances that someone had tampered with the heavy pistol.

Doc Tanner swung his sword stick, the thin steel blade hissing and whistling as he cut and parried like a fencing scarecrow, shuffling and dancing, muttering to himself from some archaic guide to fighting.

"Punto and reverso, stoccata and imbroccata. Passada. Parry and lunge. By the three Kennedys, but we'll purge this place, my friends."

Ryan held up a hand for silence. "We've been lucky so far. Let's realize that. Seems these people are too damned busy with their experiments and research to watch what's going on. But there's still a chance that someone might look at the security vid screens. So we still move quick and quiet. And from now on we take out anything and anyone we see.''

"Main thing's to get in and find what we can use to blow this mother a mile into the sky,'' the Armorer said. "We'll have to string out a little.''

"Yeah,'' Ryan agreed. "I'll go point. Krysty second. Then Jak, Doc 'n Lori, with you and Finn holding the rear. From now on there's no stopping. The security in this section is old and all fucked up. Once we reach the research sections, I guess it'll be harder.''

J.B. gave directions from his map as they moved toward the core of the complex. Each person had a favored blaster in hand, ready for instant fire. It was one of those situations, as Doc had pointed out a couple of minutes earlier, when those that weren't for 'em were ag'in 'em.

There was no danger of accidentally shooting down a friend.

There were no friends.

Just then two helmeted mutie guards stepped simultaneously from a side corridor only thirty short paces in front of Ryan. Standing close together, they began to turn slowly and awkwardly.

The caseless G-12 was already at Ryan's hip. He took lightning aim, leveling and squeezing, bracing himself even though the H&K automatic rifle was virtually without recoil. It was set on triple burst, the three bullets so close together they sounded like a single round.

Ryan squeezed the trigger twice, shifting his aim slightly from one sec man to the other. The two corpses slid and kicked on the blood-slick tiles of the corridor.

"Nice," Jak said, just behind Ryan.

The sec man on the right had been hit by all three rounds in the center of his chest, five inches below the thorax, the bullets within a finger's width of one another. The force of the impact had lifted the mutie clean off his feet, hurling him backward. Another three rounds, again tightly grouped, had hit the second guard a touch higher, knocking him sideways, his helmet rattling and spinning, still rolling after both sentries were dead.

As the seven began to move on, the loudspeaker above them crackled to life. "Sec report terminal malfunction? Query intruders? Report? Report?"

Somewhere behind them, apparently at some distance, a siren began to wail. The lights above them flickered. Ahead, a door was slammed shut.

"Chill's on," Finnegan muttered.

"Let's go," Ryan said.

Moving quickly but with stealth, they approached the nearest entrance to the research section, which was just around the next turn. Oddly the screeching siren had stopped.

Suddenly around the corner came the two pretty young women they'd seen on the day of their arrival at Wizard Island—Louella Hall and Angie Pflaug. A sec man walked behind them, carrying cleaning tools, ready for the two blue-eyed blond girls to have an antisocial accident.

"Central be with you," Dr. Pflaug said, already starting to giggle at the sight of Jak's bleached hair.

"White head was for anthrax-derivative testing at $C$ in amber," Dr. Hall said, her fingers working nervously at the collar of her cherry-red lab coat. "Why with you? And uniformwise unorthodoxy?"

Ryan had the ruthless instincts of the true killer, but even
he hesitated at chilling these poor, mentally deprived girls.
They were merely victims of a crazed policy of research
and inbreeding.

"Terminate them all," Dr. Pflaug said, hardly able to
speak to the sec guard due to her rising laughter.

"They're mine," Jak said.

And they were.

Ryan admired the careful way the fourteen-year-old
braced his right hand with his left, steadying the heavy
pistol against the inevitable kick. The boom of the shots
was deafening in the narrow corridor.

The first bullet pierced the front of the guard's helmet,
carrying splinters of black plastic with it into pulpy brain
tissue. Blood spurted all over the cream colored walls. For
a moment, as the powder smoke drifted around them, the
two young scientists continued to snigger, holding onto
each other, their laughter as bright and tinkling as drops
of crystal.

The double crack of the big Magnum drowned out their
chuckles.

One bullet went through the neck of Dr. Angie Pflaug,
sending a torrent of blood gouting from the burst artery,
patterning the ceiling in cherry-red splashes.

One bullet went through the open, laughing mouth of
Dr. Louella Hall, exiting at an angle three fingers above
her right ear and tearing away a clump of summer-wheat
hair and a chunk of bone the size of a man's fist. The force
of the impact sucked out most of the woman's diseased,
distorted brain.

"It's a good beginning," Doc Tanner said quietly.

The sirens started up again, wailing and shrieking, the
pitch rising and falling.

And rising and falling once more.

Ryan was beginning to think it was almost like some lunatic dream. They were moving through this redoubt, buried deep under the waters of Crater Lake, in what had once been the beautiful state of Oregon. They were killing security men in handfuls, even wiping out the protected scientists.

And there was no comeback.

ONLY ONE SEC MAN GUARDED the main entrance as the seven friends came within sight of it. His back was turned, a laser rifle slung across his black-clad shoulder. The dark mirrored visor stared blankly away from them, toward a moving pattern of colored lights that danced over the top of the door. Near him was a sign that read, Absolutely No Admittance Without Authorization and Accreditation.

"That one's fucking mine," Finnegan hissed, baring his teeth delightedly at such an easy target.

At that moment the speakers around them clicked to life. "All security operatives go to condition red. Repeat condition red. Weapons into full termination mode. Repeat condition red. Any person without clearance to be eradicated without warning. Condition red."

Ryan glanced at the others. "Got to be a quick decision."

"What?" Krysty asked.

"We can run for the elevator. Mebbe steal one of those boat wags. Doubt they'll come after us."

"But we must destroy this nest of evil and corruption," Doc Tanner protested.

"Sure," Ryan agreed. "But it's not up to me to order everyone to risk their lives. Chances are we can get away free if we run now."

"I never run from fucking nobody," Finnegan said. "And you don't get better chances than this, since it's a hundred to one their fucking blasters don't work."

"We go in and try to blow the complex. Or we get out now. Who stays?"

The only one to hesitate was Jak; the others immediately raised their hands. The albino sniffed. "Sure. Why not?" And he also lifted his hand.

"You don't have to, kid," Ryan said. "This isn't your fight."

Jak shook his head. "Wrong. If it's your fight, then it's mine."

"Then we go. Finn?"

"Sure," he said, hefting his Heckler & Koch submachine gun. "I'll take him out on triple-shot."

"Don't take any risks," Ryan warned.

The blaster's chubby face creased into a broad grin. "That's way weird, old friend. Have you ever known Thomas O'Flaherty Fingal Finnegan ever do anything as fucking stupid as take a fucking risk?"

"Yeah," Ryan said, grinning back. "Too many fucking times, Finn."

He watched the man move out around the corner, pausing to flatten the smooth black fur collar of his gray leather coat. The sec man turned to face Finnegan, leveling the stubby laser-blaster on him.

"Identification or termination now," the mutie's voice box croaked.

"This here SMG's all the fucking identification I need, you mutie bastard," Finnegan growled.

"Chill him now, Finn," Ryan called urgently.

"Now," Krysty cried, her voice edged with sudden panic.

Finn half turned to reassure them, just as the sec guard fired his blaster. There was a piercing hum, and a dazzling streak of amethyst light hit Finn squarely in the chest.

He screamed, something that sounded, through the shock and agony, like "Hundred to fucking one, Ma!"

# Chapter Twenty-Two

IT WAS A HIDEOUS PASSING.

Over the bloody years Ryan Cawdor had seen many men and women meet their Maker. Few of them had gone peacefully into that long night. But he had never seen anyone chilled in such an appalling way as his friend Finnegan.

The blind perversity of the fates had dictated that the laser rifle of the sec man functioned perfectly—for just long enough.

Unlike a single bullet, the beam of light from a high-power military laser acts more like a directional, narrow strip of extreme heat. A bullet drills a hole through flesh, the exit hole generally markedly bigger than the entrance wound. Not so with a laser. It is precisely the same size as it exits the human body as when it entered.

Also, light has no mass, so there is no impact. As the laser struck Finnegan, it didn't lift him off his feet, or throw him backward, nothing initially as dramatic as that.

But the power was so awesome that in the instant the blaster came to life its vivid blue beam had penetrated clean through the helpless Finn, hitting the wall only a couple of paces to the left of J.B., who immediately threw himself flat on the floor, hands over his head as chunks of liquid concrete and charred wood fell from the side of the corridor.

Along one wall, Ryan watched the termination in impotent horror, seeing that nothing could be done for the doomed man.

Stinking smoke erupted from the front and back of Finn's coat, tiny flames flaring red and yellow. Every staggering movement of the dying man only increased his horrific suffering. His skin was scorched black, the flesh broiled by the immense power of the blaster. The heat was so intense that the wretch's intestines began to explode and melt, and his blood boiled instantly where the laser had touched him.

As Finn dropped, his own blaster clattering on the tiles, the sec man kept the trigger down, almost slicing the beefy man into segments with the blaster's ferocity.

"Oh, no, no, no, no..." Krysty moaned softly, one hand resting lightly on Ryan's arm.

As the body lay smoldering on the floor, the blue light stopped as suddenly as it had started. The sec mutie looked down at the blaster and banged his fist on the control dial, frustrated that the weapon had ceased functioning.

"Mine," Ryan said. He stooped and put his G-12 caseless down, placing the SIG-Sauer 9 mm pistol alongside it. Then he moved out of cover, and walked toward the helmeted guard, loosening the white silk scarf from around his neck.

"Don't, lover," Krysty said, trying to pull him back around the corner.

"I'll chill him from here," J.B. said.

"No," Ryan said very quietly. "This is what the good Dr. Tardy might call a hands-on termination, revenge-wise. Got to be."

He shrugged off their warnings and stepped toward the sentry.

Closing in on the mutie, Ryan carefully avoided the stinking corpse, where bodily fluids still bubbled and seeped. The guard backed clumsily away until his helmet rang against the door.

Ryan looped the silken scarf in his hands carefully, his eyes locked on the reflective visor of the sec man's black carapace. The lower edge of the mutie's helmet didn't quite settle on his squat, muscular neck, leaving a couple of inches of pallid flesh exposed.

The muzzle of the blaster rose to cover Ryan's groin and lower belly. Despite his limitless courage, the one-eyed man winced. Having seen the shambles that Finnegan had become would have been enough to make any normal man fall to his knees and bury his head in his hands, weeping.

Not Ryan Cawdor.

"You just chilled one of the best, bravest men I ever knew," he said in a normal, conversational voice. "Friends are rare. Good friends rarer. And you chilled him, you heartless mutie bastard!" he shouted in sudden anger as he stepped closer.

He swung the weighted end of the scarf so that it lashed out and whipped around the guard's throat, the end coming back into Ryan's ready fingers.

The sec man tried to get his gauntleted hands up, but he was too slow. The scarf tightened and began to bite into the tender flesh of his neck. Ryan jerked hard at it, pulling the guard forward, so close he could smell the rank sweat on the mutie's body. The helmet bobbled off, and he looked into the dull eyes of the creature who had butchered Finn.

*"Die, you fucker."* Ryan kneed the guard in the groin, feeling the satisfying jarring as he caught the mutie's genitals against the bone. As the man slumped, Ryan crossed

his wrists, making the silk tighten like fluid steel, immovable, inflexible.

*"Die."*

The mutie's tongue swelled, his hands fell limp, and his eyes burst from bloodied sockets. A thread of bright crimson blood wormed from his lips and nostrils, and as the creature's body relaxed, Ryan could smell the noisome voiding of bowels and bladder.

Ryan unwound his scarf from the guard's neck, prizing it from the deep furrowed folds in the corpse's flesh. He wrapped it back around his own neck, feeling better for the killing, not stopping to mourn for Finnegan. There'd be time for that.

Later.

A PIECE OF PLAS the size of a button, a five-second fuse and a tiny copper detonator, that was all it took for the six to blast their way inside the holy of holies at the Wizard Island Complex for Scientific Advancement. The small explosion shook their ears, and then the outer door swung back.

The scientists, finally realizing they were under serious attack from the primitive outsiders, had taken precautions.

A handful of sec guards, blasters ready, were lined up to meet the intruders. There were six of them, but not one managed to fire his laser rifle. Each was gunned down on the spot in a hectic burst of shooting from the corridor.

Leaping over jerking corpses, nearly slipping in the spreading pools of turgid blood, Ryan led his friends in.

"Fireblast!" he exclaimed, stopping dead inside the doorway, the others nearly knocking him over.

They'd realized the research part of the complex must be enormous, but even in their wildest imaginings they hadn't figured on anything quite as massive as this.

Spidery scaffolding rose thirty stories high, interlocking in a delicate tracery of dulled metal. A viper's nest of colored conduits and pipes wound in and out, so far above them that they seemed like thin wires. Red and green and orange and vivid blue. There were three basic sections within the research area, marked simply Land, Sea and Air & Space. Each one seemed to vanish into the diminishing distance. Each was bigger than fifty aircraft hangars.

A long list on the wall showed the innumerable subsections of research.

A catalogue of inhumanity and megadeath:

Chemical.

Medical.

Nerve toxins.

Sight.

Audio-destroyers.

Neural synapse breakers.

RPV.

"What's that?" Ryan asked.

"It stands for Remotely Piloted Vehicles," Doc Tanner answered. "It was big around the end of the century."

Sensors.

Avoidance.

LAMPS.

"Tell me, Doc."

"It means Light Airborne Multipurpose Systems. Mainly antisubmarine stuff."

Battle-Support Missiles.

Air-Defense Missiles.

Surface-To-Air Missiles (Fixed Emplacement).

Forward-Area-Guided Projectiles.

The list was seemingly endless, and it was color-coded and had a variety of letters and numerals after each item. By far the largest number of entries was under the subhead Antipersonnel Weapons.

"Don't tell us, Doc," Krysty said in a subdued voice. "It just means lots of ways of killing ordinary people. By Gaia, but this has to be wiped clean!"

But with Finnegan dead, only J.B. and Ryan had the basic explosives knowledge to start a chain reaction that would destroy the whole complex. Jak was fine on small, localized sabotage, but nothing bigger.

"Split up," Ryan told them. "Krysty and Jak with me. J.B. to take Doc and Lori. Check chrons. I have 11:13 . . . now. Meet back at the bottom of the main elevators in. . . How long, you figure, Doc? J.B.? How long?"

The old man shook his head, as if overwhelmed by the pressure and the killings. "This gilded palace of sin, my old friend . . . It's walls of sardonyx and chrysoprase. Its mighty towers of sapphire and chalcedony, inlaid with wondrous lapis lazuli." His voice was dreamy. "Is that not the most wonderful name for a gem?" He drew it out slowly, savoring it. "Lapis lazuli."

Ryan shook him by the arm. "Don't fuck us up now, Doc. Not fucking now!"

His eyes cleared and his jaw set. The old man squared his shoulders and stared Ryan straight in the eye. "My most humble apologies, my dear friend. What can I have been thinking of? You were asking?"

"How long? How long to try and find the right places to blow this dump out of the world?"

"Their security is lax and almost useless against fighters with intent. It's odd, is it not? They have been locked

in here for a hundred years, doing nothing but research-
ing ways of killing the planet. Yet in all that time the poor
devils have quite forgotten how to fight.''

"So it'll be a slide, huh?" J.B. asked.

"I think not. They will eventually gain access to their
own defense systems. Dr. Avian spoke of hordes of sec
muties locked safely away, waiting only the press of a button to release them all. No. I think we can spare no more
than an hour."

"Where's best to go?" Krysty asked, pointing at the
massive board.

Doc sighed. "Missiles, I suppose would be best. Find
some good old-fashioned dynamite or nitro and place it
right. Should be enough. An explosion down here has nowhere to go. Could bring the roof in. Then the lake. Blow
down and set off the volcano." His eyes turned dreamy
again. "That would be a wondrous consummation—to be
born in fire and to end in fire."

Ryan turned away. "Fine, then. We'll split up like we
said. Both groups will head toward the missiles, one left
and one right. Kill anything moving. I now have . . . 11:15.
Meet back at the base of the elevator at 12:20. First there
waits, if they can, until 12:25. Then they go. Up and run.
Head back through the ville for the gateway. Wait there
twenty-four hours. Then—"

"Then, goodbye," Jak finished.

MOST OF THE NEXT HOUR passed like a dream of action
and death for Ryan and his two companions.

By his calculations they'd taken out three of the sixty-
one scientists and a sizable part of their sec men. Unless
some of the hordes of mutie sleepers had been released,
there couldn't be more than about seventy living humans

within the entire Wizard Island complex—a tiny number in that rambling techno vastness.

"Someone," Jak Lauren hissed, running a little ahead of Ryan and Krysty.

It was the frail dwarf scientist in a spidery frame of plastic tubing. Its silent motor allowed him to be suspended a few inches above the floor. Seeing them, he stopped his machine.

"Take him," Krysty said.

Ryan put the G-12 caseless on single-shot and aimed at the center of the scientist's great spongy nodding head between his moonish eyes. Just as he had when they'd last seen him, the scientist managed to control his trembling features long enough to smile at them—a wonderful, warm smile that filled Ryan with a wave of almost magical happiness. He smiled back and lowered his gun.

"Ryan," Krysty said.

"Can't. Not to...to that."

The wheelchair floated nearer, the tiny flipperlike left hand working intricate controls. The head nodded, the smile unchanging. Ryan glanced at Jak and saw him grinning helplessly at the scientist.

The delicate, harmless little...

Then there was the sharp crack from the mirrored H&K P7A-13 pistol in Krysty's right hand. A small ruby hole, black-edged, appeared miraculously in the dwarf's massive forehead above his glittering left eye. His chair weaved and stopped, and the scientist slumped dead in it, the smile still stuck in place.

"Krysty, we could..." Ryan began, shaking himself as though he were covered in cold water.

"Lover, we don't have the time," she said, pushing past him, edging Jak out of the way and taking the lead.

WORD HAD FINALLY GOT out among the scientists that death had come stalking them. Ryan and the others saw lab coats of pink, green and light blue scurrying away from them, up stairs and into rooms that opened off the main part of the complex.

Oddly they saw no more sec men.

"Here," Ryan said, pointing to a section marked with a skull and crossbones and the words over the doorway: All Personnel Caution. Explosives. Alpha-Sec Only. Others Quadruple Negative Entry.

They entered a laboratory filled with glass vials that bubbled and hissed. There was more scientific equipment in the room than Ryan had seen in his entire life. Strapped into a peculiar upright wheeled chair was the huge giant they'd seen previously, this time without his mutie escort. His face, with the distorted, swollen features of an acromegalic, turned incuriously to look in their direction. Then he glanced back to the bench where he was working on an experiment that seemed to involve whirling steel spheres in a huge vacuum jar.

"They said he was an astrophysicist," Krysty whispered. "What's he doing in here?"

"Don't know," Ryan replied. "And I don't care."

His first bullet drilled clean through the giant's torso to the left of his twisted lordotic spine. The bullet smashed into the apparatus, causing a gigantic implosion that sucked the retarded giant forward, his face and upper body almost disappearing into the whirling inferno of splintered glass and metal. They heard a bull-like roar of pain, interrupted by a choking, drowning cry as the body slumped across the bench.

Without giving the massive corpse a second glance, Ryan led them on.

"This is it," he said.

They were in a wing of the sprawling building only forty paces of so from the body of the gigantic scientist, along a corridor that ran parallel to the center aisle of the research section.

Jak smiled, running a tongue over bared teeth. "Look at that. Blow up the world with that."

"What they intended, kid," Ryan replied, shaking his head at the sight. If any baron in Deathlands had access to power like this, he could rule unchallenged. It had to be the largest collection of explosives anywhere.

Row upon row of shelves, with crates upon crates. Thousands of tons of every kind of explosive in raw and refined form, lots of it with long chemical names that Ryan didn't even recognize. Some of it, like good old unstable nitro, he knew well enough. There were miles of wires of varying thickness and hundreds upon hundreds of detonators.

"Timers," Jak said, leaping about the store like a child surrounded by a paradise of dream toys.

"Time's passing, lover," Krysty warned, glancing at her wrist chron.

"Keep watch," Ryan said. "Got to link this up with some of that napalm we saw back yonder. Get everything tied in so it blows together."

She clicked away, the heels of her designer western boots ringing on the stone floor. Watching her, Ryan felt one of those unexpected waves of great affection that come between people who are very much in love.

"Project Eurydice is under threat," the loudspeaker suddenly blared. "All personnel report to HQ section. Central must be obeyed always. Sec men reactivated. Move toward research section where intruders are believed to be." It was the unmistakable little-girl tones of Dr. Tardy. "In event of action take any steps, terminationwise, in lethal mode to protect all."

The speaker clicked off as suddenly as it had come on.

Then it returned to life. There was the noise of coughing, then labored breathing. "Ryan. Doc Tanner here. Do you read me? Over." A pause. "Sorry. My apologies. Course you can't answer, can you? No. Well, we've found what we wanted. Linked in some of J.B.'s best to some of our chum's demonic little games. See you back where we said at the exit. Over and out."

"Fuck," Ryan said, finishing looping a dozen strands of wire into one detonator. "Doc's blown our meeting. Hope nobody was listening in."

But he knew they needed an awful lot of luck for no one else to have heard.

So, with time running out, Ryan hurried Jak and Krysty along through the weapons complex. The timers had been set to go in just thirty minutes. It didn't leave them much of a margin, but it would also make it hard for the scientists to manage to defuse everything. And he'd even scattered a few clever boobies in the shelving, ready to be triggered if anyone was careless. Either way, the subterranean redoubt should go up around 12:40.

There wasn't much time for any delays.

J.B., LORI AND DOC TANNER had returned to the base of the main entrance elevator. The bodies of five sec men lay in a tangled heap at the mouth of the corridor that led toward the scientists' living quarters.

The Armorer looked carefully at his chron. "I make it 12:16. I don't hear them coming yet."

EVERYTHING WAS SET AND READY.

"Twelve-sixteen," Jak said.

If the explosives did their stuff, a devastating chain re-action would occur in the stores of lethal weapons. The first bang would lead to others, eventually spreading fire and destruction throughout the whole complex.

All the three of them had to do now was rejoin the other trio near the single exit to safety.

They were only a couple of turns in the corridor from their destination when Dr. Ethel Tardy appeared from a side door and waddled into the center of the passage. She was holding a chromed handblaster, which was connected to wires that trailed away out of sight. The muzzle was slightly bell-shaped and was pointed in their direction.

The tiny woman smiled, beaming eyes hugely distorted by her thick spectacles. Her sweet, lisping little voice showed no trace of anger.

"You have been busy, sabotagewise. We lost track of our surveillance mode operation on Dr. Tanner and the others in your party."

"Tough shit, lady." Ryan hesitated about trying to blast the diminutive scientist, the short hairs prickling at the back of his neck at the sight of the outlandish weapon she held. What was it, and what might it do?

She answered the unspoken question. "One move from you and I shall use this. It is one of our prize items of re-search, tested thus far only on our mutant experimental personnel."

"Bitch," Krysty muttered, too quietly for Dr. Tardy to hear her.

"It is listed as an emdee. Which stands for a Molecular Destabilizer. I eagerly anticipate using it upon you three and examining the results."

"What's it do?" Jak asked.

Ryan was wondering whether he should try to snap the G-12 onto continuous and rip the poisonous dwarf into bloody ribbons of flesh. But she was too far away—and her finger was on a button that had to be a firing trigger.

"Your tissue, bone, blood, skin are all composed of molecules bonded together. This will remove those fragile bonds." She could have been lecturing to a class of students.

Only Krysty had even an inkling of what she was trying to explain. "But if you do that . . ."

Dr. Ethel Tardy positively twinkled at her. "Yes, you see it! The entire structure dissolves. You melt into a billion, billion particles. Total disintegration." She smiled broadly. "And it is so painful. The element of consciousness remains surprisingly long. It is one of the best of my own inventions."

"You death-crazed lunatic," Ryan said, unable to control his loathing for the insane woman.

"No. Central bless you. We are the saviors of the world. Only through death can you come to a new life. That's how it's always been in the rules."

"You're sick," Krysty spat. "Sick and fit for death."

Dr. Tardy wasn't to be convinced. "Wrong, wrong, wrong. Quadruple negative. Central has always wanted what we can now give them. Now we can finally destroy it all. The evil will be purged, the land cleansed by fire and by the horsemen of disease and pestilence."

Now she was beginning to sound like some biblical prophet, drawing on the Book of Revelation.

"You'll wipe out the few survivors of the madness of the long chill?" Krysty asked.

"They will welcome our redemption."

"A vile death!"

Dr. Tardy shook her little Buddha-like head. "They are not worth the saving."

"Some are," Jak said, hand sliding around toward a concealed dagger.

"Move your fingers another micrometer and you're instant dusty soup," the scientist said. "Good. Now we must know what you've been doing. We know you've terminated our sec men, but we lost you as you came to the research section. What have you done? What can you hope to do? Why check us in our Central-blessed designs? Do you not see how grand is our aim here?"

Ryan took a half step forward. "Me an' my friends go around the Deathlands and there's times we do us some chilling. There's those needs it. And I like to figure the world's a touch better as we pass on by. I heard someone once talk about the darkness on the land, how he hoped to hold it back some, like carrying a sword into the sunset. Mebbe even carry it on through to a dawn. A new dawn. Sounds fucking stupid to you? Sure it does. But I'm for life. You're not."

"I'm for—" Dr. Ethel Tardy began, when Dr. Theophilus Tanner appeared like a ragged angel of vengeance and shot her carefully through the back of the head with his two-hundred-year-old Le Mat pistol.

"Rot in your own hell," he said.

# Chapter Twenty-Three

A BRIEF AND VICIOUS FIREFIGHT with a dozen of the mutie sec men slowed them a dangerous few seconds. Fortunately Ryan's party took no casualties and were finally in the elevator, climbing fast toward a fresh Oregon afternoon.

The ascent took precisely the eighty-five seconds the descent had taken. The box of dulled steel seemed to rise with agonizing slowness. Once, when they were near the top, the elevator shook, rattling against the sides of the shaft, and they dimly heard the sound of a muffled explosion. Ryan checked his chron; J.B. did the same.

"Coupl'a minutes early," he said.

"Can't trust old plas," the Armorer replied.

When they got to the top, it was a beautiful day. The sun beamed down from a cloudless sky of unsullied azure. A hawk floated majestically between the peaks away to the west. The bowl of mountains around Crater Lake was topped with a frosting of snow, but the air was warm and fresh. The main entrance wasn't guarded, and there were several of the amphibious boat wags on the ramp under the shadow of the jagged rocks that concealed the complex.

"Look at the water," Lori said. "It dances."

They looked.

The impenetrable deeps were a rich blue, normally placid and calm. Now the water was rippling agitatedly, tiny waves rising and breaking against one another and lapping at the stone ramp like thousands of little sucking mouths.

"I can feel it and hear it," Krysty said urgently, head to one side, her crimson hair like strands of fire in the sunlight.

"The bombs going?" Ryan asked.

"Sure. Can't you hear it?"

The Wizard Island Complex for Scientific Advancement was buried so deeply that not even Ryan's keen hearing could detect anything happening. But he could *feel* it. Through the thick soles of his combat boots, he could sense the faint susurration that was coming through thousands of feet of rock.

"Best go. Who'll drive?" Ryan asked.

Normally it would have been Finnegan.

"Me," Jak offered, leaping into the control seat, his snowy hair blowing in the light breeze.

Away above them Ryan noticed a small herd of deer running fast over the gray pumice slopes, their sharp hooves kicking up powder behind them. It looked as if something had spooked them.

The pink eyes of the albino spotted a faint trail that climbed the steep sides of the basin around the lake, and he aimed the amphib at it. He lowered the wheels as they reached land and gunned the motor to force the amphib up among the trees. Behind them the surface of the water was becoming more restless as whitecaps rippled the rich blue.

At Ryan's command Jak stopped the small vehicle when they crested the rise and reached the blacktop that had once carried camera-laden tourists around beautiful Crater Lake.

"Fireblast! Look at that son of . . ."

The water was beginning to bubble, almost like a monstrous caldron approaching a boil. A snaking tendril of smoke or steam escaped from the dark entrance to the complex. Even from where they stood it was possible to catch the sound of distant explosions, sounding as though they came from a limitless distance beneath their feet.

"Is it going to go?" Lori asked.

"The volcano?" Doc queried, his arm around the waist of the slim young girl as they stood on the edge of the old roadway.

"Yes. Fire mountain?"

"It just might be, the old man replied, the etched lines about his eyes showing the strain they'd all been through.

As they climbed into the amphib, Ryan glanced back once more. It had been an odd firefight. The odds and the technology had been overwhelmingly on the side of the scientists and their mutie slaves. But they had lost the art of fighting. A handful of determined people, armed with what to the scientists were primitive weapons, had utterly defeated them.

Destroyed them.

As they drove away from the beautiful country and weather around Crater Lake, they passed immense numbers of animals and birds, all fleeing south, away from the doomed redoubt. A dozen mutie timber wolves, their leader nearly as tall at the shoulder as a man, looked contemptuously at the small group of humans, then moved on at an easy lope, ignoring them.

"Wish we could've taken that molecule destroyer thing you spoke about," J.B. said sadly.

Doc Tanner heard him and grasped the Armorer's lean shoulder in a bony hand. "Don't say that, my friend. If we have done our work well, then that place of hellish enchantments will be buried forever and a day, until the dead rise gibbering from their graves. That's best.''

Lori smiled winsomely at him. "Like you said—the only good scientist is a chilled one.''

The little boat made good speed over the bumpy roads. It seemed to have a kind of floating suspension that carried them smoothly over the worst bumps. Since none of them knew how the silent engine functioned, there was a very real danger of running out of whatever fuel powered it. To be stranded in that fiery cold wilderness could have meant death.

It was near dusk when they reached the friendly ville of Ginnsburg Falls. Everyone ducked low, and Jak gunned the motor, pushing their speed up to around fifty miles an hour. They heard shouts, and what might have been a blaster, falling away behind them, but no harm was done.

"And so we say farewell to Ginnsburg Falls, nicest little town in the West,'' Doc Tanner said, his words almost whisked away by the driving wind.

They pressed on through the valley, following the blacktop as it snaked higher and higher. The skies were darkening, with deep crimson chem-clouds soaring toward them from the far west, bringing the threat of a severe storm.

"Not far to go,'' Ryan said. "Follow the trail and watch for the fork up to the redoubt. Save having to climb all around and go through those bastard tunnels.''

They were lucky. It was so dark that only Krysty's part-mutie vision spotted the blur of the road. Jak turned the amphib, angling carefully around the jagged boulders that had fallen from above. For the first time the engine was making noises, a faint angry whirring that didn't bode well for continued progress. Fortunately they reached the main entrance to the redoubt within a quarter of an hour.

The massive doors were closed, the metal scored and pitted from the efforts of generations of muties to break them down. Doc clambered out and stretched, knees and shoulders creaking.

"Hope it's the usual three-five-two code to open her up. Don't much relish making like a mole to go back into them holes."

Three, five, two did the trick, enabling them to trigger the colored lever beside the control panel. It was a tribute to the technical skill of some of the pre-Chill engineers that the door still worked.

J.B. and Lori kept watch against possible attack by the small mutie killers who'd nearly wasted them when they'd first arrived through the gateway. But the slopes of the mountains were quiet and deserted.

"Let's go in," Krysty said.

"Sure. But . . . Fireblast! Look at . . ." His voice faded away into silent awe. Everyone turned to look where Ryan stood, frozen, staring north toward Crater Lake.

The earth was exploding.

Mount Mazama had been awakened from its long slumber, provoked into a violent eruption by the bombs and fires that Ryan and his companions had triggered far below the deep blue waters of the lake. Flames and lava jetted thousands of feet into the night sky. Even at that distance they heard the bass rumbling of the mountain heaving itself into destruction.

"Hell of a funeral pyre for Finn," Ryan said. "Man couldn't ask for a better memorial."

They watched the spectacle for several minutes until the extreme cold began to bite deep. It felt like around fifty below, with the wind bringing it another twenty lower. Ryan felt the hairs in his nostrils clogging with shards of ice.

Doc Tanner shivered. "Western wind blowing, Mr. Cawdor. Time for us to hie ourselves to another place." As he spoke, his breath froze in the air, descending all around them in a shower of miniature crystals like tiny diamonds. Doc noticed it. "Sign of the cold. Hear them fall? The Russians call that the whisper of the stars. Pretty name, isn't it?"

They progressed through the long-abandoned redoubt, toward the mat-trans gateway. At the back of Ryan's mind was the staggering knowledge about Doc Tanner. About his age. About the fact that some gateways could be used for time travel if their secrets could be unlocked. It was something to think about.

Leading the group, J.B. paused as they reached the familiar sign: Entry Absolutely Forbidden To All But B12 Cleared Personnel. Mats-Trans.

The vivid red armored glass walls of the chamber glowed to greet them. The disks of polished metal glittered brightly in the ceiling and on the floor. Jak entered first, followed by Lori, both of them sitting down with their backs against the walls, legs stretched out. Doc sat next to Lori. J.B. hunkered down, cross-legged, pulling the brim of his fedora over his eyes like a man on a stoop readying himself for an afternoon sleep. Krysty sat next, resting her chin on her arms, looking up at Ryan, who stood by the door, ready to trigger the mechanism.

"I'll miss that fat old bastard Finnegan," she said reflectively.

"And me," Lori said.

"We all will." Ryan paused. "Everyone ready for the jump? Then here we go."

He pulled the chamber door firmly shut, hearing the mechanism click into action. He quickly sat down by Krysty, holding her hand. Doc had his arm around the slim figure of Lori.

The lights began to brighten on the disks, and the walls darkened.

"If they're the future, then they can fucking have it," came the quiet voice of J.B.

Ryan felt his head beginning to throb with the building pressure of the jump. As he started to slip away, he heard Doc's quavery voice singing.

"Western wind, when wilt thou blow,
That small rain down can rain?
Christ! If my love were in my arms,
And I in my bed again."

The blackness spread slowly through Ryan's brain. The last few days had been as bad as anything he'd ever known. Wherever the gateway took them, it had to be better.

As his eye closed, that was the last thought Ryan Cawdor took with him into the swirling dark.

# JAMES O. JACKSON

# DZERZHINSKY SQUARE

**Captured by the Nazis during World War II and then falsely branded a collaborator, Grigory Nikolayevich Malmudor must choose the one remaining road back to his Soviet homeland . . . as a spy for the U.S. But he is soon abandoned by his American masters in a world of deadly shadows and constant terror, faced with the promise of inevitable doom.**

DS-1

# BULLETS OF PALESTINE

## Howard Kaplan

A Kaplan novel is ''an edge-of-the-chair,
throat-grabbing page-turner! Accurate and terrifying.''
—Gerald Green, writer, NBC's *Holocaust*

His name is Abu Nidal. A breakaway Palestinian known as the
''terrorists' terrorist.'' An Israeli and a Palestinian join forces,
despite the hatreds of their heritage, to eliminate this man. Will
they ensnare Abu Nidal—or trap each other in a bloodbath of
betrayal?